Praise for Spur of the Moment

"Mystery lovers will enjoy the intelligent writing, the mix of light and dark, the astute psychology and biting social satire, and the satisfaction of a traditional (but not formulaic) mystery that's a bit of a classed-up romp."

—Jeannette Cooperman for *St. Louis Magazine*

"An entertaining mystery, full of intriguing backstage details about opera productions and introducing an appealing heroine who is feisty, funny, and deeply loyal to her shallow sibling. Recommend for fans of Blair Tindall's memoir Mozart in the Jungle and anyone who enjoys crime served up with an aria."

—*Library Journal*

"Spur of the Moment is an entertaining novel full of St. Louis references, British slang, and a dab of commentary on the state of medical research. Readers will enjoy this light, quirky tale of fictional intrigue set in our own backyard."

—Jennifer Alexander, *West End Word*

"The book sits fairly comfortably in the cosy bracket. This is by no means a criticism, but the gentle humour and thoroughly urbane style of writing point *Spur of the Moment* in that direction. Blood is shed, certainly, but not dwelt upon. It's a thoroughly enjoyable read and you might just fall in love with Renata.... I look forward to Mr. Linzee's next production starring Ms Radleigh."

—David Prestidge, *Crimefictionlover.com*

"Written with his usual elegant precision, author Linzee brings alive his city and its characters in ways that nail the reader to the page. Don't miss this one. St. Louis is undergoing a renaissance, and *Spur of the Moment* is an important part of it."

—John Lutz, author of *Frenzy*

One Fell Swoop

One Fell Swoop

David Linzee

coffeetownpress
Seattle, WA

Coffeetown Press
PO Box 70515
Seattle, WA 98127

For more information go to: www.coffeetownpress.com
www.davidlinzee.com

Cover design by Sabrina Sun

One Fell Swoop

ISBN: 978-1-60381-577-2 (Trade Paper)
ISBN: 978-1-60381-578-9 (eBook)

Library of Congress Control Number: 2016961917

Printed in the United States of America

For Pippa Bellasis

"In your house, as in a golden dream."

—*Eugene Onegin*

Acknowledgments

My thanks to Mike Giger, a real-life neighborhood savior, who gave me the job of editor of the real-life equivalent of the *Parkdale Neighbor News.*

Thanks also to Catherine Treadgold and Jennifer McCord, editors extraordinary at Coffeetown Press.

Also by the author

from Camel Press

Spur of the Moment

Prologue

Renata Radleigh was panting when she reached the top of the hill. This was the highest point in London, and a strong wind had been blowing every time she'd been here. Tonight it was bitter cold. Her eyes were tearing up and her nose starting to run as she turned in a circle, looking for Neal. The lights of the city glittered to the south, but on Hampstead Heath there was only a faint glow reflected from the overcast sky.

It was a stupid choice for a rendezvous. She would have argued with Neal the dog walker if he'd given her a chance. The hill was a wide expanse and she couldn't see very far into the darkness. She wiped her nose on her sleeve and took out her phone. Since Neal had called her, it had his number. She tried it but there was no answer. She kept the phone in hand, hoping he'd ring her.

She wandered on, turning in a circle, seeing only darkness. It was all very well for Neal; he had a borzoi to protect him. But this was no place for a lone woman, especially one who had two hundred pounds in her pocket. She was thinking of trying Neal again when her foot was yanked out from under her and she fell on her face.

Heart pounding, she twisted round to see who had tripped

her. But there was no one. She got to her feet. She had fallen over a body. She bent over it, putting a hand down to brace herself. The face was turned to the side. It was Neal. A trail of blood crossed his cheek from his ear. His cap was gone and there was something pallid showing through his dark hair. She bent close, then recoiled as she realized it was the broken edge of his skull. The palm of the hand she had put to the ground felt warm. She turned it over to see that it was covered in blood. The grass all around his head was bloody. He was dead.

Renata cried out feebly against the wind and staggered away. She must call the police immediately. But she'd dropped her phone. She had to return to the body and bend over it to pick up the phone. It was slick with blood and she had to fight not to be sick.

1

Five days earlier

RENATA WAS THE LAST SINGER of the evening. She was confident in her appearance, having worn her long black hair down so that it fell in glossy waves to her shoulders. The shimmering blue silk of her gown, along with the exaggerated eyeliner and false lashes expected of opera singers, made her eyes an almost startling shade of aqua. She felt the slow, lilting music flowing into her, relaxing her upright recital pose, making her supple-waisted. About half of her thirty-six years seemed to fall away as she became the character singing the aria, the light-hearted teenager Olga.

She was performing in the London home of Maestro Vladimir Grinevich. Brand new, it had been described in the Sunday newspapers as costing fifteen million pounds. Its interior was the work of a fashionable designer. The papers had run pictures of it, and she'd thought it couldn't look that vulgar in reality, but it did: white walls and carpets, purple furniture, steel and mirrors everywhere. Maestro had a superb ear, but not much of an eye.

Her stage was a semicircle of twenty-foot tall French windows that gave on what was called a garden, though it was mostly stone and steel. Ribbons of steam escaped from the glass lid that covered the underground swimming pool. Stairs of pure-white stone widened and narrowed in sensuous curves as they climbed the hillside behind the house. While waiting her turn to sing, Renata had been wondering what was the point of them, since they didn't seem to lead anywhere. The staircase looked like a Las Vegas stage set, and was just as brilliantly lit. It would have been appropriate for dancing girls to descend the stairs making high kicks, and many of the audience would have been grateful if they had.

This was a fundraising event to which Maestro had invited his neighbors. Since the neighborhood was Billionaires' Row near Hampstead Heath, that meant she was singing to a group of London's wealthiest residents. She'd had more attentive audiences in primary schools. Coughing was more or less continuous. Whenever the music softened, she heard the chirps of incoming calls and texts. The less inhibited were checking the screens of their mobiles, and the even less inhibited were whispering on them. Some people were waving to attract the attention of the waiters, who circulated with champagne and appetizers. Others were dozing, eyes closed and heads askew.

The rows of faces before her were Arab, East Asian, South Asian, Latin, as well as white, for the rich of all the world settled in London. But the front row was solidly Russian. The oligarchs were bulky men with knobby noses whose hair had turned gray but was still luxuriant. They were flanked on one side by their trophy wives or mistresses, who were sleepily blinking their thick eyelashes, checking their gold and diamond watches, and crossing and re-crossing their long bare legs. On the other side of each man sat his bodyguard, fashionably tight suit bulging over his shoulder holster.

It seemed to Renata that the bodyguards were more attentive than the rest of the audience. Maybe Maestro had had them in mind when he suggested that she sing Olga's aria from Tchaikovsky's *Eugene Onegin*, one of the classics of the mezzo-soprano repertoire. It reminded them of home. Or maybe they were simply used to keeping still and looking alert.

Impatient applause swallowed her final notes. She extended an arm to acknowledge the accompanist, then lifted both arms to invite the other singers to join her. Maestro Grinevich, notoriously impatient of ovations that were not for him, allowed them only one bow before lumbering to the front of the room.

"Beautiful aria, wonderfully performed, some of you are thinking. Others are thinking, last number! It's over! Whew!" He made the gesture of flicking sweat from his forehead, but in fact there was real sweat to flick away. Maestro perspired a lot, even when he was not conducting.

The audience laughed heartily. Grinevich was renowned for his outrageous and charming candor, which in a non-celebrity would have been called rudeness. He was a tall man in his late fifties with a deep chest and big belly. Graying dark hair fell over his forehead and ears, and a beard that had gone entirely gray covered the lower part of his face. His deep-set brown eyes, which Renata knew from experience could be very intimidating when he was in the pit and you were on the stage, raked the audience as he delivered his pitch. He was raising funds for his new charity, the Fidelio Foundation, which would perform operas in prisons and young offender institutions. No one in the audience would be allowed to leave without handing over a check. That got a laugh, too.

After another round of applause, in which the singers joined, Grinevich waded into the audience to begin shaking hands and collecting checks. The singers stood silently in a row, unsure what to do next. They were in a bad mood, though they covered it well. Most, like Renata, were obscure old pros. Maestro's assistants had coaxed them into performing for free with hints that the Fidelio Foundation, once it got on its feet, would employ them. Then there'd been the audience. Maintaining one's concentration amid all that coughing and texting drained one's energy. Finally, there'd been the security. Grinevich's political problems in his native Russia had followed him over here, and his house had its own team of men in tight suits with bulges under their arms. It even had a gatehouse, where the arriving singers had been detained while their papers were checked. Once in the house, they'd been escorted down corridors and watched over as they waited to perform. A baritone had muttered to Renata that he felt like a circus tiger.

Now the minders reappeared to escort them to the bedroom where they could change back into their street clothes. Renata was last in line. When a waiter passed her with a tray of champagne flutes, she surrendered to a rebellious urge. Stepping out of line, she took a glass, turned to face the room, and waited to see if anything would happen.

The guests were on their feet, making up for lost time with the hors d'oeuvres and wine, and chatting in a mélange of languages. She had read that London had more billionaires than any other city in the world, and almost all of them were foreign-born. The city offered advantages over their homes. They came from Beijing because the air was breathable, from Moscow because they could not be thrown in jail at Putin's pleasure, from Delhi because the roads were in good repair and the traffic did move—if slowly, from Sao Paolo because the lower classes were content and less likely to rob or kidnap them. And there was a good supply of beautiful houses and flats to swap among themselves, at ever-increasing prices, as well as high-toned shops and restaurants in which to fritter away surplus cash. No doubt the shopkeepers and restaurateurs were happy, but the ordinary Londoners were a bit surly about the rising prices, including Renata. She wondered if she was the only English person here.

But no: there was a blond man in a gray suit, back to her. His pose, one hand in his trouser pocket, other holding his glass by the stem, displayed that unmistakably English attitude of self-consciousness striving for nonchalance. This man seemed familiar. He threw back his head and laughed, and she recognized her brother.

"Don!"

He turned and waved. She gathered he had seen her perform, which meant he would have had time to recover from any surprise he might feel at seeing her. She was certainly surprised to see him. He came over.

"I didn't know you were in England." She breathed in enough expensive Jermyn Street toiletries to make her cough as he leaned in to kiss her on the cheek.

"Just popped over on business. Flying back tomorrow."

"Business?" The last she'd heard, he was selling houses in the suburbs of St. Louis, which didn't seem to require a trip to London. "But what are you doing *here*? I mean tonight."

His sandy eyebrows rose, disappearing under his blond forelock. She realized that she'd sounded suspicious rather than pleased. "Sorry. It's lovely to see you, but such a surprise. I mean what an extraordinary coincidence."

"Not a bit of it. I got you the job."

"Tosh! Maestro Grinevich wouldn't accept a recommendation from you."

"He would from my boss."

"Your boss?"

"My investor, more properly. My backer."

"Well … thanks."

"I enjoyed your number. Always liked '*Akh*, Tanya, Tanya.' Bright spot in such a mopey opera. Near as Tchaikovsky ever got to writing, 'Girls Just Wanna Have Fun.' "

It was unusual for him to compliment her. She recalled what she had been about to ask. "Is your backer here?"

Don glanced over his shoulder. A general drift toward the door was beginning. Guests were handing their glasses to servants, shaking hands or embracing. "Don't see him. Probably left, or stepped out to take a call." He turned back to her. "I've already asked for my car to be brought round. Can I give you a lift?"

"Mind if I change first?"

"Must you?"

"This dress marks horribly if I sit down in it. And I'm hoping to get two more recitals out of it before it goes to the cleaner's."

He reached into his pocket and pressed something into her hand. "Never mind about that. Get your bag and let's be off."

She looked down. It was a £20 note, presumably for the dry cleaner. She wanted to give it back to him, but he had turned away to say good night to someone. This bit of high-handedness was more like the usual Don. She headed for the bedroom where she had left her bag.

She and Don, three years her junior, had had a long and bitter sibling rivalry, exacerbated by the fact that they were in the same field. He had been director of development for the Saint Louis Opera, one of America's best regional companies. But he had lost the job the previous spring in scandalous circumstances. No one else would come to his aid, so Renata had, not without mixed feelings, but with surprising effectiveness.

He had never thanked her—her psychotherapist suggested that he was too deep in denial about the whole ordeal to do that—and seldom rang or texted her. But getting her tonight's gig was a good deed, as was the offer of a ride home, sparing her a long Underground journey, holding up her dress in its garment bag the whole way, trying not to wrinkle it.

The spacious bedroom was full of singers in their underwear, complaining about the audience. She found a dog—a rangy, elegant borzoi—sprawled across her overcoat on the bed. She crooned and nudged him until he moved, then collected coat and bag and returned to Don.

They followed other guests through the house and out to the tall columns of the portico. The car valets were hustling to ensure that the guests didn't have to wait too long. Don took her arm as he spotted his car arriving at the foot of the steps. She knew nothing about cars, but this was some sort of expensive sports coupe. The light from the windows seemed to flow over its curves like liquid mercury. She complimented him on it as he opened the door for her. Hiding his pleasure, he said that it was hired.

The night was cold, but the car valet had turned the heater on full blast and the interior was already comfortable. Don tipped him and got in beside her. They were off with a roar before she had her lap-strap fastened.

"I'm starving," he said. "The little *amuse-bouches* they serve at do's like this only make me hungrier. Care for a nosh?"

"Well … all right."

"There's a place in the Strand I've been wanting to try out."

"But that's miles out of the way to my flat."

"Not a problem."

And it wasn't. Renata traveled mostly on foot or by bus, and she forgot how quickly one could get about London in a car at night. Especially with Don at the wheel, jumping yellow lights, passing slower cars whether there was a passing lane or not, turning corners with squeaking tires. She knew from experience it was no good asking him to slow down, so she let him give his full attention to his driving. When they were stopped at a red signal, she asked, "What is your job, Don?"

"I'm buying real estate."

"In St. Louis?"

"Yes."

"Whereabouts?"

"Better not say, sorry."

"Well, for whom, then?"

"Again, better not say. He has a name to conjure with, and if it gets about that he's buying, prices will go up."

A few minutes later, he pulled over to the curb, where another car valet was waiting. They were at their destination already. The theaters must have just let out, because the broad sidewalks were thronged. Their car vanished as if by magic as they threaded their way through the crowd to the door of a restaurant. The queue formed immediately inside it. She took her place at the back, but Don oozed through to speak to the headwaiter. Negotiations were brief. Don waved her forward. Seeing people's expressions as she passed, she was glad the place was too noisy to hear what they were saying.

There was worse to come. Don might or might not enjoy being with her, depending on his mood, but he always enjoyed being seen with her. As the waiter pulled out a chair, he stepped behind her to remove her coat, taking his time about it, watching the people in the restaurant glance at her. Reviewers used to write all manner of nonsense about Renata, saying she was the loveliest Musetta or Dorabella ever to grace the local stage and so forth. Several years had passed since then. But tonight, when she was wearing enough makeup to cover her wrinkles and had her best recital gown on, she supposed she looked all right. Don handed her coat to the waiter and came around the table to sit down with a gratified smile on his face. It made Renata want to clatter her knife against a glass and announce to the room, "I'm his *sister.*"

He was trying to catch the eye of the sommelier. "Shall we split a bottle?"

"Just water for me."

"Oh. Still on the antidepressants?"

"A different one, but they still warn you of dreadful side effects if you drink too much."

"Hate to think of you taking a happy pill every day. In addition to the fortnightly weep-fest with your shrink. What's it all doing for you? You seem much the same."

"Let's make a deal, Don. If you'll drop the subject of my antidepressants, I won't say anything about the bottle of wine you're going to put away on your own."

They managed to smile at each other.

"You've come over to consult with your boss?" she asked.

"He has me come over every few weeks, whether we need to consult or not. Last Wednesday I was saying on the phone that St. Louis was still uncomfortably warm and stale, and he said, 'Don, you must visit your native land. It's a crisp, sunny autumn here. You need a few days' rest. You're working too hard.' "

Renata nodded and said nothing. This was typical Don. People were always saying to him just what he wanted to hear. No wonder he didn't need a therapist.

"Time before this, he said, 'Don, it's August, you must join us for grouse shooting.' So I ended up in this enormous house in Scotland, packed with billionaires armed to the teeth. The first day we bagged a hundred grouse."

"Were there enough of you to eat all these birds?"

"Nothing went to waste. The surplus was sold to a restaurant in Edinburgh."

"Couldn't you have given them to charity?"

"Renata, poor people don't want to eat grouse."

"How did you find this lovely employer?"

"He found me. On LinkedIn. His staff do everything online. You should see them, in their office in The City, searching global property markets, pouncing on opportunities. Like the world is one big supermarket, and they're strolling the aisles, eying the shelves, bunging what looks tempting into their trolley."

"And they found something tempting in St. Louis?"

"Yes. But don't get the idea it's some sort of shady speculation. This is a good thing I'm doing. You'll be proud of me when you find out."

"But you can't tell me now?"

"No."

"All right. Back to LinkedIn, then. This billionaire was looking for someone to buy St. Louis property and there you were."

"He flew me over, business class. Put me up at the Savoy. I was thoroughly vetted by flunkies. Then had to wait several days to meet the man. Would have been quite tedious if I hadn't been at the Savoy. When we finally met, we got on like a house afire. He said, 'Don, you are just the man I've been seeking.' "

"Did you make a clean breast of it?"

He rolled his eyes. "Where do you find these expressions? Old opera librettos, I suppose."

"Don, did you tell him—"

"About the spot of trouble I got into in St. Louis last spring? No need to tell them. They knew all about it."

"And you got the job anyway."

"Renata, it was a point in my favor, having been in jail."

"It was?"

"My boss and his people take a broad view. They say one can't be overawed by the laws of whatever country one happens to be operating in. Money knows no borders."

"I see. But you're quite sure this is not a shady speculation?"

He was glancing around for a waiter. The restaurant was packed, service slow. "It is *not*," he said rather huffily. "What comes out on the St. Louis end of the pipeline will be all good. What happens on the London end, though, shouldn't see the light of day."

Renata laughed. "Oh, Don. You're just trying to impress me, aren't you?"

Don's cheeks stiffened. Though cavalier about other people's feelings, he was quite touchy about his own. "I'm not one to waste time on a losing proposition like trying to impress you. I know what you think of me."

"Sorry. But it's all so sudden. The last I heard of you, you were trying to sell houses in the St. Louis suburbs. And now you pop up in London, hobnobbing with billionaires, scattering twenty-pound notes to the four winds. It's all a bit much."

"This conversation is becoming tedious. And the service in this place is not up to its reviews. Let's pack it in."

He led the way out of the restaurant. From the looks of the people waiting for a table, they thought the date had turned out badly for the two queue-jumpers and were gratified. Apart from the fact that it wasn't a date, they were right.

The Radleigh siblings had another of those partings when they couldn't wait to see the back of each other. She found Don on the curb trying to hail a cab. Her ride home was no longer on, apparently. She asked about her bag in his car, and he said he'd send it round, and she said no, he'd forget as usual. They waited in furious silence for his car to be brought round. Then he handed her the bag, got in, and roared away. So she ended up on the Underground after all, wearing her gown instead of carrying it.

2

RENATA WOULD HAVE BEEN willing to live in a slum if it meant she could afford a place of her own, but so many years into the London real estate boom, the city had hardly any slums left. She and three other skint opera singers had banded together to rent a cramped basement flat in Ladbroke Grove, a nice enough area, if a bit out of the way.

Her roommates were all absent, working at provincial opera houses, so she didn't have to worry about making noise as she settled in the kitchen. It was the largest room in the flat, but even so the fridge door banged the edge of the dining table every time you opened it. She poured herself a glass of orange juice and sat down at her laptop.

It was midnight, early evening in St. Louis, a good time to reach Peter Lombardo.

Waiting for the computer to boot up, she reflected that she was lucky to be conducting a transatlantic romance at a time when Skype had been invented but they weren't charging for it yet. Peter was on the service but not at his computer. Her screen showed her a section of the wall of his flat, with an elaborate pattern of cracks in the white plaster.

This was all she had ever seen of his place, which she feared was as dismal as her own. When they'd met the previous spring,

Peter had been living in a beautiful condominium, paid for by a cushy job in the public relations department of Adams University Medical School. He'd been dragged into her effort to rescue Don, which had embarrassed his employer. Peter stoutly maintained that he had not been fired but had quit. This did nothing to soothe Renata's guilty conscience.

Her heart lifted as he appeared on screen: mop of reddish brown hair, broad, smooth brow, hazel eyes behind steel-framed glasses, and big grin showing his white, microscopically even, all-American teeth.

"Hello, my love," she said.

"You look great."

"It's the makeup. I had a recital this evening. You're rather well turned-out yourself. That's a nice tattersall shirt."

"Thanks."

"Tell me you're not wearing hound's-tooth slacks."

He looked down. "No"

"They're glen plaid, aren't they?"

"It's a very subtle plaid."

"Peter, you really must get in the habit of looking at clothes before you put them on."

"I'm trying to maintain the sartorial standard of the journalistic profession here. How did it go? Your gig, I mean."

"All right, I guess. There was a bit of a surprise after."

"Oh?"

She hesitated and decided not to tell him about seeing Don. The encounter had annoyed her so much that she didn't want to go over it again. "Never mind. How are you?"

He said that he had enough freelance writing work to pay the bills, and all St. Louis was cheerful because the Cardinals had won the World Series. Things generally seemed to go pretty well in Peter's world. He was a wonderfully even-keeled person, not like her at all. When it was her turn, she tried to strike an upbeat note. Instead of saying that she had no opera roles, she said that she had a couple of well-paying gigs singing in churches, as well as promising auditions coming up. Opera companies all over the word sent representatives to London to hire singers. That was the main reason she was here instead of with her lover.

"Great," he said, "who's first?"

"It's Lyon on Monday."

"I thought they were last week."

"They didn't get to me. They said I could come back."

"Oh. How long had they made you wait?"

"Only six hours. Then there's Frankfurt on Tuesday."

"But you said you'd never audition for Frankfurt again."

"Did I?"

"Remember, they promised you a part last year, but the contract never arrived, and neither did an explanation, and you'd turned down other parts while you were waiting."

"Yes, well, forgive and forget is my policy. I can't afford any other. Wednesday is Buenos Aires. I have high hopes. They've hired me before."

"I remember. They put you in that awful dorm and you got head lice."

"But their opera house has such lovely acoustics."

Peter smiled—a trifle wanly. She blurted out, "Peter? How much longer are you going to put up with me?"

"I have never asked you to give up your career, and I never will."

"Yes, I know, but do you ever wonder how we're going to end up?"

Peter, who was circumspect in the Midwestern manner, held his tongue.

"You do. Of course you do. What's your idea?"

"You don't want to have this conversation now. You're tired."

"I'll make it easy for you. You don't see my career reviving. No one but myself could. In a couple of years, I'll be giving piano lessons to bored, spotty teenagers. That's taken as read. Now go on."

"That's now how I see it at all. You have friends in opera companies all over America. Sooner or later one of them will offer you a job you can't resist, in administration. And I'll move to wherever you are."

"Peter, who would put me in a responsible position? I'm so gloomy and irritable."

"The only reason you're gloomy and irritable is that people treat you like shit. That would stop if you didn't have to go to auditions."

She sighed. "I'm going to change the subject, because you're winning this argument."

"It gives me no pleasure to win it. You have a beautiful voice, and—"

"That's all right, I can always use it to sing you 'Happy Birthday.' " Renata shut her eyes. "Sorry. Not your fault. Seeing Don's put me in a filthy mood."

"*Don*? You saw him tonight?"

"Sorry again. Didn't mean to let that slip out. Yes. He's on a business trip."

"I thought he was selling McMansions in west St. Louis County."

"He's now ascended into the higher circles of international property speculation."

"Really?"

Peter had been a newspaper reporter, and his curiosity was easily aroused. She started to recount the evening's events, and once she got going, she rather enjoyed it. She'd been alone for a long time before Peter and had forgotten how it lightened the load to tell your troubles to a sympathetic ear. By the time she finished, they were both laughing.

He said, "You want me to check it out?"

"What … Don's real estate deal? Certainly not."

"Well, do you mind if I check it out?"

"Peter, this is just Don talking big, building up some mysterioso to impress me."

"I'm sure there's some of that. But I'm wondering. What do we have in St. Louis that would interest a big-time international wheeler-dealer?"

"You're much too busy to waste your time on whatever dodgy scheme my gormless brother's got mixed up in."

"He's not gormless. Assuming I'm guessing right what gormless means. He's a crafty guy. I'd like to know what he's up to. When's he coming back here?"

"Oh, Peter, just leave him alone."

"Look, I don't have to talk to him. I can find out what I need to know on the internet."

Renata said she supposed that wouldn't do any harm, and they moved on to the endearments and goodbyes, which as usual took half an hour. But she went to bed with the feeling that she wasn't going to sleep well tonight.

3

THE NEXT MORNING'S EMAIL brought Peter Lombardo a long list of questions about an article he had written from a fact-checker at the Chicago magazine that was going to publish it. He dealt with them, and by lunchtime was free to turn his attention to Don.

Before they had met for the first time, Renata had told him, in a minatory tone, that he and Don were chalk and cheese. He had no idea what that meant. Then she introduced him to Don, and the first thing the man said was, "CLH?"

"What?"

"You have CLH on your belt. Surely it should be P Something L."

Peter glanced down. "Oh. That's the manufacturer's logo, I guess."

"No, it isn't. It's the owner's monogram. You didn't steal the belt, I hope?"

"It's from the same secondhand shop where I get all my clothes."

"It doesn't bother you, wearing someone else's monogram?"

"No."

"Extraordinary."

The discussion advanced no further, because Renata was

laughing so hard that they had to find her a chair and a glass of water. In subsequent meetings, Peter had noticed that Don was always wearing a monogram, a much subtler one than the CLH on the belt. There would be a DPR above the cuff of his shirt, or on the lining of his jacket, or woven, white on white, into his handkerchief. Don thought that the world was looking at him very closely, eager to be impressed.

St. Louis seemed like a small town to Renata. She assumed that the people she knew there were constantly bumping into each other. In fact, Peter had not seen or heard from Don in months. After making himself a peanut butter sandwich, he sat down at the computer to find out what the man was up to.

It was a straightforward if time-consuming matter of going from the web page where the city of St. Louis listed real estate sales to the page where the state of Missouri listed corporations. He learned that six corporations, chartered in Luxembourg, Panama, and other countries that respected the privacy of the rich, listed as their registered agent in Missouri Donald P. Radleigh. It was impossible to find out much else about these corporations. But they had been busy lately. In the last few months, each had bought apartment buildings in Parkdale.

Peter knew Parkdale vaguely. It was an old, rather run-down neighborhood in western St. Louis, the sort of area Don Radleigh would drive through fast, with his windows rolled up and doors locked. But he was acquiring broad swaths of it. Why?

One thing was clear already. While he might have been playing up what Renata called the mysterioso in order to impress her, Don really was handling large amounts of money, on behalf of somebody who wanted to keep his name out of the transactions.

Peter sat back from the screen, took off his glasses, and rubbed his eyes. The next step was to scout Parkdale. Then talk to Don. But Don would guess that Peter had been tipped off by his sister, and wouldn't like it. Peter would have to come up with a plausible pretext.

As he plotted his next move, it crossed his mind that he'd said something to Renata about confining his research to the internet. But he was sure he hadn't actually promised.

The afternoon was warm and sunny. November had begun, but Indian summer was lingering, as it often did in St. Louis. Peter was grateful; last month several paychecks had been delayed, and he'd been forced to sell his car to pay the rent. He was now getting around on a bicycle.

In Parkdale, he pedaled slowly up and down the streets, looking the neighborhood over. This part of St. Louis had been built up in the first two decades of the twentieth century. Parkdale would have started out as a solid but not fancy middle-class neighborhood of small apartment buildings, mostly three- and four-story walk-ups. They had held up well, being built of the excellent local brick, in shades of red ranging from rust to burgundy. Tall old trees, mostly pin oaks that retained their dead brown leaves, shaded small crabgrass lawns.

Some of the buildings were well maintained. Hedges were trimmed. Light-colored cement between bricks indicated recent tuck pointing, and the stained-glass windows in the stairwells had been preserved. But other buildings showed peeling paintwork and broken windows, and on every block were uninhabited buildings with boarded-up windows, their lower walls covered with squiggles of spray paint. Peter couldn't tell if it was gang graffiti. Here and there roofless brick walls stood amid tall weeds, and there were quite a few vacant lots.

The people he saw were mostly African American. Carpoolers were returning from work: old cars chugged up to buildings and weary people got out. Neighbors sitting on the front steps of buildings exchanged waves with them. At curbside, men conferred over the open hoods of ailing cars. Children ran around, shouting and laughing.

Earlier, Peter had found the website of the Parkdale Neighborhood Association, and their efforts were apparent. There were no abandoned cars on the streets. In most vacant lots, the trash had been picked up and the weeds cut. One lot had even been converted to a community garden, burgeoning with vegetables awaiting harvest. A single gardener was at work as Peter coasted by, a white woman who was ripping bindweed out of a sage plant with such vigor that he wondered if the plant would survive. Parkdale was trying, but as to why it had attracted the interest of a London speculator, Peter was none the wiser.

He had sent a text asking for an appointment with the president of the neighborhood association and been told to come around anytime and look for a green Ford pickup with a lot of junk in its bed. He spotted it parked in front of one of the well-tended buildings. The front door opened, and a man came out, bald on top, long gray hair at the sides pulled into a ponytail. He was not tall, but his well-perforated Grateful Dead T-shirt revealed a muscular chest and arms. Segments of heavy metal tube held together by a chain were draped over his shoulders: Laocoön with a plumber's snake, thought Peter. He was always coming up with classical allusions, which were not welcomed by the editors of the publications he wrote for.

"Mr. Rubinstein?"

"Even tenants who are behind on the rent don't call me 'Mister.' It's Joel."

"I'm Peter. We've exchanged texts."

"Oh yeah. Walk with me to the truck. I don't want to set this thing down and have to pick it up again."

"You're editor of the newsletter, right? In addition to being president of the association?"

"I do all the jobs no one else will."

"It's a good newsletter. I checked it out online. In fact, I've got an idea for it."

With a grunt, Joel shrugged off the plumber's snake, which

landed with a clatter in the truck bed. "You mentioned that in your text. Do you live in the neighborhood? I don't recall seeing you around."

"No. I'm a freelancer."

He cocked his head and gave Peter a sideways look. "You think we *pay*? Sorry, but—"

"Pay would be nice. But I'm willing to do the article just for the exposure."

"Just to get your byline in the *Parkdale Neighbor News*?" Joel leaned his elbow on the gate of the pickup truck and put his other hand on his hip. He gave Peter an appraising look. "I googled you."

"Oh?"

"You used to be on the Springfield *Journal-Register*, over in Illinois. You covered the state legislature."

"I covered everything. We were short-handed toward the end."

"Good paper. I was sorry when it went under." Joel was feeling the sun on his bald head. He pulled a battered ball cap out of his back pocket and put it on. "What I'm getting at is, you're a pro. Why do you want to write for our newsletter?"

Peter considered. Joel Rubinstein seemed to be a shrewd fellow. Honesty would be the best policy with him. "I'm interested in what's going on here. Don Radleigh's purchases, to be exact."

"Don Radleigh. Charming guy. Everybody loves his accent. But I've never been able to get him to sit still long enough to answer questions. What makes you think you can do better? You know the guy?"

"He's the brother of my girlfriend."

"Oh. So he'll be willing to give you an interview."

"On that account, no. But if I tell him I'm writing a very positive piece, to show him to the neighborhood in a favorable light, omitting anything controversial—"

"What you journalists call a blow job."

"Well, yes."

"That would be just right for the *Neighbor News*. I'll hire you to write that piece. How's three hundred dollars for six hundred words?"

"That's generous."

"Oh, I want more for my money than the article."

"More than the article?"

"See if you can find out what the guy is *really* up to."

"Deal." They shook on it. Then Peter pulled out his long, narrow reporter's notebook. "Mind being my first interview?"

"Sure. I'll give you a quote. Mr. Radleigh is welcome in the neighborhood. I hope he'll accept the invitation I sent him to join our association."

Peter nodded as he scrawled shorthand. "How long have you been in the neighborhood, Joel?"

"I grew up in an apartment in that building over there. My father owned it. That's the way it was back then, a working stiff would save enough to buy a building, then live in one apartment and rent out the rest. Made for a nice neighborhood, mostly Jews but lots of *goyim*, too. Everybody got along. Then came the sixties. A few blacks moved in and everybody panicked. But my dad didn't want to up stakes. Buildings fell in his lap 'cause no one else wanted them. When I got back from Vietnam, I started working for him."

"You formed an association to bring the neighborhood back."

"In the eighties. By then, I owned so many buildings that self-preservation required it. I've got a dozen or so other landlords in the association. People who are on board with me, I mean. We're trying a lot of community-building measures—"

"I noticed the garden. How's it going?"

"Off the record?"

"You're the boss." Peter put away his notebook.

"The neighborhood has improved. A little. But I can't say it's turned the corner. St. Louis isn't Austin or Seattle. We don't have droves of young people rushing in, looking for somewhere, anywhere, to live. Neighborhoods in a growing city can come back in a couple of years. Takes a lot longer in St. Louis. Several times I've thought, we're about to turn the corner. I can hand responsibility for my one hundred and fifty-seven toilets over to someone else and retire. But then there was a change in the tax law that made apartment buildings a less attractive investment, or a murder in the neighborhood that got too much media attention, and back we slid."

"Don Radleigh could be a boon to you."

"Well, yeah. He's bought up a lot of buildings very quickly. Frankly, though, the guy makes me nervous. He's a mystery to me. The kind of investors who ordinarily buy buildings in Parkdale, they come to me for help. They need bank loans. Government grants. It's a slow process. But Radleigh? He just writes a check. I sure wish I knew where his money comes from."

"I'll do my best to find out."

4

THAT EVENING, PETER CALLED Don's cellphone. He picked up at once: he was at O'Hare Airport, homebound from London, and thoroughly befuddled by jet lag and in-flight liquor. He said he would call back tomorrow.

He didn't, and was unresponsive to Peter's messages. The day ended with no appointment made. Peter was unfazed. This was typical Don. The next morning, he mounted his bike and headed back to Parkdale.

Reaching the neighborhood, he pedaled up and down its grid of streets. Don had a conspicuous car, an old maroon Jaguar sedan. It was not long before he spotted it, parked by the curb with its trunk open. Don was nearby, hammering a "For Rent" sign into the front yard of a building. He was wearing jeans, but they were expensive designer jeans, and his denim work shirt had sharp creases and probably a monogram, if you looked closely enough. It was a sunny day but he had no cap. Vain of his thick blond hair, he never wore hats. A pair of sunglasses rode the yellow waves atop his head. When Peter called his name, he advanced with a puzzled expression.

"Peter? What brings you down here?"

"We talked on the phone, remember?"

"No, sorry. Head like a sieve these days. What did we talk about?"

Don's bad memory provided his friends and acquaintances with much amusement. It also provided Don with a pretext for stalling or getting out of commitments. Peter asked, "Do you know the *Parkdale Neighbor News*?"

"That rag. I'm always picking them up from the yards of my buildings. Nobody reads it."

"They'll read the next one. It's going to carry an interview of you. By me."

He waited for the reaction. But if it occurred to Don that Renata had sent Peter, he did not let on. "Oh. You got an assignment from that Rosenthal fellow?"

"Joel Rubinstein."

"Well, I hate to cost you a paycheck, Peter. I know you're unemployed."

"I'm freelance."

"Right. But I'm afraid I haven't the time to sit for an interview."

"Fine. Go about your business. I'll tag along. It'll make for a better story."

"What's your slant?"

"A day in the life of a socially responsible, community-building landlord."

Don lowered his sunglasses to his nose. Behind them, he made unhurried calculations. Finally he said, "All right. Lock your bike to yonder lamppost."

Peter did so. As he got in the Jaguar next to Don, he was thinking that this had been a bit too easy.

"First off," Don said, "you can't use the word 'landlord' in the article."

"I can't?"

"Sounds so medieval. As if I'm going to be exercising *le droit du seigneur*. The modern term is property owner. And I am the very model of a modern property owner." He began whistling the Gilbert and Sullivan tune as the Jaguar pulled away from the curb. After the initial hesitation, he seemed to be looking forward to the interview.

"How many buildings do you own in the area at present?"

Don worked his eyebrows, looking straight ahead. "A lot."

"But how many?"

"Let's leave it at that, shall we?"

"Don, anybody who's willing to do some internet research can find out that you own eighty-nine buildings."

"Why ask me, if you already know?"

"How come you've bought so many buildings, so quickly?"

"Because I have boundless faith in the future of Parkdale." He glanced at the blank page of Peter's notebook, lying on his thigh. "Come on, start writing. Don't you know a quote when you hear one?"

Peter obeyed. Don continued, "We're well located. We have excellent housing stock. Just blow off the dust and these buildings will shine. Parkdale was a flourishing neighborhood once and will be again."

"A lot of St. Louis neighborhoods were flourishing once and are borderline slums now. What's different about Parkdale?"

"It has Joel Rubinstein and his friends in the association. And now it has me. You know, I was making a packet selling houses in the suburbs. But I wanted to do something that would make a difference. So I went looking for a neighborhood to rehab, and chose Parkdale."

"*You* chose Parkdale?"

"That's what I said. Am I going too fast for you?"

It was the London moneyman who had chosen Parkdale, but Peter couldn't say so without bringing up Renata. He continued writing.

"This'll be the easiest article you've ever written," Don said.

They turned onto Parkdale's main drag and parked. Don led the way to a bare shop front. The door was open and he called out, "Ethan!"

A wiry young man advanced from the dim interior, blinking

at them. He had close-cropped dark hair and a ring through his left nostril. "Peter, this is my new tenant Ethan, proprietor of what will soon be the well-known ice cream emporium Cold Comfort. Peter is a journalist who's profiling me. How's it going?"

"There was a shooting last night."

"Yes. Dreadful business. LaToya Robinson is her name. I reached her at Granger Hospital and you'll be happy to hear she's on the mend."

"It happened practically in front of this store. If I'd been here, I coulda got shot, too."

"If you'd been here, and open for business, it wouldn't have happened, because there would have been lights and people. That's how we're going to drive crime off this street."

"Channel Five News called. They want to do a story. Which will scare people off."

"Refer them to me. I've an idea for an afterschool program I want to talk about, get the kids off the streets and out of trouble. Keep your pecker up, young Ethan, customers are coming."

Don clapped him on the shoulder and turned away, ignoring Ethan's plaintive, "They better. My kitchen cost as much as a car. A *nice* car."

Peter followed Don out, scrawling shorthand. "Uh, Don? I love your act, but aren't you overdoing it?"

"Hmm?"

"Suppose I call LaToya Robinson?"

"Suppose you do?"

"And find out you never spoke to her?"

"Then you'll have wasted your time. Because you wouldn't be able to use that in a *Neighbor News* story."

Next door, a man was standing on the sidewalk with hands on hips, frowning. He was a tall, narrow-shouldered, big-bellied man with a moustache and bags under his eyes.

"Herb, how are you?" Don said.

"The zoning board is giving me grief about my sign." He

pointed upward, at the black skeleton of an unlighted electric sign, outlining a jowly pig, grinning in anticipation of being killed and devoured. "Too large for a sign that's perpendicular to the building, they say."

"I'm afraid that's true. You'll have to install it flat."

"But nobody'll see it. Cars whiz by at forty."

"They'll slow down when we widen the sidewalks and put in landscaped medians."

"When's that gonna be?"

Don laid a hand on Herb's shoulder, a gesture the other man didn't seem to welcome, and turned him to look at the other side of the street.

"This whole block will be transformed. There's a farmer's market coming to that vacant lot, locally sourced organic produce only, of course. Where the muffler shop is now, there'll be an artisanal bakery. The pawn shop's due to be replaced by a micro brew pub, and as soon as I get the chop suey joint out, a high-end tattoo emporium is taking its place."

Herb looked sideways at Don, stroking his moustache doubtfully. "I sure hope things improve," he said. "You know how much it's costing me to rent my smoker?"

"Buy it," Don said. "You'll save money in the long run. You're going to be here for years."

They got back in the Jag and turned onto a residential street. Peter asked, "Have you inked the deal with this artisanal tattoo emporium?"

"It's the bakery that's artisanal; the tattoo parlor is high-end. Do try to get this right."

Abruptly he stopped and got out of the car, leaving the engine running. Peter watched him use his phone to take a picture of a "Kitty Lost" sign taped to a telephone pole. Returning, he handed the phone to Peter. "Help me keep an eye out for this cat."

"Oookay," sighed Peter. "You spend a lot of time looking for lost cats?"

"Sometimes I'm able to find them. Hang on … if I find this one, you can take a picture of me returning it to the tearful owner. Front page of the *Neighbor News*!"

They were coming up on the vacant lot that held the community garden, and Don said he had to pop in. Gardeners of various ages and hues were spreading woodchips in the paths between the raised beds. A woman, the one Peter had seen yesterday, came toward them. She was wearing a T-shirt that said, "People who think they can run the world should start with a small garden." Her long, fair hair was bound in a loose kerchief. Her sturdy physique and stern expression, and the hose looped over her shoulder like a belt of machine-gun ammunition, made Peter think of a Soviet poster. She might have been a comrade leaving her crops to fight the Nazi tanks.

"Don! Jill and Bob had their tomato plants stripped bare last night."

"How wretched for them. After all their work."

"Somebody needs to explain to these jerks that 'community garden' doesn't mean just anybody can harvest vegetables."

"I'll call the police. Ask them to swing by more often. How's the workday going otherwise?"

"Turnout could be better. Especially among the males. You know, I was really happy when so many men joined the garden."

Don raised his eyebrows. "Hannah! You actually had hopes for our sex?"

"Males have upper-body strength, which is useful in garden work. Now, if only they had enough lower-body strength to move their asses out of their chairs …."

"Pack of damned layabouts, eh? Well, you'll motivate 'em."

He leaned down to put his arms around her and kiss her on the mouth. She reciprocated with enthusiasm. *Hmm!* thought Peter. Was this part of the act, too?

"Peter, this is Hannah Mertz, Queen-Empress of the

Community Garden. And Hannah, this is Peter, who's writing about me for the *Neighbor News*."

She fixed him with a level gaze. "Be sure to write that Don is the best friend the community garden has."

"Naturally." Peter flipped a page and started scrawling. "Please spell your last name for me."

After Don accepted an invitation to dinner at Hannah's, he and Peter got back in the Jaguar. Its old engine was not appreciating all this stop and go, and Don had to manipulate the manual choke to get it going again.

"Hannah's one of my tenants," he explained as they drove away. "When she moved to Parkdale, she was a bird with a wing down. She'd been married to a student at Adams U. She supported him through business school, and once he had his MBA he divorced her and married a classmate. Right bastard, if you ask me. But it's funny, she never says a word against him."

"Just says all men are bastards. Meaning her ex couldn't help it. She doesn't want to have to hate him personally."

Don laughed. "Bollocks! You just met her. What could you know? Honestly, you and my sister are two peas in a pod. She's always coming out with blazing insights like that."

They drove a block in silence.

"Mind you," Don resumed, "maybe you're on to something. For all the anti-man talk, she's dead easy on me. Never nags me about doing the dishes or lowering the toilet seat. Anyway, I suggested Hannah take over the garden, which was languishing. She's done wonderful things for it. And vice versa. Oh, hello, there are the Hrebecs. My newest tenants. Just moving in, in fact."

He pulled to the curb behind a U-Haul trailer attached to a car. A wizened couple were standing beside the car. Its interior was packed to the roof with boxes. Don said in an undertone, "They came here as refugees from the Bosnian war. Years ago, but they told me every time they pack up and move, it stirs bad memories. They do look a bit down in the mouth. Let me see if I can cheer them up."

The old couple, it developed, were not experiencing post-traumatic stress but simple fatigue. They had loaded the furniture themselves and couldn't face unloading it.

"And more's the pity, it's a third floor," said Don. "Well, let us help with the heaviest things. You don't mind, Peter?"

"C'mon, Don. Landlords don't help tenants move in."

"Property owners do. Let's start with the sofa. Grab the back end."

It took two hours. The Hrebecs were so courtly and grateful that Peter could not be annoyed with them. He was annoyed with Don, who took a lot of cellphone calls, absenting himself from every third or fourth trip up the stairs. Peter was sweaty, sore, and exhausted when he sank back into the Jag's leather seat. Don invited him home for a beer, saying it was the least he could do. Peter could only agree.

It was five thirty, and already darkness was falling, a reminder that despite the warm temperatures, autumn was far along. Don switched on his headlights. He drove a few blocks and turned into an alley.

"You live in the neighborhood?"

"Right here."

He pointed at a small brick apartment house, typical of Parkdale. They turned into an alley. A row of garages sat behind the building. Don pulled into one and stopped short. A man was lying on flattened boxes against the far wall. He put up a hand to shield his eyes. Don leaned out the window and said, "Sorry, Wayne. I'm going to have to ask you to get out of the way while I pull in. For your safety."

Wayne was encumbered with so many layers of clothes that he looked like the Michelin Man. He lumbered to his feet and backed against the wall. His gray hair was lank and disorderly. He watched in silence, eyes wide, as the Jaguar pulled in. Still without a word, he scrambled back to his bed under its front bumper.

As they got out, Peter noticed the line of beer cans and empty Everclear bottles along the wall. He said, "Does Wayne sleep in your garage often?"

"When it's chilly or rainy. One can't converse with him. It makes him nervous. But he's very considerate about his toileting, so I don't call the police."

"Another great touch for the article," said Peter ironically.

Again, Don topped him. "Be sure to add that I'm worried about him now winter's coming. I'm going to have to persuade him to go to a shelter."

They climbed the fire escape at the back of the building to the second floor and went in. When they were settled in the comfortable living room with bottles of Schlafly IPA in hand, Peter looked Don in the eye and said, "Where's your financing coming from?"

"People I've talked to about the bright future of Parkdale."

"How many backers do you have?" According to Renata, there was only one.

"Several. I'm quite persuasive."

"Who are they?"

"I've just told you."

"What are their names?"

"Rather slow on the uptake, aren't you, old son? That's all you get."

Peter snapped his notebook closed and put it away. "If we go off the record, will you be honest with me?"

Don smiled triumphantly, and Peter realized that this was the point he'd been driving Peter to all day. Don said, "If you'll be honest with me."

"All right."

"What really brought you to Parkdale?"

"Renata told me you were buying property in St. Louis. It

was my idea to pursue it, so don't blame her. The rest I got off the internet."

"I figured it was something like that."

"Your turn. This isn't the real Don Radleigh I just spent the day with. What are you up to?"

"Actually, it is." Seeing Peter's expression, Don held up a placating hand. "I won't deny I was having a bit of fun with you. But I *have* changed."

"Quite a change. You've never shown a scintilla of social conscience."

"After what I went through last spring—"

"You mean, when your sister got you out of jail?"

Don blinked and started again. Peter had never heard him acknowledge that Renata had saved him. "After the ordeal I went through, I began to question my values. The way I'd lived my life up to then. Does the name John Profumo ring a bell?"

"Tory cabinet minister in the '60s. Caught sharing a call girl with a Soviet diplomat. Resigned in disgrace."

"Got it in one. I forgot what a history boffin you are. Do you know what he did after he resigned? The very next day, he went to a homeless shelter in East London and asked if he could make himself useful. They gave him a broom and he started sweeping. Spent the rest of his life there, ending up as president of the charity."

"You're saying you're like Profumo?"

"I was caught in a sex scandal and resigned in disgrace, so yes. I got myself a real estate license and started selling houses in the suburbs. But something kept gnawing at me. I thought, anyone can do this. I'll try to do something harder. I'll try to do good."

"Don, Joel and his friends have been trying to bring Parkdale back for thirty years."

"Well, now I'm in it with them. For as long as it takes."

5

INSTEAD OF GOING HOME, Peter cycled over the highway to the fashionable neighborhood called the Central West End, where he went to the local branch of the public library, borrowed a laptop, and set to work. He hoped to get the article done before his beer buzz wore off. As Don had promised, it would be a very easy article to write, provided Peter did not dwell on the fact that he didn't believe any of it. He was most suspicious of the "sincere" part at the end.

He felt sheepish about admitting to Renata how far he'd gone with his inquiries. He was relieved it was too late to call her. She would be sound asleep after a long day of rushing around London doing auditions.

Rushing around London. Peter had never been there—he had crossed an ocean only to visit Hawaii, left the country only to see Mexico—but he had majored in English literature, so he imagined Renata rushing around Charles Dickens' London. Fighting her way through ankle-deep mud and fog and rain, jostled by Cockneys, pick-pocketed by street urchins, elbowed into the gutter by rich, mean lawyers. Lost among crowds of people who didn't know how special she was. If only somebody would give her a job today.

Half his mind occupied by such musings, he knocked the

article off and called Joel Rubinstein. As he was mentally composing his message, Joel picked up. He invited Peter to bring the article right over, and gave an address.

It was a chilly night with a scent of impending rain. The streets of Parkdale were deserted, except for cars going very fast and playing rap very loud. Some floated on eerie purple light. Peter's destination turned out to be a four-story apartment building on an intersection a block up from the main drag. He locked his bike to a fence and rang the bell. Over the intercom, Joel told him to climb to the top floor.

Joel was waiting to wave him in. The lights were off in the sparsely furnished apartment. A man was standing at each window, looking down through binoculars. A video camera stood on a tripod in the middle of the floor.

"Some of my fellow landlords in the neighborhood association," Joel explained. "We're looking for drug dealers."

"The streets are pretty empty."

"Oh, the usual action is going on. You just have to know where to look."

"You've been doing this for a long time?"

"Dealer vigil is a regular activity. We use a different apartment every week. We all have plenty of empty ones. When we see a deal going down, we videotape it. When we have enough tapes, I take 'em to the city prosecutor. Try to persuade him to encourage the police to arrest a few dealers."

"They're reluctant? Are they being paid off?"

"Nah. Just can't be bothered. The jails are full of dealers already."

There was a distraction as one of the men at a window called for the camera. Peter moved to the window to see a car pulling to the curb and a thin, hooded figure emerging from the shadows to lean into its window. But drugs and money had changed hands and the car pulled away before the camera could be set up.

"Car buys are no loss," said Joel with a shrug. "The prosecutor always says the driver was just asking for directions. Want to show me what you've got, Peter?"

They went into a windowless kitchen, where Joel turned on the overhead light. Peter noticed the new fridge and stove and the granite counter. "This is nicer than my apartment," he said.

"You're welcome to it. Doesn't do me much good having nice apartments, if people have to walk by drug dealers and burned-out buildings to get to them."

Peter laid a print-out of the article on the counter. Joel put on his glasses and read it carefully. "The *Neighbor News* will be delighted to publish this," he pronounced.

"Thanks."

"What else did you find out?"

Peter said miserably, "Nothing."

"He just bullshitted you?"

"Yep."

Joel folded his bare, muscular arms and gave Peter a hard stare. "In that case, I'll just have to cut your pay."

"Fair enough."

"That's not the answer I was looking for."

Peter gave him a questioning look.

"How about this. I'll pay you the full amount, and you keep digging."

"I don't know what else I can do."

Joel pulled two stools from under the counter. Sitting on one, he offered the other to Peter. "This Radleigh guy has me worried. Has us all worried. He's been buying too many buildings, too quickly. I can think of only two explanations."

"What are they?"

"Radleigh and his backers just aren't very smart. They don't realize how much it costs to rehab buildings, especially the really beat-up ones he's buying. They don't know how low rents are around here. The profit margins are paper-thin. They're gonna lose their money."

"Which will be bad for Parkdale."

"The other possibility would be worse. You know what Section 8 housing is?"

"Vaguely."

"The feds pay most or all the rent for poor people. Good idea, but there's a problem. Since the rent's guaranteed, landlords don't bother to screen tenants. They let sleazy people in who trash the places. They deteriorate until no one's willing to live in them anymore. In this neighborhood, we have too many empty buildings already. And Radleigh is buying them up."

"So you think he's going to spend the bare minimum to bring them up to code, then rent them to sleazebags and cash the government checks."

"A landlord can make money that way. For a while."

"But the neighborhood goes downhill fast."

"If Radleigh's working for a slumlord, we're fucked. So we'd be very grateful for any information you could provide."

Peter thought it over and said, "I'll see what I can do."

6

In London the days were growing noticeably shorter. Dawn was coming later, and getting up was harder. Renata was luxuriating guiltily in bed when her mobile pinged. It was a text message from Peter, asking her to turn on Skype. She booted up her laptop, which told her that it was two a.m. in St. Louis. Something had to be wrong. She drummed her fingers nervously while waiting for the computer to find the satellite.

At last Peter came up on the screen, leaning on an elbow and hanging his head. He looked both stubborn and contrite, the way he'd looked when she took him to *Der Rosenkavalier,* and he told her at the interval that wild horses couldn't drag him back in for Act II.

He said, "Has Don called to complain about me?"

"What? No, I haven't heard from him at all. What would he be complaining about?"

"My prying into his affairs."

"He *knows?* But you said you were only going to look on the internet."

"What I found there was disturbing enough that I had to go on."

"Oh, lord. Is Don in trouble?"

"No. The Parkdale landlords are."

"What's Parkdale?"

He explained. She was a bit annoyed with him for breaking his promise to her to leave Don alone. But it seemed that Don had already punished him for it. The Skype page had a small window that showed her own face, and she was struggling to hide her amusement as Peter recounted how Don had toyed with him. Once he got into his talk with Joel Rubinstein, she no longer felt like laughing.

She said, "I can see you've taken a liking to this Joel bloke."

"He and his fellow landlords spend their days patching the wounds of these old buildings with their own hands, their evenings keeping drug dealer vigil, and their nights worrying about their bank loans. And the neighborhood is balanced on a knife edge."

"Sounds like you're writing the story in your head already."

"I've already turned in the story."

"And you hate every word of it. I am sorry my brother was so exasperating to you."

"Not your fault."

"Do you really think Don's working for a slumlord?"

"I have my doubts about Joel's theory."

"You don't think Don could sink so low?"

"Sure he could. But I don't think his boss would bother. A London billionaire, setting up as a St. Louis slumlord? There can't be enough profit in it to justify his trouble. No, this is something bigger. But I can't imagine what."

"Possibly even Don doesn't know what his boss has planned."

"What?"

"Well, maybe he's being used. Why are you staring at me like that, Peter? Is there a reception problem or something?"

"No. I can't believe what you just said. You actually think he believes he's going to save the neighborhood?"

"I admit the Profumo bit touched me."

"It was bullshit."

An equally curt retort leapt to her lips, but she kept them

clamped tight. She and Peter had never had an all-out row. They were bound to someday, but she'd resolved it was not going to be about her brother. She asked a neutral question. "What about the gardener? Do you think she's really his girlfriend?"

"I think she thinks she is. But Don in love with a woman who has dirt under her fingernails?"

"Not his usual form."

"But you think he's changed."

"He has," Renata said, "in some ways. He's much less nasty to me. He doesn't say those things he used to say, like you're an aging journeyman, or you're past your sell-by date."

"What a prince. Maybe someday he'll manage to thank you for getting him out of jail."

Her temper threatened to flare again. This was her brother he was talking about. Time for another neutral question. "What are you planning to do next?"

"Follow him."

"Peter, you don't know how to follow people."

"As a matter of fact, I do. When I was on the paper, one of the investigative reporters had me following a bagman for a corrupt politician. I got pictures of him collecting bribes. After the story ran, he went to prison and the politician was kicked out of office."

"And what are you hoping to do to my brother?"

It brought Peter up short. "This is not personal, Renata."

"It is to me. Naturally, I feel loyal toward him."

"Why?"

A reporter to the core, Peter was fond of the blunt question. She said, "He wasn't always like this. I have fond memories from when we were children."

"Like what?"

"Well … there was a time … when I was eight, I believe, and Don was five. We shared a bedroom. Our flat was on a high floor of a tower block. There was a terrific storm. The thunder was coming simultaneous with the lightning, and I was just old enough to know that meant the storm was right on top of us. I thought a bolt of lightning was going to blast through the window and hit me. Don heard me whimpering. He asked if I wanted to come in with him. I hesitated, because I was the big sister. But in the end I did. I still remember how warm and safe I felt under the duvet with him. It makes up for a lot of irritating behavior."

"I can understand that, I guess. When did he begin to develop into the Don of today?"

"Things changed before we got much older. It's hard to believe now, but people made a terrific fuss over me when I was a young pianist. Then a young singer. Our parents were always driving me to competitions. Don was still too young to be left home alone, and of course he was bored frantic. And if I won, the local newspaper would send a photographer 'round. It was hard on Don."

Peter smiled. "So Don turning out the way he did is your fault. He's your responsibility through life."

"No, of course not. I'll be quite happy to let the chips fall as they may in Parkdale, and I wish you would, too." She glanced at her face in the little window. Her eyes were widening dangerously. Her nostrils were actually flaring. Any more mockery from Peter and she'd lose her temper.

But he backed off. Literally. He leaned away from the screen and dropped his gaze. He was sensitive to her feelings, in a way none of her previous boyfriends had been. In fact, she used to wonder if men went in for sensitivity at all.

He said, "Renata, let's say for the sake of argument—"

"I don't want to do argument any favors. I want to slam the door in its face."

"So do I. But let's say you're right about Don. He wants to do good in Parkdale. This London billionaire has other plans and is using him. You really want to let the chips fall?"

She thought it over and sighed. "No, I suppose not. All right, do your Philip Marlowe routine. But be careful."

7

RENATA HAD A BUSY day ahead. After her usual breakfast of an orange, a banana, and a cup of tea, she fell in with the rush-hour crowd headed downhill to Ladbroke Grove Station. Her brain was busy.

No wonder Peter found it hard to understand her contradictory feelings about Don, how he annoyed her when they were together, worried her when they were not. The Lombardos were a big, robust Italian-American family, even if some of their old-country traits, like love of opera, had faded.

He had three siblings. All his parents and grandparents were alive. He had uncles and aunts, nieces and nephews, cousins and in-laws. In the usual American fashion, they were spread across their vast country, from Montana to Florida, and seldom got together, but Facebook and phone calls regularly brought news of weddings, decisions to move in together, and births. The Lombardos were being fruitful and multiplying.

The Radleighs were dwindling. In fact, they were an endangered species.

Once they'd been a prolific and energetic Victorian family. Renata had visited country churchyards where their headstones stood in rows, driven through suburbs they had laid out and named the streets for themselves and their in-laws, rented storage lockers for their diaries and letters home from the colonies. Radleighs had been quite keen on serving the Empire, and two world wars had taken a shocking toll on the men. The family was knocked off balance. Temperance and common sense deserted the Radleighs, along with luck.

Growing up, Renata had noticed that where other children had relatives, she had stories. The grandfather who embezzled a small fortune from his firm and simply disappeared. The uncle who got drunk and drove his Jaguar off the Hammersmith Flyover. The cousin who was murdered because of a gambling debt. The aunt, who after a scandalous divorce moved to Australia and never sent back so much as a picture postcard.

Renata's father had died when she was in her twenties. After pursuing a clandestine affair with his dentist's secretary for twelve years, he had finally run away with her. Their plane, bound for the Costa del Sol, had crashed in France. Three years later her mother, who had taught maths at a comprehensive all her life and hated it, dropped dead of a brain aneurysm in front of her horrified class.

Renata's therapist had told her that, in his professional opinion, her anxious, gloomy disposition was not neurosis. It was justified.

Now, aside from a great-aunt she visited in the nursing home and a couple of cousins with whom she exchanged Christmas cards, she had no one but her brother. His feckless, antic, self-deluding behavior constantly reminded her of all the dead Radleighs. She felt she owed it to their ghosts to pull him back from the brink.

If possible. Why did the fool have to get Peter's back up, and enjoy doing it so much? Don took other people too lightly. It had cost him dearly all his life. As a boy, he used to come home from school battered and bruised, having taunted a classmate too long and too cleverly. As a teenager, he had occasioned several mortifying phone calls to their parents, from the parents of girls who had not welcomed his attentions as much as he'd thought they had.

Now he had ignited the fire in Peter's belly. He'd become the crusading reporter, standing up for the little guy against a malefactor of great wealth. The fact that he no longer had a newspaper to write for had slipped his mind.

Once the planet revolved a bit more and daylight came to the Midwest, Renata's boyfriend was going to start "tailing" her brother. This was bound to turn out badly.

She came out of her reverie to find that, on autopilot. she had made her way to the station, through the ticket gate, and down the escalator to the platform. The train swooshed in, raising a warm wind that lifted the litter. As usual, not enough people alighted, and too many boarded. She resigned herself to standing.

Then a blond boy in a blue school blazer rose and offered her his seat. She thanked him and took it, with the usual mixed feelings. She was glad chivalry wasn't quite dead in Albion, but why *her?* Did she look that old, or that woebegone?

She'd resolved that if she got a seat, she would spend the ride studying her solo. She opened the bag and took out the score of the Haydn High Mass she was on the way to rehearse at the Brompton Oratory. But it was simply not on. She stared blindly at the notes while her mind churned away.

Peter was right. If Don meant well but his boss did not, trouble lay ahead. Much depended on the sort of person this billionaire speculator turned out to be. It was maddening that she had been in the same room with him on Saturday night. Had seen his face, if only in the unfocused way she saw any of the faces of the audience she was performing to. But he had slipped irrevocably away.

The next moment she said to herself, *Why irrevocably?* She knew Maestro Vladimir Grinevich, and Grinevich knew Don's boss. Maestro would tell her his name. Then she could find out if he was lying to Don and manipulating him. She could warn

Don to bail out before he did something criminal and wound up in jail. Again.

It would be easy to get in touch with Maestro. He was in rehearsal at Covent Garden. She could go there now. It would mean missing her own rehearsal, but she'd just have to lump it. When the train reached Euston Station, she alighted and headed for the Piccadilly Line.

The narrow lanes of Covent Garden were not as packed with tourists as usual, for it was a wet, cold day. She had a clear view of the big white opera house with its red awnings and row of Corinthian columns supporting a noble pediment. She walked by it, noting the posters for Maestro's new *Eugene Onegin* opening tomorrow, and turned the corner. A wet gust of wind hit her full in the face. She pulled down her hat brim and wiped her eyes. At the stage door, Maestro's car, an especially hideous and hulking American SUV, was waiting. So were the demonstrators.

Vladimir Grinevich was popular in the West, applauded as he mounted podiums from Berlin to Los Angeles. But he insisted on hanging on to his primary job as music director of the Maryansky in St. Petersburg, which meant publicly supporting Putin. So wherever Maestro went, he was pursued by small but bitterly determined groups of demonstrators, who reminded him of Putin's latest outrage, and of Grinevich's own statements of patriotism and personal loyalty.

This lot looked pretty miserable, hunched in their soaked anoraks, holding signs hooded with protective plastic bags. But they had an air of anticipation. The car had been summoned, which meant that rehearsal was about to break and Grinevich would soon appear.

At the desk inside the stage door they knew Renata, but extra-tight security was in effect when Grinevich was in the house, and she had to pass through a metal detector. After she was judged to be harmless, she walked down narrow backstage corridors and emerged in the famous auditorium. Its rows of red seats ascending steeply heavenward looked even plusher when they were empty.

Wave upon wave of Tchaikovsky at his most anguished surged and crashed onstage as Onegin pleaded and Tatiana resisted. Renata took a seat down front and watched Grinevich at work.

He was one of those conductors who wanted the audience to be in no doubt about who was in charge. He did not use a baton, so he could have both hands free. He pointed at a singer when it was her turn to sing, a mannerism that annoyed Renata, who knew her cue perfectly well, thank you. To the various sections of the orchestra, he made gestures as if clawing the music out of them. Throughout a performance, he would teeter on tiptoe, crouching, lurching. Some day he would fall off the podium and many musicians would rejoice.

Gymnastics indicative of Russian soulfulness accompanied the final crescendo. Silence fell, but only for a moment. Then Grinevich released Tatiana and held Onegin back. Renata knew why. In an earlier part of the scene he had been just a fraction of a beat behind the orchestra, and Grinevich, whose musicianship was impeccable, had noticed. With Grinevich it wasn't enough to hit the note, you had to hit the center of the note. A perfectionist herself, Renata respected him for that. He made Onegin repeat the passage, which the baritone did resentfully, singing of love and despair while standing with his hands in his pockets as if waiting for a bus. Satisfied, Grinevich released everyone.

He stepped down from the podium, looking like a boxer who has won on points. His cheeks were flushed above his gray beard, his forehead beaded with sweat. Damp ringlets of graying dark hair were plastered to his neck and ears. He took a deep breath and buried his face in a towel.

When he lifted it, he saw Renata and smiled. Whatever his political sins and personal quirks, he had done her a few good turns over the years and always remembered her name. He waved off a worried-looking young man who was holding out a phone to him and sat beside her.

"Morning, Maestro. It seems to be going well," she said.

"We open tomorrow. Too soon. This part is all right, but Act One has problems."

"Olga?"

He nodded. "The mezzo cannot sing "*Akh* Tanya, Tanya." I mean, she can hit the notes, but the character has eluded her. I wish I had you in the part, Renata."

It was an indiscreet remark, but Renata wasn't complaining. For the next three quarters of a minute, Maestro talked knowledgably and appreciatively of her performance of "*Akh,* Tanya, Tanya" on Saturday night at his house. Every word engraved itself in her memory. At discouraging moments over the next few years, she would recall them.

He toweled his face again and said, "Anyway, thank you for coming and giving us that lovely number. Sorry about the audience."

"They were your neighbors?"

"Mostly." He made one of his expressive Russian gestures, hunching his shoulders and turning down his lower lip. "London is getting as bad as Moscow. And it's the same people making it that way. My neighborhood is going downhill."

It was a curious thing to say about Billionaires' Row. She raised her eyebrows.

"My so-called neighbor two doors down? I've never met the man. He's in Monaco. He only bought the house as a way of laundering money. Has no plan of living there. Doesn't maintain the place. It can fall down for all he cares. He can still sell the land for more than he paid."

Now she remembered reading about the derelict houses of Billionaires' Row, which were the cause of considerable indignation among Londoners like herself, living four to a basement flat. She asked, "Did you know most of the people at the party?"

He shook his head. "My staff made up the guest list. The only criterion was having a lot of money and maybe being willing to donate some to the Fidelio Foundation."

"Maestro, I was wondering if I could see that list."

He did not reply at once. Raising his arm, he ran a hand through his hair. His bare forearm had left a sweat stain on the armrest. She wondered fleetingly if tonight's patron would be indignant to find a stain on his three-hundred-pound seat. He might be consoled if he knew it was Grinevich's sweat.

"Why do you want to see it?" he asked.

"Well … this is going to sound odd. I unexpectedly met my brother that night. And he told me he'd got me the job by asking his boss to put in a good word for me with you. I was just wondering—"

"Not true. My staff picked the singers. I have no time for things like that." Realizing this sounded a bit graceless, he recovered handsomely. "If I was doing it, I wouldn't have needed a hint to invite *you*."

"Thanks. Can I get a look at this list?"

Grinevich gave signs of Russian indecision, wagging his head and stretching his full, ruddy lips this way and that. "Maybe best not, Renata. These people are touchy about their privacy."

"Well … all right. In fact, I don't need to see the whole list. I just want to see who brought my brother, Don Radleigh."

Grinevich glanced at his aide, who was still waiting tensely a few feet away, the mobile clutched to his breast. Somebody important and impatient was probably on the other end. "Why do you want to know this man's name?"

"Um … again, this is going to sound odd. Don's acting as agent for this man in a big land deal in America. I'm curious about him."

"Why don't you ask Don?"

"I have. He won't tell me."

Another moment's hesitation, and Maestro turned to her and smiled. Grinevich's charming smile was famous in the opera world. It was what he gave you when you weren't going to get anything else.

"Peculiar business, Renata. I would feel uncomfortable getting involved."

Heaving his bulk out of the chair, he went to his assistant, who held out the mobile. As Grinevich took it, other people who had been loitering around the stage approached. Soon there was a solid ring around him. Renata gave up.

Outside the rain had stopped, but the overcast had not thinned. She walked slowly toward the station, feeling dissatisfied with herself. She should have thought this through beforehand. Only now did she realize she'd been hoping that Grinevich would say he knew Don's boss and the man simply wasn't the sort to set up as a transatlantic slumlord. Renata could read all about him in the *Economist* or the *Financial Times* and put her mind a rest.

Instead, what Grinevich had to say about his neighbors only gave her more cause for worry. Maybe Peter's suspicions were justified. He himself had no doubts about that. In a couple of hours, he would wake up, put on his mackintosh and false mustache—or whatever—and begin following Don. No matter what Peter said about his expertise, she felt certain that Don would twig and the escapade would end with her lover and her brother brawling in the street.

She'd skipped rehearsal for nothing. Even if it was just a church performance, Renata felt guilty. The last time she'd missed a rehearsal—three years ago—she'd been down with pneumonia. She simply had to do something productive with the free morning she had given herself.

She paused to call and deliver a plausible lie about why she had missed the rehearsal. A friend who had been robbed was distraught. She would do whatever was necessary to atone.

By the time she stepped through the gate at Covent Garden

Station, she had worked out a plan. She'd had dealings with Grinevich's staff before. Maestro's professional life was as chaotic as his personal one. His staffers spent their days dealing with one cock-up after another. They were permanently frazzled. If she caught one of them at a distracted moment and asked nicely, the girl might just hand her the guest list.

8

On Saturday, she had arrived after dark, in a taxi full of singers, and hadn't got much of a look at London's most expensive street. Arriving now after a long walk from Hampstead station—proximity to the Tube obviously wasn't something billionaires looked for in a residence—she strolled along it slowly and found it an odd sort of place.

It didn't feel spacious. The lots were enormous by London standards, but the houses were, too. Bounded on all sides by high walls or fences, they looked pent up. And jarringly diverse. Unlike the rich of the past, who'd had to live in Belgravia in identical attached houses, the rich of the present were free to indulge their architectural whims. She walked by Palladian colonnades next to Queen Anne turrets next to Dutch gables. As Maestro had said, she passed several derelict mansions, with "no trespassing" signs on their chained and padlocked gates.

Grinevich's house was in eighteenth-century style. It had no street number but a name, on a placard attached to the black, cast-iron fence. It was called Whitecroft. The house certainly was white. It looked the way Buckingham Palace would have looked, if the palace had been built yesterday.

She approached the high gates and the security kiosk. It

seemed excessive to have a gatehouse only fifty feet from one's front door. Grinevich must be more worried about the anti-Putin demonstrators, or somebody, than he let on. A man in a dark generic uniform, with a short haircut and flat eyes, saw her and slid the glass pane open.

"Help you?"

From his tone, "help" was the last thing on his mind.

"I'd just like to pop in and see Antonia for a moment." She hoped Antonia was still here. Turnover was rapid on Grinevich's staff.

"Name?"

She gave it.

The guard glanced at a clipboard. "You're not on the list. Sorry." The apology was about as heartfelt as the offer of help.

"Can't you ring through to Antonia and say I'm here?"

"No point. She's not allowed to put people on the list if they're not previously authorized."

"I am authorized. I must be. I was here Saturday, and you lot checked my ID and photographed me and did everything but give me a DNA test."

"It doesn't work that way."

"Then how does it work?"

But he was already sliding the pane closed.

Renata spun on her heel and stalked away. She was annoyed—but a fat lot of good that did her. She thought of Peter, who had much more experience than she of pestering important people and being turned away by their gatekeepers. He dismissed such rebuffs as lightly as they were dished out. By now she was across the street, and she stopped walking and asked herself, *What would he do now?* He'd wouldn't stalk away in a huff. He'd hang about for a while. It was almost lunchtime. Antonia or someone else she knew might come out. Or the kiosk shift could change, giving her another guard on whom to try another story.

She walked down the street until she was out of sight of

the kiosk and found a wall to shelter her from the wind. She leaned against the cold brick surface and buttoned up her coat. She did not feel too conspicuous, because Billionaires' Row was no quiet by-way. It was a wide, straight, busy street. Vans from FedEx, UPS, and DHL passed on the way to make deliveries, along with the smaller, more chichi vans from Asprey's, Fortnum & Mason, and Berry Bros. and Rudd, Wine Merchants by Appointment to Her Majesty the Queen. There were also long limousines and sleek sports cars with loudly gurgling exhaust pipes.

Renata's toes were going numb with cold, and she was thinking of giving this up, when she saw someone approaching down the empty sidewalk. It was a young man, pulled by an unruly team of large dogs. He crossed the street toward the gate of Whitecroft. Renata followed at a distance. The unhelpful guard came out of his kiosk all smiles. He took charge of the dogs, and the dog walker went up to the house. The front door opened and a teenage girl appeared with the lean borzoi Renata had met on Saturday. She handed the leash to the dog walker. The man reclaimed his pack and set out in Renata's direction.

"Oh, hello," she said as he drew near. "I think this is an old friend of mine. Is her name Katya?"

"His name is Pechorin," said the dog walker gruffly, but he pulled in the reins like a charioteer. This allowed her to get close to the borzoi, who was used to admiring humans and permitted Renata to stroke his floppy ears and silky fur.

"But surely this is the Grineviches' dog?"

"It is, but it's Pechorin."

"Of course. My memory's at fault." Down on one knee, she continued to stroke the complaisant dog and tried to think of what to say next. Peter would have prepared a story for every contingency while he was waiting.

"Look. I'm paid to *walk* 'em."

"Sorry." She jumped to her feet. "Mind if I walk along?"

"Suit yourself."

"Do you take them out on the Heath and let them have a run?"

"Have a run? Not likely. They'd take off in all different directions and I'd be the rest of the day chasing 'em. And God forbid I came back without one of 'em."

"Dogs are rather doted on, are they?"

"Too right. They've got their grooming sessions and their nail-clippings and their play dates. I have to make an appointment to take 'em out for a shite."

Renata laughed. She recognized it as the carefree trill of Musetta in *La Bohème*, a role she had sung for Opera North last spring. It caused the irritable man to glance at her for the first time, so she followed it up with the direct look and shameless-flirt smile Musetta gave the audience before launching into "*Quando m'en vo*."

The dog walker smiled back, uncertainly. He had a long, sallow face, and eyes so close together they seemed crossed. She supposed he didn't get much attention from the Musettas of the world.

"I'm headed for the Heath, too. Mind if I walk with you?"

The smile vanished. He blinked and tucked his chin into his collar, like a child expecting to be hit. "Best not."

Not knowing what to make of that response, she walked on beside him, wondering what to say next. They were passing along the wall of one of the empty houses. As they neared the gate, the dogs picked up their pace. Moving as one, they veered toward it. The man clucked his tongue and tugged at their leashes in vain. In front of the gate they sat down, their long bushy tails sweeping the ground behind them.

"You go ahead," he said to Renata. *"Go!"*

She twigged. "You bring them in here, don't you? Let them off lead, sit and have a fag while they do their business." He was a smoker; she could smell it on his jacket. "Saves you a quarter-mile walk to the Heath."

He blinked and ducked again. "It's not the walk I mind.

But the bleedin' dogs—one of 'em squats in the middle of somebody's driveway, and some guard sees it on CCTV, and before the turd has dropped, he's out there waving his Kalashnikov in my face and telling me to clean it up."

The dogs were looking up at him with large, hopeful eyes. Pechorin was whimpering with excitement.

"We can't just stand here," he said. "Clear off, why don't you?"

"I'll go in with you."

He was in no position to argue. Grasping the padlock with one hand, he pulled a key out of his pocket with the other.

"How'd you get the key?"

"Friend at the security firm gave it me. Same one who told me this was all bollocks." He nodded his head at the no-trespassing sign, with its warning that the grounds were regularly patrolled and under constant CCTV surveillance.

He pushed open the gate and the dogs bounded through. Renata followed, looking around at the forlorn grounds. The concrete drive was coated with green moss, the lawn overgrown and dotted with fallen tree limbs. The house itself, a handsome redbrick Georgian, showed long rows of boarded-up windows. The dogs, frantic with impatience, were circling the man as he locked the gates behind them. Then he unleashed them and they scattered into the undergrowth, noses to the ground, snorting and panting with canine happiness.

The man came up to her. His head was down, too. "You said you're a friend of the Grineviches?"

"Don't worry, I won't grass on you. I work for Mr. Grinevich, too. I'm a singer."

He looked relieved. "Should've figured you for a musician, with a coat like that."

Letting the insult to her well-worn Marks & Spencer's anorak pass, she said, "My name's Renata, and I should like to ask you a favor."

"I'm Neal." He gave a noncommittal shrug and offered her a cigarette. They sat on a noble balustrade that was cracked and chipped, on either side of an urn that had lost both handles. Neal smoked and Renata held her cigarette at arm's length.

"Do you know Grinevich's staff?"

"What, the girls in the office, ground floor at the back? There's always a flap on in there, and they're running about with two phones to their heads, but we nod to each other."

"I'd like you to ask one of them for a paper. A guest list for the party Grinevich held on Saturday."

Neal gave his blink and duck. "Don't know if I can do that."

"It's *terribly* important. The party was a sort of concert. I sang. Bloke came up to me afterward, said he ran a small opera company and might have a job for me. And I lost his card. *Such* a fool."

She was rather proud of this tale, which she had made up on the spot. Peter himself couldn't have done better. Neal seemed to accept it without question. But that didn't mean he'd help her. He sat in silence for a while, nervously picking shreds of tobacco from his lips.

Finally he said, "Couldn't do it now. Pechorin's the first dog I drop off. If I go in the house with him, it'll mean leaving the rest of 'em with Sean at the gate for too long. One of 'em's bound to leave his calling card, and that'll put Sean in a rage. He can be a surly bastard."

Taking another leaf from Peter's book, she kept silent, giving him time to talk himself into helping her.

"On the six o'clock round, though, Pechorin's my only dog. I could maybe nip in the house then. Say I needed the loo. They always send me to the one at the back. Near the office. Girls'll still be there. That's when they get the calls from America."

Renata smiled but kept her silence. He'd almost talked himself 'round. But abruptly he tossed away the cigarette and sat up straight, giving her a hard, sidelong glance. "Look here. How do I know you're not one of that anti-Putin lot?"

"The demonstrators? No."

"We've had them in front of the house, waving their signs and shouting all sorts of rubbish."

"Neal, all I want is the guest list."

"Maybe that's not what you're after at all. You know I bring the dogs in here. Now you're trying to get something else on me. What's your game?" His chin had sunk into his collar and he was blinking rapidly.

"I'm a *singer*. Looking for a job. That's all."

"Sing something then."

"No. That's ridiculous. I can show you ID—"

"What'll that prove? You say you're a singer. Prove it."

"Oh … very well. What would you like to hear?" She searched her memory for the shortest aria she knew that would sound passable sung a capella. "How about '*Voi che sapete*'?"

He wrinkled up his nose. "None of that foreign muck. Sing 'Memory.' That's a good one."

Her heart sank. She had never seen *Cats*. Like everyone, she'd heard 'Memory' countless times in cars and waiting rooms. But she didn't really *know* it. All she could do was an imitation of Betty Buckley, or Barbra Streisand, or whoever was singing it in her head. And it wouldn't sound like them. She was a trained singer, and had never really figured out the crossover thing—not that anyone else had done it totally successfully, except maybe Frederica von Stade or Dawn Upshaw.

Neal lit another cigarette. Folded his arms and looked at her. Impatiently. Suspiciously.

Renata stood up, faced him squarely, breathed in, and launched into "Memory."

It was acutely painful. Her breathing was off. She couldn't quite recall where the key modulations happened. Sometimes she even failed to remember a word and had to slur her way through. And, unable to shake the voice of Barbra Streisand in her head, she could hear herself doing strange pop singer swoops that would make any other classical singer shudder. She hoped he would be satisfied and tell her to stop. But he made her go on to the last note. Perhaps she was butchering the number so badly he didn't believe she was a professional.

She'd ended up gazing heavenward, which she hoped was an appropriate bit of characterization. Lowering her eyes, she found that Neal was standing with his back to her, shoulders hunched, both hands gripping the balustrade, like a passenger about to be sick over the ship's rail.

"Sorry," she said.

Neal turned to her. His eyes were full of tears. A moment passed before he was able to choke out, "That was … beautiful."

9

Renata spent the rest of the afternoon at the National Theatre. A friend who was an assistant stage manager there had offered her a gig as a light walker, which meant she filled in for a performer while they set the lighting cues. It didn't pay much, but it paid at once. She would be handed a check before leaving the building. Considering her current cash-flow crisis, the check would be most welcome.

For a couple of hours, she stood, sat, or walked slowly up and down the stage of the Olivier Theatre, while at the back of the empty auditorium, the boffins on the lighting board tried out various hues, angles, and intensities. Since all she had to was reflect light, she had time to think. Far too much time.

She was afraid that Neal the dog walker was going to get cold feet. If she never heard from him again, it would put paid to her attempts to find out whom Don was working for. She had no other ideas for preventing him from being deceived and manipulated. And Peter was on his trail. Literally. If Don caught him and they got into a fight, who would win? Renata was wonderful at coming up with questions she could fret pointlessly about, and this one tormented her for a good half-hour before she reached the satisfying conclusion that Peter was stronger and faster but Don would fight dirtier, and they would both end up in hospital.

The boffins were at last satisfied. She filled out the paperwork and collected her check. Climbing the steps to Waterloo Bridge, she set off across the Thames. It was dark now, and much colder, but even so, she had to stop for a moment, lean her elbow on a parapet, and take in the sweep of the riverfront. The floodlights did wonderfully by it.

Parliament stood forth in warm brown, highlighted in gold. She turned the other way, to the colonnade of Somerset House, the spire of St. Bride's, the dome of St. Paul's. Lights glittered in the glass skyscrapers of The City.

Ordinarily she took her native town for granted, abandoning its splendors to the tourists. But she had been feeling a renewed loyalty ever since Peter had suggested that her future lay elsewhere. She would inevitably be offered an administrative job in an opera company somewhere *in America*, he had said. She'd been arguing with him in her thoughts ever since. She was a Londoner. She was not going to leave the greatest city in the world for Minneapolis or Sarasota.

Renata did not need her therapist to tell her that this was avoidance. She did not want to think about retiring from the stage. A pessimist about most things, she had boundless hope for her career. This bad patch would end. The jobs would start to come. The ring of her mobile banished these pleasant musings. *Peter*, she thought, *calling from the emergency room of Granger Hospital*. She put the phone to her ear and said hello. The voice was so soft she couldn't make out what it was saying. She covered her other ear with her hand. "What? Say again, please."

"I said I've got it."

"Neal? Oh, well done. Where are you?"

"Just left the house. I'm taking Pechorin to the Heath."

"Ah, doing what you're supposed to for a change."

He did not respond to this sally. It seemed Neal wasn't in the mood to join in her festivities. She said, "Did you have a hard time getting the list?"

"No. New York was on the line about some change in Grinevich's schedule they hadn't been told about. The whole office was at sixes and sevens. I grabbed this one girl by the elbow, told her about the list and why you wanted it, and she found it, made a copy, and handed it to me."

"Oh, you gave them my name."

"That was the idea, wasn't it?"

It had been the idea. She wondered why it made her uneasy now. The anxiety in Neal's voice must be catching. She said, "You've got the list. All's well."

"Not so sure. Don't know what kind of reception I'll get when I take Pechorin back. Grinevich's usually home by then."

"The girls don't tell him half the things they do to smooth his path through life. Not to worry."

"Look, I'm the one whose job's on the line. If Grinevich sacks me and the other dog-owners hear why—"

"I'll get there quick as I can and take the list off your hands."

"Bring money."

"What?"

"I'll need money if I'm sacked. Bring two hundred pounds or it's all off."

That was more than the check she had just received. Her cash-flow crisis would worsen. Renata swallowed hard. "All right. Where do we meet?"

"Hampstead Heath. Top of Parliament Hill."

He rang off.

Forty-five minutes later she emerged from a grove of trees and began to climb the grassy, steep slope of Parliament Hill. It was the highest point in all London, someone had told her, and soon she was breathing hard. Her nerves were taut. The journey had taken much too long. She'd had to locate a cash point, then a second one, because the amount was over the limit. She considered a cab, but it was rush hour and the streets were clogged, so she took a crowded and halting underground train. The wind grew stronger and colder as she climbed. She hoped Neal hadn't given up on her, that his greed was holding fast against his nerves.

But all the while, in the darkness atop the hill, Neal was lying dead.

10

Renata stared down at Neil's twisted, bloody form and bashed-in skull. She brushed in vain at the blood on her skirt. She had banged up one knee while tripping over the corpse, but other than the bloodstains on her clothing, she wasn't much the worse for wear. Swallowing hard, she touched in 999 and said, in a voice she hardly recognized, that she had found a dead body on Parliament Hill. The calm woman said a car was on the way and began to ask her questions. They quickly became too complicated for Renata. She said she would stay here and rang off.

She had wandered a long way from the body while she talked. She forced herself to return to it. Should she search it for the guest list? The idea filled her with revulsion, and the 999 operator had just told her not to touch anything, but—

She broke off these pointless thoughts. How stupid could she be? She wasn't going to find the list. Whoever had killed Neal had taken it. The list was the reason he was dead.

The blood-slick phone was still in her hand. She wanted to throw it away, but there was another call to make. She scrolled until her brother's name appeared on the phone's bright screen and pressed the call button, setting off the many digits of his mobile number. What time was it in St. Louis? The simple calculation was beyond her. The phone rang and rang. Then the recording.

She said, "Don, you are working for a murderer. Stop doing what he tells you. Get right clear of him. Now."

Appropriately for the neighborhood, Hampstead Police Station was old-fashioned and rather high-toned. It had cream-over-light green paint on its walls, hissing radiators, and stout wooden doors with frosted-glass windows. Renata gave her statement to a young policewoman seated at a computer. Looking at the screen rather than at her, the woman asked innumerable questions, many of which seemed pointless. The police seemed to be keenly interested in Pechorin. Had she seen his leash? What about paw prints?

The paw prints of a gigantic hound, Renata said to herself, quoting Sherlock Holmes, and had to stifle a giggle. Her nerves were shot.

Finally, the interview was finished, and the policewoman left her sitting beside the desk. She waited for a long time. She wished that she could call Peter, but the police had taken her mobile. Its bloody state made it part of the crime scene.

At length, a portly man with gray hair, tufted eyebrows, and a ruddy face sat down behind the desk. He was wearing a tweed jacket and tie and carrying several folders. His manner, as he introduced himself as Detective Inspector McAllister and ranged the folders across the desk, was so deliberate that she felt he ought to be wearing a cardigan and smoking a pipe. He opened a file and began to read. Minutes passed. It was as if they were two strangers sitting next to each other in a train.

She could stand it no more. "I know I've behaved very stupidly," she blurted out. "I got that poor man killed."

"Don't be too hard on yourself, Ms. Radleigh. You may have had little to do with Marsh's death."

This statement baffled Renata. She said, "Marsh?"

"Neal Marsh. He was known to police, as the saying goes.

Only small stuff—drunk and disorderly, passing bad checks, that sort of thing."

Renata blinked and shook her head. The police seemed to be awash in irrelevance. "You have read my statement, Inspector?"

"Oh yes."

"The list I was talking about—the guest list—it wasn't found on the body, was it?"

"No."

"That means that the killer took it."

"Or that Marsh never had it at all."

"Of course he did. He got it from someone on Grinevich's staff."

"We've interviewed the young ladies. They all denied giving Marsh papers of any sort."

"One of them is lying. She doesn't want to get in trouble."

The jutting eyebrows rose. "Lying to the police in a homicide investigation is one sure way of getting in trouble," he said. "We rather think they're telling the truth."

"Then you think I'm lying."

He shook his large pink-and-gray head firmly. "I'm making no such accusation, Ms. Radleigh."

"Neal … Marsh … he told me he had the list."

"In the course of maneuvering you into a pretty desolate locale, with a large amount of cash in your pocket. And he's a man with a record. You may have had a narrow escape this evening."

"You seem to think I'm quite stupid. You're not taking my statement seriously."

"Of course we are. But there's little in your statement to concern the Metropolitan Police. You—or in fact it seems to be more your friend Mr. Lombardo—think that your brother is involved in some sort of dodgy real estate transaction in America. It doesn't seem to me that Mr. Lombardo has evidence laws are being broken, but I'm the first to admit, I don't know American laws. I would advise him to contact the local authorities. That's really all I can say about your statement."

She swiveled in the chair so she could look him full in the face. "The man my brother is working for is *here*. He wants to keep his name secret. He found out somehow that Neal was going to give me the list with his name on it. And he had Neal killed."

"It's a terrible shock to come upon a corpse. Please don't think I'm condescending if I say you're overwrought."

"Condescend to your heart's content. Just tell me. If Neal wasn't killed for the list, what was he killed for?"

"The dog."

"Oh," Renata said, after a moment of stunned silence. "So that's why there were all those questions I couldn't answer about leashes and paw prints."

"Don't worry. Your statement helped us establish that Marsh had the dog with him when he headed for the Heath."

"I'm so glad you accept one thing I said. Inspector, Pechorin is a fine animal. But do you really think he's worth killing for?"

"We don't think the assailant meant to kill Marsh. Just hit him harder than intended. No doubt that's what his barrister will say in court, if it comes to that."

"You have a suspect?"

"Not as yet. But this latest incident fits a pattern."

"A pattern. You mean somebody's been assaulting people and stealing their dogs and … what, selling them?"

"Holding them for ransom."

"Ransom?"

McAllister sat back, crossing his legs and folding his arms. He really did seem to need a pipe to fiddle with. "There are some very wealthy people in this district."

"I've noticed."

"The house prices have been going up astoundingly. With them the cost of goods and services and everything else. Early in the summer, we noticed a trend in the posters people put on fences and telephone poles, offering rewards for their lost dogs."

"They're going up?"

"It was when a Chinese gentleman offered three hundred pounds for information leading to the return of his King Charles spaniel that we decided to take action. Held meetings, sent out circulars, warning people that they were letting themselves in for trouble. Villains can read, too."

"I see."

"And sure enough, September third, a shih tzu is taken from a car parked in Frognal Road. The owner receives a demand for three hundred and fifty pounds. He cooperated with us and we caught the man. But the local villains were undiscouraged. September twenty-seventh, Golders Hill Park, a man demands a woman's Staffordshire bull terrier at knifepoint. Passersby intervene and he flees.

"October fifteenth, a van pulls up beside a dog walker in Gresham Avenue. He has an Irish wolfhound, a Bichon Frise, and a Bernese mountain dog. Men jump out, knock him down, try to force the dogs into the van. The dogs ran off, but the dog walker had a concussion. Note the pattern of escalation, culminating in tonight's incident. The media will give it full play. We'll have people ringing up in droves, saying they're afraid to walk their dogs."

"No wonder you're not interested in my story," Renata said.

McAllister frowned. His eyebrows seemed to bristle. "We are not disregarding you, Ms. Radleigh. Mr. Grinevich is cooperating fully. Soon we expect him to receive a ransom demand. That will of course confirm that we're dealing with dognappers. If there is no call, of course, you'll be hearing from us."

Renata sighed. She'd heard those last five words countless times, at the end of auditions. Invariably meaning that she was *not* going to hear from them.

* * *

IT WAS VERY LATE by the time she got home. She went straight to the answering machine. There was nothing from Don. He'd never been good about returning calls, but surely he couldn't ignore her last message. He must be calling her mobile. It would be ringing unheard in a bin in an evidence room somewhere in north London. She rang Don's number, got the recording, and left her landline number. Then she called Peter. His phone was off, too.

She looked at her watch. It was five p.m. in St. Louis. Early evening was Peter's favorite time to Skype with her; it wouldn't be long. She put the laptop on the night table, booted up, started Skype. Then she fell back into bed. She thought she was too keyed up to sleep, but exhaustion got the better of her. When Skype's merry electronic tones roused her, she felt as if she had been asleep for hours. She pulled herself upright and reached for the keyboard.

Peter's face popped up on the screen. She gasped. His left cheek was grotesquely swollen and mottled with bruises, so that his eye was almost closed. He noted her reaction and said, "I've had an interesting day."

11

Peter had set out early that morning. He biked to the Central West End and into one of the capacious underground garages of Adams University Medical School. Locking up the bike, he went to the row of WeCars—Toyota Priuses that the university rented at cheap rates to students and employees. Peter was no longer an employee but had kept his ID. Swiping it, he chose an inconspicuous light-green car and drove across the highway to Parkdale.

Don's Jaguar was parked in its garage. Wayne was presumably still asleep under its front bumper. Don seemed to be asleep, too. The curtains of the second-floor apartment were closed. Peter found a parking space on the street with a view of the building and alley entrance. Then he put on his Cardinals cap. He also had a fisherman's porkpie and a floppy-brimmed sunhat; the investigative reporter who had taught him how to tail people had said wearing a hat helps to alter your profile. He'd also told him that you had to be alert at all times, so he had no books or magazines, and his cellphone was off. For two hours, nothing happened, except that Don appeared briefly at his window as he opened the curtains.

Peter was prepared for this. Surveillance was stupendously

dull. It might be hours, even days before Don let slip the mask of the socially conscious property owner.

Finally Peter heard the morning coughs of the old Jag, and a moment later it appeared, coming out of the alley. He started the Prius and followed.

Don spent the day looking after his buildings. Peter learned only that he was a sloppy painter, spattering paint across windows, and that he disposed of the fallen leaves he raked from his yards into alley Dumpsters that were marked "No Yard Waste." Peter was bored, but Don looked far more bored. Whatever he said, it was impossible to believe that he intended to spend years tending his properties and hoping the neighborhood would improve.

Sitting in the Prius as the hours crawled by, Peter began to develop fellow feelings for the drug dealers. Like him, they were waiting around. Black teenagers with pants sagging and ballcap visors askew, they leaned against lampposts on street corners or lolled on the front steps of abandoned buildings, watching for a car to pull up at the curb and a customer to wave them over. Peter also saw Joel Rubinstein's green pickup several times. Once Joel drove right by him, recognized him, and gave him a surreptitious wave. He knew what Peter was doing.

At five o'clock sharp, Don called it a day. He drove out of Parkdale and over the highway bridge. Peter assumed he was heading for one of the Central West End's numerous bars. Instead he turned into the garage entrance of Lindell Terrace, a luxury condo tower with big windows commanding handsome views of the dome of the New Cathedral. *More Don's style*, Peter thought. This was where he really lived. The Parkdale walk-up was part of his community builder act.

Turning into a side street, Peter parked. Slumping in his seat, he kept his eyes on the rearview mirror, watching the garage entrance. Half an hour later, he was startled when Don walked by the car. He hadn't seen him coming out of the lobby door.

Don passed within five feet of Peter, but luckily it was dark by now and he continued on his way, oblivious. Peter stayed put until he was a hundred paces down the street, then got out of the car and followed him. It felt good to be on his feet after so many hours behind the wheel and he strode briskly, closing the distance slightly. Don had changed to a blue blazer and gray flannels. He was walking at a quicker than normal pace, as if late for an appointment.

Sure enough, someone was waiting for him. A woman. She was standing under the awning of a restaurant, smoking a cigarette, which she threw away to extend a hand to Don. He took it and kissed her on both cheeks. They went into the restaurant.

Peter slowed his steps. As he approached the restaurant, he looked in the windows. It was reassuringly dim. He decided to risk going in. A long bar lined with patrons was on his left, the tables to his right. He stepped up to the bar and ordered a glass of wine. It took several over-the-shoulder glances to spot Don and the woman.

They were seated at a table in the rear of the restaurant. Don's back was to him and the woman was facing him. She was a notable beauty, with a bell of dark hair framing a heart-shaped face. She was leaning forward, talking, her expression intent, her gestures emphatic. Peter wished he could hear what she was saying. The conversation went on long enough for him to finish his wine and order another. Don and the woman, he noticed, had hardly touched their glasses.

Abruptly the woman stood. Don half-rose, politely, then resumed his seat. Peter turned his back as the woman walked past him. She continued to the door and went out.

She was wearing a short skirt, dark hose, and high heels. Her hips swayed beguilingly.

Don stayed only long enough to drain his glass. Peter hunched his shoulders and bowed his head as he went by. Once he was out the door, Peter got up and resumed following him. He walked back to Lindell Terrace. Peter got back in his car. Ten minutes later the Jag drove out of the garage entrance.

They returned to Parkdale. A wiry, bearded man in maroon scrubs, probably a nurse or doctor from nearby Granger Hospital, was waiting for Don on the curb. They shook hands and went into an apartment building. Peter debated with himself. Don was obviously back in property owner mode, showing an apartment to a prospective tenant. Could Peter safely call it a day? He hadn't packed a lunch and was starving. Also, he was looking forward to Skyping with Renata and telling her about the Lindell Terrace apartment and the Dark Lady of the Central West End.

He had just about decided to head back to the medical center and turn the Prius in when a big black SUV slid slowly past his window. It pulled into the curb ahead of him. Its back-up lights came on. It kept on reversing until its bumper almost touched his. Headlights were glaring in his mirror: another car, coming up close behind him. He was boxed in.

Peter was paralyzed by disbelief. He shook it off and threw open the door. His seatbelt held him back. He scrabbled the buckle open, jumped to his feet, and started running. But an escape attempt on foot had been anticipated. A man materialized out of the darkness ahead. Peter recognized him as one of the street-corner dealers. The skinniest one. Peter went straight at him, thinking he could knock him aside.

The kid dropped into a crouch worthy of an NFL lineman. He hit Peter low and came up fast, upending him. His glasses spun off into the night as he landed hard on the pavement, flat on his back. The kid could have finished him off with a kick to the head, but he missed his chance. Peter scrambled to his feet and swung. The kid ducked the blow. His fist flew at Peter's face. An explosion of pain, and the lights went out.

HE CAME TO IN the back of a moving car. His tender cheekbone was resting on the bristly carpet, and every bump jolted him painfully. He swiveled his head so the uninjured cheek was against the carpet. That was all he could manage for a while.

The car stopped. The tailgate opened. He gazed up at a blurry figure silhouetted against a brighter background.

"Put on your glasses," the figure said.

Peter lurched onto an elbow. His glasses, neatly folded, were lying beside him. Odd that his kidnappers had taken the trouble to retrieve them from the street. He put them on.

"Come on out. You're okay."

That was odd, too, and patently false. He managed to get his feet to the ground, but when he tried to stand, dizziness overcame him. The man caught him. It was the same skinny teenager. He had a harder time holding Peter up than knocking him down. They staggered across what seemed to be a big garage, with bright overhead fluorescents and machine noise echoing off the concrete walls. They went through a door into a small storeroom, where a lone man was sitting on a stool.

He was a middle-aged African American, with an eroding hairline and a stomach that pushed out against his green warm-up suit. He watched in silence as the teenager settled Peter on another stool and stepped back. The older man's gaze shifted to follow him. Only the right eye moved. The other, Peter realized, was glass.

"Sorry you got hurt." He was addressing Peter while glaring at the teenager. "I only wanted to talk to you. But I got niggers working for me who don't know how to do what they're told."

His expression was so fearsome that Peter took pity on the teenager. He said, "I didn't give him much chance to explain."

The man was unmollified. He said, "Get out," and the teenager hurriedly obeyed, closing the door behind him.

The man's right eye joined his left in gazing at Peter. He said, "I'm Tavon Jackson. You heard of me?"

"Read about you. The *Post-Dispatch* calls you the Drug Kingpin of the West Side."

"Kingpin," Jackson repeated. The word seemed to amuse him. "Who are you?"

"Peter Lombardo."

Jackson rose and advanced, putting out his hand. Shaking it felt odd. When it was withdrawn, Peter saw that it was missing the little finger and half of the ring finger.

Jackson resumed his seat. "My corner boys tell me you been following Radleigh all day. But you're not police."

"No."

"Reporter?"

That was close enough. Peter nodded.

"Why you interested in Radleigh?"

Peter closed his eyes tightly, then opened them. He wished he wasn't still feeling so woozy. "Let me get this straight. You brought me here to ask me about Don Radleigh?"

Jackson folded his arms. His sleeve rode up and Peter noticed that he was wearing one of those expensive Swiss watches that told the phases of the moon. There were no gold chains around his neck or rings on his fingers. He said, "Week ago, he caught one of my boys sitting on the steps of a building he owned. Told him, 'Clear off! And tell your boss his days in Parkdale are numbered.' "

The imitation of Don's crisp, upper-class accent was so perfect that Peter had to laugh. "What did you make of the threat?"

"I've heard scarier threats, you know what I'm saying? Even if I got to pull my operation out of Parkdale, there's other neighborhoods. Moving product on the street, that the easiest part of this business. Tough part is, what you do with all the cash coming in? We got fucking *bales* of ten and twenty dollar bills rolling in every day. We got to turn that into capital. You know what I'm saying?"

"Capital," Peter echoed.

"Right. I'm always looking for investments. If the 'hood is coming up, I want a piece of it."

"You mean you want to buy some buildings. Did you talk to Don about this?"

"I was driving through Parkdale, saw him mowing a lawn. So I waved him over. When he heard who I was, he about pissed his pants."

"I bet."

"But I convinced him I only wanted his advice. He got up in the passenger seat and we had a talk." Jackson paused and gave Peter a long, appraising look. "You called him Don. You know the guy?"

"Yes."

"Trust him?"

It was strange being asked to vouch for Don, especially by a drug dealer. But there was no doubt about the answer. "No."

Jackson shrugged. "I asked him did he think property values in Parkdale was going to rise. He said yes."

"Did he say why?"

"I asked that too. He did an awful lot of talking without answering my question. You know what I'm saying?"

"Don's good at that."

"He trying to be helpful, though. Told me if I wanted to buy a building, I couldn't do it with bales of tens and twenties. Nobody could know the money was coming from me. He told me about shell companies. Offshore accounts. All that shit. Then he stopped talking. I can see him thinking. Figure now I'm really gonna hear something. And he say, 'I'm *terribly* sorry, but it's too late for you to get in on the deal.' "

Again, he caught Don's accent perfectly. Then he looked hard at Peter. "So. What that mean?"

Peter considered. "I guess that this spectacular rise in property values is going to happen in the next few days."

"This guy Radleigh. He crazy?"

"No, I don't think so."

Jackson waited for him to say more, and when it wasn't forthcoming, he glanced at his watch. "I'll get somebody to run you back to your car. I'm not sorry I didn't get in on this deal. Something wrong with it. You know what I'm saying?"

"I know exactly what you're saying."

12

Peter finished his story. Renata watched him on the screen as he put an icepack to his cheek and winced.

"Have you been to the hospital?" she asked. "Are you sure you're all right?"

"At the moment, I feel like I'll never chew again. But once the swelling goes down, I'll be okay."

"What do you make of the woman?"

'The Dark Lady of the Central West End?"

"Yes. Is she Don's bit on the side?"

"She's certainly more his usual type than Hannah. But I'm not sure."

"Because they didn't snog?"

"Just exchanged Frenchy air kisses."

"And she left him in the bar?"

"Right. On the other hand, their conversation was intense."

"Oh, Peter. What do you make of all this? How can real estate values in Parkdale skyrocket in the next few days?"

"Don and his boss have been tipped off. They know something nobody else knows."

"That there's a lake of oil under Parkdale?"

"Not likely in eastern Missouri."

"Or a gun will go off and there'll be an Oklahoma land rush?

Thousands of middle-class people stampeding into Parkdale to rent apartments."

Peter smiled. "I saw that movie, too. It's not going to happen. Tell me about your day."

"*My* day? Not so good. I got a man killed."

"What?"

She told him everything that had happened, ending with, "I think the police are wrong. What do you think?"

"Of course they're wrong. And we now know how far Don's boss is willing to go to keep his name a secret."

"So I'm not crazy. Splendid. But I have no idea what we should do next."

"I know what you should do. Stay home. Keep the doors locked."

She looked at his grave face on the screen. "You mean you think I'm in danger? I suppose it's possible that this billionaire could find out about me, from Maestro or even the police—"

"Renata, he's already found out about you. From Don."

"Oh."

"That's why Don hasn't called you back. He called his boss instead."

She had not thought of this before. But the moment she heard it, she knew it was true. The realization hit her with sickening force. "He wouldn't deliberately put me in danger. He doesn't know what his boss is up to. He's being used."

"You still think so? I think he's in it up to his neck. Whatever the scheme is, it's coming to a head in the next few days. Be careful."

After they finished Skyping, she turned off the light and put her head on the pillow. But she could no more sleep than fly. Neal Marsh was on her conscience. She went over every moment of their brief acquaintance, thinking about how she might have been more clever, or more cautious, or just luckier, and he would still be alive.

Her thoughts wandered round and round this maze without a center. Finally she could bear it no more. It occurred to her that there might be a way out. Other people existed who were guiltier of Neal's death than she was. She had to turn her thoughts to them.

Opening her eyes, she found that it was light in the room. She washed and dressed, made a cup of tea, and put in a call to DI McAllister.

After a long wait, he came on the line. "Yes, Ms. Radleigh, what is it?"

The brusque tone, after his ruminative manner last night, caught her by surprise. "I was just wondering if you'd be wanting to talk to me today."

"If that becomes necessary, we shall be in touch."

"But you don't think it will?" He said nothing. She was afraid he was going to ring off, so she rushed on, "Has there been a ransom demand, then?"

"Yes."

"Have you made an arrest?"

"Not as yet. You will be notified."

"But Grinevich is working with you? You're going to trap this man when he comes to get his money?"

"Mr. Grinevich has made his own arrangements," McAllister said bitterly.

"You mean he paid the killer off without telling you? But he can't do that!"

"It's up to the crown prosecutor's office to decide how to proceed against Mr. Grinevich. We'll continue the homicide investigation."

"What does that mean? You'll wait for the next dognapping?"

"I'm not going to discuss the case with you, Ms. Radleigh. Goodbye."

"You were quite happy to discuss it last night," Renata said, but the line had closed. She replaced the receiver. She was sitting at the kitchen table, and she looked at the windows, high up on the wall. Beyond them, she could see the litter-strewn area and the low iron fence that separated it from the sidewalk. People's legs were passing back and forth. Peter had told her to stay home today. But he seemed to think she lived in a citadel, not a basement flat. Anyone who wanted to get at her had only to break one of those windows.

That made it easy to disregard his advice. She put her teacup in the sink and reached for her coat.

13

THIS TIME THEY DIDN'T give Renata any trouble at the Whitecroft gatehouse. Grinevich, a late riser, was still at home, and gave the order to admit her.

She was shown in to the big room overlooking the garden, where Saturday's recital had been held. A few staffers were perched on purple chairs, with papers on their laps and phones at their ears. They gave Renata empty smiles as she passed. Maestro had the pages of an orchestral score spread out across the gleaming parquet floor and was prowling among them, frowning. He did not notice her at first. Beyond the windows, the sky was gray. The gas fireplace was on. It was a six-foot-broad open trough of flame that would have done the job at a crematorium. On the rug before it, the borzoi sprawled and dozed.

"How's Pechorin?"

Grinevich looked up. "As well as can be expected, considering his ordeal."

She picked her way among the pages of the score and sat down on the sofa. "The police are cross with you."

"Yes. When I admitted what I'd done, they were very unpleasant. Even made threats. But my solicitor says there will be no charges."

"Because of your celebrity and connections?"

Grinevich smiled. "Because this is a dog-loving country."

"Ah."

His expression changed. He came and sat on the sofa beside her, a little closer than she would have liked. "I'm not proud of myself, Renata. I feel terrible about what happened to Neal. I wish I could have kept my word to the police. But the phone rang in the middle of the night, and the voice on the other end was very scary. He said I had to bring the money at once or he would cut Pechorin's throat."

Pechorin seemed to sense that they were talking about him. He raised his elegant head and regarded them with large, shining eyes. Grinevich smiled at him.

"But that's all bollocks, Maestro, isn't it?" said Renata. "There was no ransom demand."

He turned to her, eyebrows raised. He seemed more interested than offended.

"You returned yesterday evening and one of the girls in the office told you Neal had just been 'round, and somebody'd been fool enough to give him a copy of the guest list. You remembered our conversation of the afternoon. You looked at the original to see which of your guests had brought Don. Then you warned him."

Grinevich was no longer looking at her. After a moment, he said, "Are you waiting for me to confirm or deny these speculations?"

"Not necessary. I've given thought—hours and hours of thought—to how Neal ended up dead, and that's pretty much the only way it could have gone. You must be very afraid of this man."

One of the girls was approaching, heels clicking on the parquet. She had a phone in her hand and an urgent look on her face. Grinevich waved her away. This surprised Renata. She thought he would welcome the interruption. But evidently he had something more to say to her.

"Afraid?" he repeated. "No. At this moment, I am feeling no fear whatever. And that's a happy state. I grew up in the old Soviet Union, Renata. I know just how happy." He eased himself back into the sofa and crossed his legs. Again she wished he wasn't sitting so close to her. "Growing up there, you learn to avoid 'brave' people. They care only about their consciences. When they fall, they pull you down with them."

She could feel on her face the heat from the inferno of a fireplace. Grinevich had beads of sweat on his forehead but didn't seem to mind. "So," she said, "brave people are selfish."

"You could put it that way."

"You're not selfish. Who were you thinking of last night when you made that phone call? Your children and ex-wives? Your mistresses and friends? The world's classical musical fans?"

"Yes. And I was thinking of you."

"Me?"

"I've always liked you, Renata. You're very talented. And unlike most talented people, you're nice. You deserve better in life than you're getting."

"Very gallant of you, Maestro, returning compliments for insults. Or are you trying to throw me off?"

He shook his head. "I'm not playing games with you. I have no idea—none whatsoever—what this man is doing in America, but it's safe to say that he's going to make some money. Well, a very great deal of money. Don't get in his way."

"Or I'll end up like Neal?"

"If he wants to threaten you, he can do it himself. This man—he's not like those selfish people I was complaining about earlier—when he makes money, his friends make money, too. That's the force that moves the world, Renata. Don't defy it."

14

She had just enough time to make it to the Brompton Oratory for rehearsal. If she missed another one, they would sack her, and she couldn't afford to lose the paycheck. So she went, with the hope that music would do for her what it always had—fill her head, cast out her worries.

Not this time. The act of pushing air over her vocal cords to make them vibrate had never seemed so pointless. She was distracted and irritable. She wanted to snap at the choristers for singing so badly as to throw her off, at the music director for imposing his odd ideas about Latin pronunciation, at Franz Josef Haydn for writing notes that were difficult for her to reach.

Finally, they were released, and she went over the road to catch the Fourteen bus. She had booked a rehearsal studio and an accompanist at the University of London, to work on "*Una voce poco fa*." With the help of a coach, she had recently revamped the ornamented sections to show off the agility of her middle range. Sopranos had largely taken over the role of Rosina in Rossini's *Il Barbière de Siviglia*, as they had Carmen, and they could put in flashy high notes, but they had trouble moving their voices in the middle range and lower sections, and some traditionalists still preferred a plummy mezzo quality overall. Renata still had the chops to handle the lightning-fast fioratura sections. She had almost finished memorizing the entire role. You never knew when the scheduled Rosina would fall ill, leaving an opening for a last-minute replacement to save the day.

What ambition and discipline she used to have, as recently as last week! Don liked to make fun of her for frittering away her life making pretty sounds. She knew nothing about how money was made, he said, how things really worked in the world. She'd never been so close to agreeing with him.

She boarded the bus and mounted the spiral stairs. It was her habit to sit near the front of the upper deck. Buses made very slow progress through London, and it helped her be more patient if she was above the traffic. Approaching her stop on the Tottenham Court Road, she looked down on a strikingly fashionable woman waiting to board—a tall, slender Indian in a well-tailored pearl-gray trouser suit, with a deep-burgundy purse and matching high heels. Her beautiful, dark-brown face, with its large black eyes, high cheekbones and long, high-bridged nose reminded Renata of Maestro's borzoi. Her hair was covered by a fine foulard scarf. Only the way it was bound tightly round her neck indicated that it was a religiously mandated head covering and not a fashion accessory.

The bus was juddering to the curb, and Renata made her way down the stairs and out the door. The Indian woman was not boarding. She was waiting for Renata. She smiled and waved, then approached with hand outstretched.

"Hello, Renata. My name is Jhumpa."

Renata automatically took the offered hand. It was slender, almost bony, and the grip was light.

"I'm happy to meet you," Jhumpa went on. "I've heard so much about you."

"From whom?"

"From Don. We work together."

"Oh."

"I've spoken to Don, just this morning. I'd like to tell you what he said. May I walk along with you?"

Renata hesitated, glancing around. It was mid-afternoon, and the sidewalks were thronged with people. This lovely young woman seemed to mean her no harm. Don was talking to her and wasn't talking to Renata. It was irresistible to hear what she had to say.

"All right." They turned and set off down a side-street named Torrington Place. Jhumpa seemed to know where she was bound. Renata said, "May I ask you something?"

"Of course."

"Are you having me followed?"

Jhumpa laughed. "Oh, no."

"But you were waiting for me."

"Well, I knew your schedule."

"That I was going to the rehearsal studio? How did you know?"

"That's another department. I don't know how they find out these things."

She spoke softly, and Renata had to strain to hear her on the noisy street. Renata was very good at accents—at anything to do with voices—but so far could not place this woman. The way she pronounced her name, *Jooompa*, sounded more North of England than Indian, and she pronounced "schedule" the American way, *skedjl*. Don had told her that his boss employed people who belonged to no particular country.

"What did my brother say to you?"

"First, let me say, I am entirely on your side."

"You are?"

"Yes. Don is quite maddening. He's acting the way my brothers do, telling me bits and snatches of what they're up to, leaving me worried sick. I really do feel for you." She was twisting at the waist, turning not just her face but her whole upper body toward Renata as they walked. Now she reached out and stroked Renata's sleeve.

"I appreciate that," Renata replied, though she was more puzzled than reassured.

"But really, you needn't be concerned. Our boss has given Don a great opportunity, and he's handled it brilliantly so far."

"You know what he's doing, then?"

"Well, not all the details."

"But you know why your boss is so interested in Parkdale."

Jhumpa lost her smile. Only for a moment, then it was back. "Don didn't tell you that. You found out on your own. Aren't you clever?"

"Not especially. The information is all on websites." She did not know if Don had told Jhumpa about Peter. Best leave him out of it. "But why is your boss interested?"

Jhumpa replied, but her words were obscured by a car's bleating horn.

"Sorry, what?"

Jhumpa took her arm and steered her into a narrow mews that dead-ended against the back of a high building. It was lined with parked cars, but there were few people about, and it was quieter.

"I said, property values in Parkdale will go up."

"That's hardly worth the sotto voce."

She laughed again. "No. What we do in our office is ordinary business. Buy low, sell high. Or try to. But that's not what I want to talk to you about. I want to explain why Don hasn't called you back."

"I'll be fascinated."

"He is resentful that you're bothering him. He's involved in delicate negotiations. Carrying a lot of responsibility. This is his big chance."

"You said that already. This is all rather vague. Have you really talked to my brother?"

They had come to a stop and were facing each other. Jhumpa said, "I'll tell you his exact words. He said, 'Last spring when I was in trouble, Renata saved my arse. I don't pretend otherwise.

But now she thinks it belongs to her. That I'm incompetent to manage my own life and she has to do it. Well, I want my arse back.' "

Renata sighed as her doubts disappeared. That was Don, all right. He had his blinkers on, eyes on the prize, blind to all else. "Did he tell you what I said?"

"Well, in general, he said you were worried—"

"Did he tell you I said his boss was a murderer?"

Jhumpa looked away. She wasn't just avoiding Renata's eye. Renata followed the gaze and saw a man coming up beside them. He was an Indian, too, with the gleaming black hair and mustache of a '30s movie star. His fashionably tight suit showed a powerful physique. He walked right up to Renata and grasped her arm. Jhumpa had the other one. They dragged her along toward a parked panel van. Its rear door was sliding open.

Renata tried to dig in her heels, drew in her breath to scream.

A man came around the van, bent down, swept her feet out from under her. They quickly bundled her into the van. She was crying out for help, knowing as she did that the cry would not reach the mouth of the mews and penetrate the din of the street beyond. The door slammed shut.

The three sets of hands settled her in a bench seat and let her limbs fall. The mustached man opened a jump seat and sat facing her, within arm's reach. She heard the other man sit down behind her. Jhumpa was standing, bent over, talking on her mobile in Hindi. She ended the call and said, "He's on his way." Then she maneuvered her slender, long-limbed body into the van's front passenger seat.

Renata was afraid they were going to tie and gag her. But there was no need. The van had no side windows. She could see out the windscreen, past Jhumpa's scarfed head, but beyond was only the back of another parked van. She could no longer hear the traffic from Torrington Place, fifty feet behind her. There was only the breathing of the people in the van.

For the next twenty minutes, all anyone did was breathe. Jhumpa kept her back turned. The mustached man watched Renata's hands, which were lying in her lap. She could feel the gaze of the man sitting behind her. She was too frightened to move a muscle. The others, she supposed, were just used to waiting for their boss.

She heard a car pull up beside the van. The front door opened and a man sat in the driver's seat. The springs shifted under his weight. He brought with him a faint, citrusy scent of expensive aftershave lotion, and something else. The atmosphere changed. She could sense the alertness of the three Indians. The man did not turn his head. She could see only his dense gray hair, long enough to cover the tops of his ears, a roll of brown skin at the nape of his neck, the white collar of his shirt, the shoulders of a dark, pinstriped business suit. He reached up to adjust the driving mirror. As it swiveled, she caught a glimpse of the lower part of his face, heavy jowls pulling down the corners of a wide, thin-lipped mouth, bending it in the sickle shape of a shark's. He settled the mirror so that he could watch her face. She could no longer see his.

"I enjoyed your number on Saturday." It was a deep voice and the Indian lilt was strong. " '*Akh* Tanya, Tanya.' I go to Covent Garden frequently. I was surprised your name was unfamiliar to me. I told Don, perhaps I can do something for your career."

He sighed heavily. "Now look where we are. What a sad state of affairs. Jhumpa?"

"She knows it's Parkdale." Jhumpa was turning to face her boss and Renata could see her profile. No trace of a smile now. Her voice sounded anxious. "But she says she found out on the internet."

"That's true, I expect. They're very public with this sort of information in America. And of course she'd have no difficulty accessing their websites from here."

Again Renata thought, *They don't know about Peter*. Don must not have mentioned him. He felt he'd handled Peter well, with his suave performance in their interview. He hadn't noticed Peter following him the next day. Didn't know he'd seen the Dark Lady, talked to Tavon Jackson.

"What else?" the boss said.

"That's all," Jhumpa replied.

"That's enough. I don't want her interfering in Parkdale, not at this time."

Jhumpa leaned toward him urgently. "Sir, what can she do? Make phone calls? No one in America will take her seriously."

The young woman's friendliness to her had not been entirely feigned, Renata realized.

"But I don't want to have to *think* she may be interfering in Parkdale." The deep voice sounded weary and irritable. "You pulled me out of a meeting to deal with this, Jhumpa. The one with Nigel and Jeremy."

"I'm sorry."

"Now I've come halfway across London. I don't want to waste all this time and not come to a decision."

"We can let her go," said Jhumpa. "I'm sure of it."

"Did she mention the dog walker?"

Jhumpa dropped her eyes.

"Ah," said the boss. He seemed gratified to have scored this point against his overeager assistant. "Well, that's it, then."

His head turned slightly as he raised his eyes to the mirror to look at Renata. "You have a difference of opinion with the police. Is that right?"

Renata was too frightened to answer.

"Sir, again, it doesn't matter," said Jhumpa. "The police aren't listening to her."

He was shaking his head. "Jhumpa, enough. I've gone sour on this business."

Jhumpa swung around in her seat to face Renata. Her black eyes were very wide. "If we let you go, you will go straight home. Right? You will stay in. For the next three days, you will make no phone calls. Answer none. If you don't cooperate we will find out. You must do exactly what I say."

Renata swallowed hard and found her voice. "I'll do what you say."

Jhumpa turned to look at her employer. She waited.

He sighed and said grudgingly, "All right."

Jhumpa gave a curt order in Hindi and the mustached man grasped the handle and slid open the door. Jhumpa looked Renata in the eye again. "Remember. Three full days."

Renata nodded and jumped out the door. She didn't even look at the long, gleaming car parked beside the van. She ran to the mouth of the mews, slowing down only when she reached the crowded sidewalk of Torrington Place.

She was too nervous to stand in the street, hailing a cab. She walked on until she came to Euston Station. It was necessary to change trains, and she kept looking at her watch. It seemed important to get home before dark.

15

WITH A HERD OF homeward-bound office workers, she climbed the steps of Ladbroke Grove Station to the street. They trudged under the A40, elevated by stout concrete piers daubed with graffiti. Renata slowed down as she began the slight but long uphill slog. Eager as she was to get home, she was very tired.

The overcast sky had formed a lid over London all day. But now the sun slipped below the cloud layer, making its only appearance of the day a moment before it set. Slanting golden light bathed Ladbroke Grove. Along the row of old houses with columned porches and bay windows, colors brightened and shadows deepened. In front of Renata, a curtained window turned into a mirror, reflecting her and the pedestrians behind her. One of them caught her eye.

He was a fireplug of a man, short and solid, straight up and down from shoulders to waist. He was dressed nondescriptly, in baseball cap, windcheater, and jeans, except for new trainers in flaming orange.

She had seen those trainers before, as she was gazing down at the floor of the train car fifteen minutes ago. The man had gotten off at her stop. That didn't mean he was following her. She moved closer to the street-side of the pavement, so that she could look into the wing mirrors of parked cars as she passed. The angles the first three gave her were wrong, but the fourth yielded a glimpse of a bland face under a cap. They passed a cross street, then another, and she continued to catch reflections of him. When she crossed the last street before her flat, he was still with her.

She told herself firmly that he had not been sent by Don's boss. Jhumpa had won her the right to go home. If the boss did have men following her, they would be subtler. And they would be sleek Indians like the mustached man. Not this clumsy bloke.

He belonged to a more common species—the domestic perv. Like any woman who traveled alone around London and was even moderately attractive, Renata was occasionally followed, remarked upon, accosted. But what a day for this perv to pick to make a nuisance of himself. If he followed her through her gate, approached her while she was fumbling with her keys, she simply wouldn't be able to cope. So she walked by her house.

She reached the top of the hill and her neighborhood's leading landmark—a Sainsbury's that was as big as an American supermarket, with a car park to match. She headed for it. Before sliding back, the automatic glass doors gave her a glimpse of Orangefoot. He was following her in. The huge place was filled with people doing last-minute, pre-dinner shopping. The crowds and bright overhead lighting and shelves full of brightly packaged goods made her feel more comfortable. She began to walk faster, zigzagging through the aisles, dodging shopping trolleys and the people pushing them.

As she approached the doors on the other side of the store, she had a good view of the interior behind her reflected in them, and she did not see Orangefoot. Perhaps some other woman had snagged his attention and he was chatting her up. Or, one appetite succeeding another, he was queuing for a sandwich at the takeaway counter.

It was perceptibly dimmer outside. The sun had dropped

below the horizon. *He'll never find me again*, she thought, and set out to flank the building and retrace her steps back home. A row of bollards marked off the car park. A man was sitting on one of them, smoking a cigarette. As she approached, he threw it away and stood. She couldn't tell if he was looking at her. The visor of his flat tweed cap obscured his eyes. He had a narrow face and craggy features. He was a tall, thin, and long-limbed.

He took a step toward her.

That broke the spell at last. *Idiot*, she said to herself, *fool*. Tired and dejected, she had reached for the least troubling explanation. Now the truth hit her. Flathead was the partner of Orangefoot, and they had been sent by Don's boss. He had changed his mind. He didn't want to have to worry about her after all.

She was backpedaling toward the doors of the supermarket. She heard them swish open and turned to see Orangefoot come out. Veering away from him, she went the only way she could—through the gate and down the steps to the towpath of the Grand Union Canal. But that was all right; there would be plenty of cyclists and joggers. She used to jog here herself.

Jogging sounded a good idea right now. She broke into a run, her handbag flapping against her hip on its strap. There was no phone in it. The police still had her mobile. The waters of the canal reflected the light remaining in the sky so she could watch her footing. The paving of the path was uneven and the edge of the canal only a pace to her right. The grumble of traffic faded behind her and the only sound was the cawing of the crows in the tall bare trees of the cemetery across the canal.

She risked a glance over her shoulder. The men were pursuing at a run. Flathead was closer, only twenty paces or so behind. Orangefoot was almost invisible in the gathering dusk. She had only an impression of movement and flashes of his orange trainers. Flathead was moving along easily, long legs striding, arms pumping, torso straight up and down. Anyone seeing him would think he was just out for a jog, which was probably what he intended.

It seemed to be growing darker by the second and the path was not as populated as she had hoped. She passed two elderly joggers and a cyclist going the other way. What if she grabbed somebody and begged for help? He'd probably struggle out of her grip and run away—which would be the smart thing to do. These men were probably armed.

She glanced back again. Flathead was still keeping his distance, jogging easily. He looked like he could close the gap anytime but was waiting for full darkness to come and potential witnesses to dwindle to none. Which they would do: there was a stretch of wasteland ahead. It was a long way to the next road crossing the canal, to traffic and streetlights. If she veered left off the path, there was only bare ground and the fence surrounding the towering round grid of the natural gas storage tanks. Nothing to do but keep running.

Now she was passing a moored longboat. It wasn't showing any lights. But the next one on had people living in it. There were lights in its narrow windows and smoke curling from a small funnel. Running along toward the bow, she saw a man standing on deck. The smell of sizzling meat came to her. He was barbecuing and talking on his mobile. Renata could leap aboard. She wanted to, but that would only put the man in danger with her.

She was passing him now, only feet away. If there was one thing she knew how to do, it was modulate her voice, and she said, distinctly but she hoped not loudly enough for her pursuers to hear, "Those men are chasing me. Call the police. *Please!*" For a split-second they were face to face, hers imploring, his dumbfounded, then she was past him.

She faced front to find a cyclist about to collide with her. He was coming on fast, standing up on the pedals, in an American-style helmet and striped spandex outfit. She veered one way and he veered the other. He grunted "Stupid cow!" as he passed.

As soon as she had her feet under her, she looked back. Flathead sidestepped gracefully to let the cyclist by.

She faced front and put on speed. Reminded herself that years of voice training had given her capacious lungs and this sense of being out of breath was only fear. *Just run for all you're worth*. No more looking back.

The instant she made that resolve, a noise made her glance over her shoulder—a heavy splash. Orangefoot was in the canal, shouting and thrashing. He too must have sidestepped to avoid getting hit by the cyclist, but not as sure-footedly as Flathead. The cyclist was still upright. His elbows wagged wildly as he pivoted the handlebars, trying to recover his balance. Flathead had stopped and was looking back.

Renata stopped too. The man in the cold, filthy water was shouting for help. There was almost an arm's length between the water level and the top of the canal wall. He'd need a hand to scramble out. The demon cyclist recovered his balance and disappeared into the darkness. "He's no use," Renata heard herself mutter. "It's on you. Help your mate. Go *on*."

Flathead turned his back on his mate and started after Renata. She swiveled on her heel and lurched into motion. Worrying about secure footing was a luxury she could no longer afford. She picked up her pace. Her labored breathing filled her ears. To her left was a stretch of waste ground with rubbish heaps and dead scrub and bushes. She thought of trying to find a hiding place. But she wouldn't be able to control her gasping and it would betray her.

She ran on. Now there was a chain link fence on her left. It was fully dark and no joggers or cyclists were in sight. No choices left, not even bad ones. She would not look back again. She was running full out, her whole torso shuddering with the effort to pull in more breath.

Ahead, a solid form materialized out of the darkness, a

bridge over the canal. She recognized it and knew that if she could get to it, there would be a road with streetlights, people, and traffic. But it was too far away. The man behind her would be closing the distance. Any moment she would feel the blow at her back as he tackled her and slammed her to the pavement under him.

A car pulled onto the bridge and stopped. Red and blue lights on its roof were spinning. The police. The barbecuing man, bless him, had done as she asked.

Hope made Renata risk a backward glance. Her pursuer wasn't giving up. He bent at the waist and bounded forward, putting his all into one last effort.

She did the same. She felt new strength in her legs, new breath in her lungs. She went up on her toes and sprinted, risking a headlong tumble into the canal.

A light shone out at her, close enough to dazzle. It was on her level—a policeman was down on the path in front of her. Not far away at all. She was safe.

Renata stumbled to a halt and looked back. Yes, the bastard had had enough at last. He'd taken to his heels. She turned toward the approaching copper. It was a woman—a rather pudgy Indian, not as tall as Renata's shoulder. The nightstick secured to her belt was swinging, the handcuffs jangling, as she pounded past without a word, eyes and torch beam fixed on the fleeing Flathead.

In a moment, another copper approached, a gray-haired white man. "You all right, miss?"

Gasping for breath, she nodded.

"I have to go after my partner," he said. "I must ask you to go with me."

Renata nodded again. They set off at a brisk walk.

"Is he armed?"

"I don't know," she managed to say.

"Stay behind me."

She didn't mind that at all. He was a tall man, a reassuring bulwark. He muttered into the radio clipped to his jacket as they walked.

There was a sharp, dry crack. A gunshot. The policeman broke into a run. Renata followed. "Amital?" he said into the microphone, and when there was no response he shouted, *"Amital!"*

Exhausted, Renata fell behind as the cop ran on, playing his light over the path and the canal. A woman's voice came out of the darkness. "Here! In the water."

The policeman's torch beam found Amital. Her long black hair had come unfastened and covered half her face. She was side-stroking toward the bank, one arm crooked across Orangefoot's chest. She had him in a lifeguard's carry so that his body was atop hers and his head above water. She knew what she was doing, but Renata could not tell if Orangefoot was in any condition to benefit. The visor of his cap covered his face.

"He shot him," Amital said. "Bloke was shouting for help and the bastard just stepped to the edge of the canal and shot him. Then he ran off."

The policeman crouched by the edge of the canal, setting down his torch and reaching out both hands.

"There are steps," Renata said, suddenly remembering.

The policeman turned his head and gave her an incredulous look. "*Steps?*"

"They put them in when they dug the canal. In case a horse fell in." She picked up the torch and shone the beam to her left. "There."

The policeman went down the steps cut into the canal wall, wading in waist-deep to take Orangefoot from Amital. As he did, Orangefoot's cap fell off, revealing the bullet hole in his forehead. He was dead.

16

THE OFFICERS WHO HAD saved her life were PC Amital Singh and PC Neville Hillman. Renata shook them by the hand and thanked them when they parted at Ladbroke Grove Police Station. She had never felt so kindly disposed to the Old Bill.

Then DI Ian McAllister arrived, having been summoned from Hampstead Station. Over the next four hours, her opinion of the police sank steadily. He was as sluggishly methodical as before, questioning her, leaving her in the interview room for long periods while he was presumably making calls or consulting with other detectives, returning to ask her the same questions again. He wouldn't respond to her demands to know whether he believed her story, grasped that the attack on her was connected to the murder of Neal Marsh.

During one long wait, her thoughts turned to mundane matters. She picked up the phone on the desk and rang a friend who was also an impecunious mezzo-soprano. Renata asked if she would like to sing a Haydn High Mass next Sunday. She leapt at the offer. Then Renata left a message on the machine of the music director at the Brompton Oratory, explaining that she was indisposed and had found a replacement.

Finally, McAllister returned. He opened the door of the

interview room but did not come in. "You're free to go. A police car will take you home. Or … you said that you live alone, Ms. Radleigh?"

"My flatmates are away."

"Do you perhaps have a friend you could stay with?"

Renata smiled wanly. "Would that be a precaution against Flathead coming after me again? Or against my doing myself harm while the balance of my mind is disturbed?"

The tufty brows lifted. McAllister sat down across the table from her. "I have never said or implied that you're insane, Ms. Radleigh."

"No. But I get the impression you think I ran away from a couple of muggers and the rest is my overwrought imagination."

He sat back and crossed his legs to consider her words. He had the air of a chess player with plenty of time on the clock.

"That would be a possibility," he said at last, "except that the man you call Flathead shot and killed his accomplice. That's extraordinary behavior."

"It's bloody terrifying. Orangefoot was going to be arrested. Flathead shot him to prevent that—prevent his being questioned. That's how important it is to the Indian billionaire to keep his identity a secret."

McAllister folded his arms and meditated.

"Do you believe *any* of what I've been telling you?" she asked at length. "They were sent by the same man who had Neal Marsh killed last night. Tonight he tried to have *me* killed."

"We can't assume that was their intention."

"What?"

"The one you call Flathead was armed. He could have shot you."

"Perhaps I was too far away. Or it was too dark."

"Or perhaps they only intended to rough you up. Or throw a scare into you."

"Only." She suppressed an urge to slap his bland, pink face. "Can we at least agree that their intentions weren't friendly?"

"Most definitely." The eyes under the tufts turned kindly. "You've had a very frightening experience. That's why I suggest you stay with a friend for a while."

"Inspector, please tell me. Do you believe my story?"

"In police work, it's not a question of belief or disbelief. We will find evidence to support your assumptions, or not, as the investigation develops. We have a procedure we follow in a homicide."

"Would you mind telling me what it is? What you're going to do next, I mean."

"It's standard procedure, no secret about it. We start with the body. Identifying the body, in this case. The man you call Orangefoot had no ID on him. Either he wasn't carrying a wallet or it's at the bottom of the canal. We'll drag the canal tomorrow. Or we will use fingerprints or if necessary DNA tests to find his name. It is likely he's known to the police. The file on him will tell us his address and associates, and we will use the information to find the man you call Flathead."

"That could take some time."

Unperturbed, McAllister nodded.

"And you're not even going to look for the Indian billionaire meanwhile?"

"Come in tomorrow and we will sit you down with an artist. Try to come up with a sketch of this woman you call Jhumpa."

"It's not a question of me calling her that. Jhumpa is her name."

"How do you know?"

"Right. She didn't show me her passport. What about Grinevich then? He lied to you."

"I've already put in a call. Grinevich is in the pit at Covent Garden now, conducting *Eugene Onegin*. I left a message for him to call me tomorrow. He won't, of course. It will be his solicitor. In any case, I would like to have more leverage when I talk to Grinevich."

"Leverage?"

"Once we have your man Flathead in custody, facing charges for the murder of the man in the canal, he'll tell us who he's working for."

"And while you're looking for him, this deal will be going forward in America. They wanted me to keep myself incommunicado for three days, remember? There simply isn't time. Can't you ring the police in St. Louis?"

"The crimes have been committed in London, Ms. Radleigh. Not St. Louis."

Her tired mind grappled with this bald statement. Was it possible McAllister was inadvertently giving her cause for hope? She folded her arms and bowed her head. Let him wait while she thought things over, for a change.

Don hadn't broken any laws yet, as far as she knew. Not important ones, anyway. He didn't know what kind of man he was working for. He was keeping himself willfully ignorant of what was going on in London. Maybe there was still time to stop him before he went over the edge. If only she could go to see him, face to face, and convince him of what she knew ....

Anyway, she longed for the sight of Peter's face and the touch of his hand. She was in dire need of cosseting.

"Going back to your original question, Inspector," she said, "I do have a friend that I can stay with."

17

When he got up that morning, Peter found on his phone a text message from Renata saying that she was on her way to St. Louis and would arrive tonight. His joy at the message was clouded by worries about the medium. Why hadn't she called? This news was worth waking him up for, wasn't it? And why did she have a new phone number? He sent her a reply, asking if anything had happened.

There was still the whole day to be gotten through before he saw her. He went to his desk and made a freelancer's usual round of phone calls, begging some editors for work and politely reminding others to pay him for work already done. Then he got out the mop and broom. His apartment wasn't much—one dingy room with a kitchenette and small bathroom—but at least it would be clean for his guest.

By the time he was finished, he had another text. She was at Heathrow, waiting to board. Something had happened. She would tell him about it when she got there. She was fine and had learned nothing new. This enigmatic message set his nerves to jangling. He called Renata immediately. Her phone was off. The flight must be airborne.

Keyed up and frustrated, he decided to go out. He shouldered his bicycle and went down the stairs, headed for Forest Park.

It was another of those pleasant but eerie between-seasons days St. Louis got in November. The grass was covered with dead leaves, but the temperature was in the sixties. Trees stretched their bare gray limbs against cloudless blue skies. His phone chirped: a call, not a text. He put his feet on the ground and took off his helmet. The screen of his phone showed an Adams University number. Peter hoped they hadn't caught on that he had kept his employee ID so he could borrow WeCars.

"Peter Lombardo? Please hold for Roger Merck."

It turned out to be a long hold. He swung off his bike and propped it against a tree as he wondered what this could be about. Roger Merck was his former boss, the Associate Deputy Vice Chancellor for Public Relations. Peter liked Roger—he was an affable man—but they had been happy to see the last of each other. During *l'affaire* Don Radleigh last spring, Peter had been compelled to do things that embarrassed Adams University.

The deep, mellow voice came over the line. "Pete! How are you, young man?"

"Fine, Roger. How are you?"

"Couldn't be better. Say, I want to see you about a job."

"A job?"

"You're a free-lancer, aren't you? I want to hire your lance for a week or two. Can you come see me?"

"At your office?"

"No, I'm at the medical school. Your old stomping ground. How soon can you get here?"

"Well, I'm in Forest Park—"

"Excellent! I'm in my car, parked at Euclid and Clayton. See you in a few minutes."

"More than a few. I'm on a bike," Peter said, but Roger had hung up. Peter mounted up and headed east. Soon, over the trees, the bulky form of Granger Hospital, the medical school's teaching hospital, came into view, along with the familiar towers of its labs and clinics nestled among the luxury apartment buildings of the Central West End. He hoped Roger wouldn't mind that he was in T-shirt and shorts. And that he'd be rather sweaty by the time he arrived.

As it turned out, Roger, climbing out of his Volvo and waving to Peter as he arrived, was in athletic gear himself, all of it prominently stamped with the Adams name and shield. He was an African American of about sixty, with café au lait skin, dense, pure-white hair, and gold-framed glasses that glinted in the sun as he put out his hand.

"You're looking well. Lock up your bike and come with me."

They headed not toward any of the buildings, but the tennis courts atop one of the medical school's large underground parking lots. "Now for the job," Roger said. "Let's talk money first."

"You must have dealt with free-lancers before."

Roger laughed, his familiar deep-in the gullet rumble. "You'll be writing press releases and fielding calls from the media, probably a lot of them. So let's not bother doing it piecemeal. A set fee okay with you? Ten thousand."

"That's okay with me," said Peter, who had not seen a check that big in a long time.

"We'll throw in a little extra for expenses. We may have to set you up with an office and a secretary, depending on the volume of queries."

"If you must. Uh, Roger, mind if I ask ... why me? Considering my role in last spring's shit storm?"

"Some shit storms can't be helped. We didn't blame you. And you have familiarity with the subject matter already."

"I do?"

"Joel speaks highly of you."

"Joel Rubinstein?"

"Yes."

"So the subject is Parkdale?"

"Yes. But the chancellor wants to tell you about it himself."

To avoid further questions, Roger forged ahead, leading him

along the fence of the tennis courts. They were surprisingly busy for a weekday, but it was easy to spot Philip G. Reeve, chancellor of Adams University, because he had only one arm.

As they approached, Reeve was walking back to the service line. He was dribbling the ball with his racquet. Peter had read somewhere that it was his right arm he had lost and he had been right-handed, but neither that nor anything else had stopped him. "Hello, Roger," Reeve called out. He added, "Hello, Pete," though they had never met. "Be with you in a sec."

Standing behind the service line, he let the ball roll off the racquet. It bounced, and he gave it a hard tap with the racquet. The effect was the same as when an expert player tossed it: the ball ascended to its predetermined height and seemed to hover there. Reeve coiled and sprang. With a crisp *pop*, the ball rocketed across the net.

The rally was a long one. The chancellor's opponent was also a strong player, covering court effortlessly, hitting drives that passed only a couple of feet over the net and landed deep in Reeve's court. But Reeve had no trouble dealing with them. Peter had not realized before that he had lost his entire arm: not even a stub protruded from the short sleeve of his shirt. He used a Continental grip, so he did not have to shift it between backhands and forehands, and he put his racquet head to the ground to help him keep his balance when he changed directions. His lopsided silhouette emphasized the grace and power of his movements.

Various explanations—surgical, neurological, and immunological—circulated about why he did not use an artificial limb. Some suspected that the real explanation was political. To the right, he was a wounded warrior. To the left, a man who had overcome a disability.

Much speculation, friendly and unfriendly, centered on Philip G. Reeve. He was the biggest celebrity in St. Louis who was not a Cardinal, and his fame extended far beyond the town. Adams University, an ambitious institution, had gone out and acquired a star as its leader. Reeve was the scion of an old Virginia family. Like many of his forebears, he had gone to West Point. Then he had studied engineering at MIT. As a young officer fighting in Iraq, he had been badly wounded in an IED blast.

The book he had written about his long, difficult recovery had become a bestseller and a television movie. Reeve had served in high posts in the Veteran's Administration and Defense Department, then become dean of the engineering school at Purdue, where he demonstrated a magic touch as a fundraiser. When Purdue made the mistake of not elevating him to the presidency, Adams pounced.

He had been here three years, generating controversies that gained national attention. When the helicopter parent of an undergraduate had written to complain to him about her darling's disappointing B- in organic chemistry, Reeve's scolding reply had gone viral. He had ejected from campus a fraternity notorious for drunken parties. He had promulgated tough policies against date rape that had won him plaudits from feminists. At the moment, he was in the news for raising Adams' international stature with a new campus in the Gulf States of the Middle East. New York University had a campus in Abu Dhabi, the University of Missouri had one in Dubai, and the former president of Cal Tech had gone to Saudi Arabia to found a new university. Adams would not be left behind—not with Reeve at its head. It would become a university to the world. The next generation of the world's leaders, he promised, would include many Adams graduates. Still, some complained that he was more interested in his own career than in the university, and that he had one ear cocked toward Washington, for a call to take up a Cabinet seat.

Naturally Reeve kept Roger's department busy. Peter gradually realized that this was not a tennis match but a PR event. The players on the bank of courts were all medical students, warming up while waiting to take their turn with the chancellor. Each one got about ten minutes. If they just wanted to rally, he was gentle with them. But if they were good and wanted to play games, he played with fierce concentration.

Recognizing him, people were coming over from the street to watch and take pictures with their phones. Peter noticed some of his former colleagues at work, keeping them on their side of the fence. Other PR people were shooting photos and video, or interviewing whichever student had just played the chancellor.

A van from one of the local TV stations pulled up, and a woman jumped out. She strode toward the courts but was intercepted and politely repelled by another of Roger's minions. Peter said, "Does the chancellor do this often?"

"Phil likes to be accessible to students. He plays touch football in the quad on the main campus, too."

"Touch football? Really?"

"He makes amazing catches."

Reeve hit an overhead smash that almost bounced over the fence. It must have been the last point of the game, because he put down his racket and waited at the net for his opponent to come up. No exulting or fist-shaking, but he looked pleased. Since Peter was going to have to shake hands with the chancellor soon, he watched how it was done. The answer was with the left hand.

Aides flocked around Reeve as he crossed the court, throwing a jacket over his shoulders, taking his racquet and offering him a towel. He patted Roger's shoulder, then offered his hand to Peter.

"I know your byline from the alumni magazine," he said. "You wrote that profile of the heart surgeon. Doctor …."

"Vaughn."

"Excellent piece." Reeve was average height, with a wiry build. His hair, dark brown with just a little gray at the temples, was cut very short, which emphasized the angularity of his face. He had a lined forehead, long, straight, thin-bridged nose, and cheekbones so sharp they seemed to threaten to break the skin. His eyes were a brilliant blue—the same color as Renata's, Peter realized with a start. The face of Philip Reeve made you think it might be true that suffering ennobled.

"Excuse us, guys," he said to his entourage, as he took Peter's elbow to lead him a few paces away. Roger trailed behind.

"We've got a great story for you, Pete," he said. "We—that is, the medical school—are buying some buildings in Parkdale."

"Oh, really," said Peter. He struggled to keep a straight face. "Uh … how many buildings would that be?"

"Two hundred."

"Two hundred thirteen, to be precise," Roger put in.

"But … that's all the buildings there are in the neighborhood," Peter said. "You're buying up Parkdale, in one fell swoop."

"Yes."

"How much money are we talking about?"

The chancellor and Roger shook their heads in unison. The latter said, "We don't want you to put an exact figure in the press release."

"I'm afraid it's the first question reporters will ask me."

"What we want you to emphasize is that this is a great thing for the medical school. It will quadruple the amount of housing we can offer to students and employees."

"Do you actually need that much housing?"

"No, but we have to own the neighborhood to bring it back. It's a good thing all around for the med center to be surrounded by healthy communities. And we're going to invest the effort and the funds to make Parkdale what it used to be." The chancellor had been briefed on the high spots of Parkdale history, which he rattled off. It had one of the first synagogues in western St. Louis. Graduates of its public high school included a Hollywood director and a Yankees short stop. Eighty of its sons had served in World War II. "Please mention those facts in your release. Roger will give you the file. We'd like you to get started on the release right away, though of course it will be embargoed until the public announcement."

"When will that be?"

"Five p.m., in Parkdale."

"Five p.m. *today*?"

"Yes. All the details are in here," said Roger, handing him a bulky manila envelope.

"Look forward to seeing you there, Pete," said the chancellor.

On the way back to his bicycle, Peter reflected that there was one thing he knew: why the university was hiring him. Joel had told them he'd written about Parkdale, and they thought he might have picked up rumors about the impending sale. They wanted him on the payroll, writing an embargoed story, instead of going to the newspapers.

The papers would be interested. He recalled joking with Renata about how it would take an Oklahoma land rush of middle-class renters descending on Parkdale to turn the neighborhood around quickly. And that was exactly what was going to happen.

The sale was good news for Adams U and good news for Parkdale. It was absolutely wonderful news for Don Radleigh and his mysterious investor, who were about to sell, at a handsome profit, all the eighty-nine buildings they had just bought.

The news was not going to be a surprise to them.

18

PETER SPENT THE AFTERNOON at home, working on his embargoed press release. It wasn't long before his phone began to ring. Word was leaking out. In St. Louis, the usual pattern for big real estate deals aimed at saving urban neighborhoods was that they be talked about for years but never actually happen. The Parkdale buy, which nobody had heard about until it was a fait accompli, was exciting keen interest and a certain amount of suspicion. There were going to be plenty of reporters at the announcement. At four o'clock, he donned tie and sport coat, stuffed his pockets with press releases and business cards, and set off.

The event was staged with typical Adams U munificence. A vacant lot, freshly mown and devoid of litter, was hung with banners, ribbons, and balloons in the Adams colors of green and gray. Posters on easels showed how the lot was going to look after Adams transformed it to a park with a playground, fitness trail, and water feature. Bleachers were set up to face a dais, and as five p.m. approached, associate provosts and vice-chancellors—including Roger—mounted it and took their seats. Peter was willing to bet there hadn't been so many men in dark suits in Parkdale since the synagogue had closed.

At five sharp Chancellor Reeve bounded onto the podium

and stepped up to a lectern bearing the Adams seal. His speeches were much admired in the public relations and development departments, and this one did not disappoint. It was short and punchy, packed with sound bites that Peter scrawled in his notebook. Amid the crowded bleachers, he felt that Reeve was speaking directly to him—more than he had earlier, when the chancellor had in fact been speaking directly to him. For a few minutes, all the unanswered questions about the Parkdale deal fell away, and there was only a man burning with zeal to save a once robust, now battered neighborhood, as well as make life more agreeable for students and employees. By the time he finished, Peter was ready to pick up a broom or shovel and join in the effort.

Reeve did not take questions but said he would be available, and as he stepped down, reporters and photographers mobbed him. Peter knew he wouldn't be able to get close enough to hear, so he wandered among the associate provosts and vice-chancellors, who were also answering or avoiding questions from reporters. Some of them were about Don Radleigh and his fortuitously timed buys.

Everybody seemed to be enjoying the party. A line had formed for barbecue, and a man in a pink pig suit, complete with floppy ears and curly tail, was dishing out ribs. Peter guessed that it was Don's tenant Herb, who was probably grinning behind his mask as he thought about all the potential customers soon to move into the neighborhood. At a table next to him, the skinny, nose-ringed Ethan was handing out ice cream cones, looking much happier than he had the last time Peter had seen him. The Adams University student band was playing bluegrass. Peter saw Don ringed by reporters, three or four deep. He was wearing a handsome, tan gabardine suit. Sunglasses were perched atop his head. His eyes were bright and his cheeks flushed. Renata had said once that he enjoyed attention so much that he couldn't tell when it was hostile. Peter edged into the outer ring and listened.

A reporter—probably not the first to do so—was asking when Don had heard that Adams was buying his eighty-nine buildings.

"Late yesterday," he replied. "It knocked me for six."

"Does that mean you were surprised?"

"Absolutely."

"*Completely* surprised?"

Don missed the insinuation. "I didn't before, but I realize now that it was I who gave Adams the decisive nudge. They were impressed by the confidence I showed in buying so many buildings—including the derelict ones, even those that were just empty shells."

"But they're still derelict and empty shells," said a woman Peter knew was from the St. Louis *Post-Dispatch*. "How many of your buildings have you actually had time to rehab?"

"Not as many as I'd like. I love these old buildings. I was looking forward to renovating them. But I had to give them up … for their own good, as it were."

The reporters exchanged sidelong glances.

Don went on obliviously. "In future years—well, not even years, months—I'll be walking these familiar streets admiring all the improvements Adams is making. To the buildings themselves, of course, but there will also be bike lanes and racks, security phones on every corner, new trees and parks, and it will give me deep satisfaction to think I played a small part in—"

"What do you say to the rumor that one of these parks will be named after you?" drawled a man from the *West End Word*. No such rumor was in circulation, and there were chortles and even an outright guffaw as the unsuspecting Don preened himself.

"What's your reaction to Chancellor Reeve calling you an urban pioneer?" asked a woman from the NPR station.

"Well, I'm quite—"

"Don't you think 'urban profiteer' is more like it?"

A hard blow from the side sent Peter staggering. The man standing next to him had fallen against him. Somebody was pushing roughly through the crowd. It was a short, rotund man, with a few wiry black hairs crossing his bare pate. He closed in on Don, shouting at him in English so strongly accented that Peter couldn't get what he was saying. Don was backing off, raising his hands palms out. The man grabbed his collar with one hand and punched him with the other. The punch knocked off Don's sunglasses but did no other damage.

Four Adams security men were on the assailant now. They forced him to the ground, cuffed him, and dragged him away. Hanging his head, he went quietly. Don was denying to the reporters that he knew what that was about or who the man was. Peter followed the security men, hoping for a word with the assailant.

He assumed they were going to escort him out of the party and release him, but instead they turned him over to some St. Louis cops, who put him in the back of a patrol car. Joel Rubinstein sidled up, hands in pockets. He spoke quietly to one of the cops, who shook his head and got behind the wheel. The patrol car drove away.

Joel watched it go, frowning. He was dressed up for the occasion. His jeans were clean, his T-shirt had no holes in it, and his ponytail was bound in a ribbon rather than a rubber band.

"You know that guy?"

"Oh … hi, Peter. Yes. His name's Mohammed Qasedi. He's one of those landlords I was telling you about, who rent to Section 8 tenants."

"A slumlord."

"More of a slum peasant. He was an optician in Cairo. Came over here when the troubles began a few years ago. His credentials were worthless here, so he took out a loan and bought a building. He didn't know what he was doing, and he wouldn't listen to us or didn't understand us—his English isn't too good. He ended up with tenants who trashed his building even faster than usual. It was uninhabitable. He sold it to Don for twenty thousand dollars. Don just sold it to Adams for three or four times that."

"Oh. Of course, there's nothing illegal in that."

"No." Joel gave Peter a keen look. "You know, you never did report back to me about who Don's backer is."

"I never did find out. I know only that he'll go to any lengths to keep his name a secret."

"It doesn't matter anymore. To me, anyway. My worries about Parkdale are over. And I'm rich."

Peter nodded. "I'm benefiting from a bit of Adams U largesse myself. Thanks for recommending me to Vice-chancellor Merck."

"I just said you were poking around the neighborhood, and he decided to bring you onto the reservation."

"How long have you known Adams was going to buy up Parkdale?"

"Only since yesterday. Of course I've been trying to talk Adams into buying some buildings from me for years. Telling them Parkdale had potential. They would listen, but it always turned out they had other priorities."

"Why move now? And buy up the whole neighborhood?"

"You know what they say about gift horses. All I know is I'm rich."

"You don't sound happy."

"Well, I'm not as rich, or as happy, as Don Radleigh. And whoever he's working for. Such lucky guys."

Raising his eyebrows, Joel turned away. Peter realized that he had failed to get a quote from him, one he could use in a press release. Time to get to work. Looking around, he spotted a good prospect for a quote: a tall black man, with a chest so broad he couldn't button his suit coat. Revealed in all its glory was a "power tie" in glowing yellow.

"Frank Muldaur," Peter said, approaching. "Still a haberdasher's nightmare, I see."

Muldaur looked down on him with hooded eyes. "Do we know each other well enough for you to insult my taste?"

"Come on, Muldaur, you know me. Peter Lombardo of the Springfield *Journal-Register.* Whenever I wanted an interview with the Mayor of St. Louis, I knew I could count on you not to help."

"It's the Chief of Staff's job to see his boss doesn't waste his time on small-town Illinois papers. *Journal-Register* went bust, didn't it? What you doing now?"

"At the moment, I'm working for Adams U."

"PR? Guy who enjoys being obnoxious as much as you?"

Peter poised his pen over his notebook. "What do you think of the Adams purchase of Parkdale, Mr. Muldaur?"

"The City of St. Louis has long regarded Adams as a partner in urban progress. The Medical Center is the top employer in the city, and this property acquisition is a good thing all around."

"Very nice," said Peter, scrawling. "What about the tax angle?"

"I don't know what you're referring to."

"Sure you do. Adams is a non-profit. Doesn't pay taxes. That means a lot of buildings would drop off the city's tax rolls. You can't be happy about that."

"There you go being obnoxious again. I gave you your quote. So long."

"Come on. You must have a real answer."

"I'll save it for the real reporters." Muldaur moved off with this stately walk, his arms swinging at some distance from his broad torso.

Peter moved on. He saw Don, who had recovered from his encounter with the slum peasant and was now sipping lemonade and chatting with Roger and a couple of other vice-chancellors. He considered joining them, just to see how Don would react. But his attention was drawn to a woman sitting in the otherwise empty rows of chairs facing the podium.

It was the woman Don had met for a drink in the Central West End. She was not looking at him, or at anyone, just smoking a cigarette with an unalloyed enjoyment one rarely saw these days. Peter glanced around. Hannah was about twenty paces away, studying one of the posters for the proposed park.

He approached the woman, smiling. "Evening."

She did not smile back. She gave him that special look—a combination of raised eyebrows and lowered lids—that beautiful women mastered to discourage troublesome males.

He resorted to his job to avoid a brush-off. "I'm from med school PR. Mind if I talk to you for a moment?"

She held out her cigarette menacingly, as if it were garlic and Peter a vampire. "What's your problem? This is usually enough to guarantee me some privacy at an Adams event."

"I'm hoping for a quote."

Seen close up, she looked a little older, with a few more lines around her eyes and mouth, but the heart-shaped face framed by the bell of dark hair was just as beautiful. Her legs, in dark-toned hose, were elegantly crossed. Her perfume blended agreeably with the smell of smoke.

"Oh, you don't want a quote from me. I work for a part of the university that the chancellor, and therefore your department, has little interest in."

"And that would be?"

"The College of Arts and Sciences."

"The chancellor isn't interested in arts and sciences?"

"He prefers engineering and business. Disciplines that quickly convert students to generous alumni donors."

"Before we go any further, may I have your name and title?"

"I've already gone too far to give them to you. Are you trying to get me in trouble?" She gave him a direct look and a smile, a charmingly lopsided one that brought out a long dimple in her right cheek. He didn't think she was much worried about getting in trouble.

"Off the record, then. What's your response to the Parkdale acquisition?"

"Complete surprise. I'd heard nothing about it."

"And now that you've had time to think it over ...?"

"Complete bafflement. The chancellor has never shown much interest in St. Louis. I don't know why he'd want to rescue a neighborhood."

"Well, maybe he's thinking of the students. He wants them to be well-housed."

"He's never shown much interest in our students, either. He thinks they're a bunch of pampered degenerates who ought to be in boot camp."

Peter sat down beside her. "You know, you really make it worthwhile going off the record. What is Reeve interested in, in your opinion?"

She flicked away her cigarette with red-nailed fingers. "He makes no secret about it. At a faculty meeting once, one of my colleagues said he was afraid that Reeve wanted to change Adams too much. Reeve replied, 'I'm not interested in changing the university. I want to change the world.' "

"The 'global networked university,' " Peter said. "The 'university to the world.' "

"So you do know his buzz words. He doesn't like our campus, with its musty buildings and students reading old books, sitting around talking about them, trying to figure out what's important in life ... I mean, where does that get you? His vision is a brand-new campus, in a desert, with clean, disciplined students learning to be docile technocrats, and not daring to have a thought of their own, lest they lose their scholarships or get thrown in jail."

"You're talking about the Mideast campus."

"Yes. We have a delegation from the Sultan of Kutar arriving later this week. I'm surprised the chancellor can spare a thought for anything else."

"Would you say there are a lot of people on the main campus who share your views?"

"I'm not alone."

"Any chance you'll be going on the record soon?"

"Perhaps." She uncrossed her legs and leaned forward, letting him know his time was about up.

Time for the key question, then. "Do you know Don Radleigh?"

"I know who he is, but we've never met."

This was untrue. He gave her a doubting look, but she'd already turned away. She sauntered off, slender hips switching under her short black skirt.

He stood and looked around. Chancellor Reeve had left, and so had Don. In fact, the party was visibly winding down. He had better wrap up his PR duties. He distributed press releases to reporters, took down quotes from a couple of vice-chancellors, consulted with the staff photographer about identifying subjects and cut-lines.

Feeling he had earned his barbecue, he headed for the stand, where Herb had taken off his pig head. His sweat-soaked moustache drooped as he filled plates. Peter got in line. Ahead of him was a man with dreadlocks reaching to his shoulder blades and an expensive tweed sports jacket. The combination was incongruous but familiar.

"Imani?"

The man turned. His broad-browed, handsome face was the color of sourwood honey. He smiled and offered his hand. "Hello, Peter. How are you?"

When Peter had been a full-time PR man, he'd written a piece for the alumni magazine, singing the praises of the med school's new minority scholarship program. Associate Professor Imani Baraku of the School of Public Health had responded with a letter to the editor, demolishing Peter's article, point by point. Roger skillfully made the incident go away, leaving Peter still feeling angry and embarrassed. It surprised him that when they met, Imani Baraku was perfectly affable, and that for the rest of Peter's stay in PR, he went out of his way to be helpful and pleasant.

"You here for the ribs?" the professor asked.

"No, I'm working."

"Oh, you're back with PR again? Glad to hear it."

"Only temporarily. I'm the public info officer for the Parkdale buy."

Imani's eyebrows rose, clearing the top of his horn-rimmed glasses. "Really? What can you tell me about it?"

Peter pulled a piece of paper out of his pocket. "It's all in my press release."

"Thank you, but I've already read it. Didn't notice your byline. Forgive me. Now what's not in there?"

Peter smiled and looked down.

"Come on, you can tell me. You're only a temporary Adams slave."

It always disconcerted a white person when a black person used that word, and Imani knew it. He was expert at throwing you off balance and making you blurt things out.

"Nice try, Imani. But in this case, I really don't know much that's not in the release."

"But you have a personal connection to this Radleigh guy, right? His sister, to be exact."

"And you have a long memory. Uh … Imani? The line's moved."

The professor looked around and saw that a gap had opened in front of him. He closed it, then turned back to Peter. He wasn't done probing. Peter decided to speak first. "What's your interest in Parkdale?"

Imani swept a hand across the scene. "You notice who's not here?"

"Who?"

He raised his chin. Peter looked up.

People were leaning out and looking down from the windows of the buildings around the vacant lot. They were almost all black.

"Everybody's having a good time and saying how great this

is for the neighborhood, except the neighbors," Imani said. "Didn't notice, did you?"

Well, he hadn't. Stung, he said, "There's nothing to prevent them coming down and joining in."

"They're too busy wondering how long till they're evicted and where they're going. You got to love that Adams U style. Settle their fate without consulting them. Then they're welcome to some ribs. This is just urban removal all over again."

"You'll recall that in my release, I mentioned that the university is going to offer some apartments to non-students at subsidized rents."

"That paragraph was a bit short of detail. Like how many apartments, how much rent, and where the people are to live while the buildings are being renovated. A careful writer like yourself would have included those details, if they'd been available to him."

Peter's cheeks felt hot. It was so irritating, having to argue with people when you suspected they were right and you were wrong. Now he remembered why he had gone freelance. "All of that will be announced."

"I can't wait."

"Imani, are you going to criticize this deal? Publicly?"

Chuckling, Imani put his hands in the pockets of his tweed jacket. "I'm planning to do more than criticize it. I hope I can undo it."

"But it's a done deal."

"The papers aren't signed yet. The money hasn't changed hands."

"Next!" Herb called out.

It was Imani's turn. He smiled pleasantly at Peter and turned with appetite to the spread of ribs, beans, and potato salad.

19

All the traveling she had to do had not served to make Renata a good flier. For one thing, there was the discomfort—her femur was a bit too long for the space available between seats—and for another, there was her certitude that the plane was going to crash. So, at no point in this long journey had she managed to get any sleep. She did finally drop into a stupor, from which she was jolted awake by the impact of the wheels on the runway, and the realization that this was St. Louis. Peter would be waiting in the terminal, only a few hundred yards away.

Glad to be on her feet and off the plane, she strode down a long corridor, trailing her carry-on behind her. The whirring of its wheels on the floor was audible. Lambert-St. Louis, the fourth airport she had passed through on this journey, was by far the quietest. That was something that always struck her about St. Louis: its emptiness. Where was everybody? For a Londoner, it was almost eerie. There didn't seem to be enough people here to keep a city going.

She debated popping into one of the loos she was passing and putting on some makeup, for Peter's sake. By now her face must look a fright—worn, lined, pallid. But she was too eager to see him to stop. So she strode on, pace quickening all the time, half-running by the time she passed the TSA barrier, and there he was, with his tousled red-brown hair, hazel eyes behind gold-framed specs, and broad smile. She abandoned her suitcase to run the last few steps and throw herself into his arms.

After a few minutes of billing and cooing, he retrieved her carry-on. But instead of heading for the parking lot, he let go of its handle and faced her squarely. "Now. I've waited long enough. Tell me what happened in London that you've been holding back."

"Oh, Peter. It's so embarrassing. I was stupid and careless, and you're going to be very cross with me." She told him about the chase by the canal. He was not angry. He took her in his arms and hugged her tight. For a long time neither of them moved or spoke. This was well worth flying the Atlantic for, Renata thought.

At last she patted his shoulder and stepped back. "Right. Must get going. And meantime you can bring me up to date on your end."

But Peter was white-faced and glassy-eyed. He said, "I'm … having a hard time focusing. In fact, I really don't care about Don and his problems. He almost got you killed."

"His boss gave the order. Don has no idea what's really going on."

"I don't forgive him that," said Peter stonily.

"Let's find a place to sit down and have a coffee." She grasped the handle of her suitcase with one hand, Peter's hand with the other. It took a hard tug to get him moving. They went into a Starbuck's where they were the only customers and ordered large, strong coffees. Then they sat down on straight chairs with a table between them.

Renata said, "It was a horrible business. The worst part was that man in the canal getting shot. He'd outlived his usefulness. There was a danger he'd talk. So his mate just executed him. Horrible."

"I'm finding it hard to feel sorry for this son of a bitch who was trying to kill you."

The blood was coming back into Peter's face. In fact, he was looking rather scary. She reached across the table for his hand. "Something good can come of this. We're going to see my brother. Right now. I'll look him in the eye and he'll tell me what he's holding back. It's worked before, remember?"

"Then he was in jail. He knew he needed you. Now he thinks he's on top of the world. Doing the big deal that'll make him rich."

"I'm going to tell him, you have no idea what kind of man you're working for. He tried to have me killed. That's bound to shock some sense into him. He'll level with us. And then we can talk sensibly with him about how to get out of this mess before it's too late."

"Renata, I'm afraid it's already too late."

"What?"

"Don is in too deep. He can't be as blameless as you're hoping he is."

"What's happened? Tell me."

"The sale has been made. All of Don's buildings. All of Parkdale. To Adams University. And Don knew it was going to happen." He filled her in on the details.

Renata thoughtfully sipped coffee gone cold. She said, "Well, one thing is becoming clear."

"Is it? That's good. Tell me."

"Put two and two together. The Indian billionaire has to keep his identity secret *because* he committed some crime to find out that Adams was going to buy Parkdale. He must have bribed or blackmailed somebody close to the chancellor."

"That makes sense. Except for one thing. The billionaire is in London. Don is here. If bribing or blackmailing was done, Don's the one who did it."

"No."

"Why not?"

"Because Don wouldn't do anything like that. I know he's silly and shallow—"

"Don't forget selfish, while we're on the S's."

"But he's never hurt anyone. Except himself."

"Naturally you find it hard to accept that your brother—"

"Yes, I do. I've known him from birth, and he's not a criminal. He's being used. Remember what he said. That he's doing good. Saving the neighborhood."

"He's happy then. So let him be. Let's go home and to bed and stay there for a few days."

"Peter, he's on the spot. The moneyman's hidden behind his shell corporations and so forth. Don's here taking the heat, because everybody thinks he had inside knowledge."

"And their suspicions are justified."

"It's not as bad as it looks."

"Dear, I'm afraid you're going to find out things you don't want to know."

"Well, I'm *not* afraid. Let's go find Don."

20

THEY DROVE STRAIGHT TO Don's condo tower in the Central West End. Peter assumed that now the deal was done, he wasn't going to pretend that he lived in Parkdale any longer. But the doorman told them that Mr. Radleigh was not in and had not been in all day.

They got back in the car—another rent-by-the-hour Prius—and drove over the highway to Parkdale. It was late, but there were many cars driving around, some of them patrol cars, from both the St. Louis Police and Adams U security. Lights were on in most windows. Little knots of people were sitting on the front steps of the buildings, talking. The neighborhood had an unsettled feeling. Peter remembered what Imani had said.

He parked in front of Don's building. They got out and walked around it. No lights were showing in his apartment. They went up the fire escape, rang the back doorbell, and knocked on the door. Renata called out his name. No response.

Back in the car, they compared telephone numbers. Peter had no number for Don that she did not have, and she'd tried them all frequently without response. It occurred to Peter that Don's fellow landlords might know where he was.

He drove to Joel Rubinstein's building, the tall one at the busy intersection where the landlords kept watch for drug dealers. The light was on in their top-floor aerie. He explained to Renata as they climbed the stairs.

Joel opened the door to his knock. "Oh. Hi, Peter."

"Hi. This is Renata Radleigh."

Joel looked at her. His eyes widened. Peter had never had a drop-dead gorgeous girlfriend before, and he still wasn't used to the way other men reacted to her and the way it made him feel, the one-two punch of atavistic emotions—possessive pride and irrational jealousy. Even after a transatlantic flight, Renata was a traffic-stopper. Her own belief that whatever beauty she'd possessed had long ago faded made her even more attractive. Aside from her recital gowns, her clothes were old and plain, and she had no theatrical mannerisms whatever. But you could tell from the way she held herself and the light in her eyes that she was no ordinary person. She smiled and put out her hand.

With difficulty, Joel pulled himself together and shook it. "Come join the celebration."

"Of the sale?" Peter asked.

"Of not having to spend our nights watching drug dealers anymore. They're the university's problem now."

There were open pizza cartons and Styrofoam chests with the necks of beer bottles poking out of the ice, but the men around the table, most of them Joel's age, had their heads down and were talking quietly. It didn't look like much of a celebration.

They brightened when Renata was introduced. They crowded round to take her hand and asked questions to hear her accent. Peter ran the gamut of caveman emotions again.

Eventually Joel was able to pry her loose and take them into the kitchen for a talk. Peter explained, "Renata's come to see her brother. But we can't find him."

"Probably lying low," Joel replied. "He's tired of being asked questions he doesn't want to answer."

"Is that all?" Renata asked. "Peter told me about the assault at the party."

"Don't worry about Mohammed. The cops have let him go, but he's not looking for a rematch with Don."

"There are others, though, who have hard feelings?" she asked.

"Some. Those of us here, however, have no cause for resentment. We're going to be rich."

"So why's everybody so down at the mouth?" Peter asked.

"Yesterday I was responsible for one hundred and fifty-seven toilets. Now it's just the two at home. It's all happening too fast. Maybe you haven't heard the latest?"

Peter shook his head.

"We're all going over to the Adams campus tomorrow morning. To close the deal. Which is totally screwy."

"It would normally take weeks, wouldn't it?" Peter said. "They'd inspect every building, negotiate a price for each one."

"I hear the word has come down from the chancellor himself," Joel said. "Get it done."

"So you're going to be overpaid. That's not so bad."

Joel, looking no happier, did not reply.

Renata said, "Don will have to be there, then. At the meeting on campus tomorrow."

"That's true," Joel said. "You'll be able to find him there for sure. Come at noon. I'm sure lunch will be up to Adams standards."

21

THE WARM SUN ON her face awakened Renata. The window by Peter's bed was open, and she lay listening to that wonderful American creature, a mockingbird, running through his repertoire of impersonations of lesser birds, adding ornamentation with a brio few bel canto singers could match. It crossed her mind that she had traveled a long way south. It was like summer here.

After leaving the landlords, they had gone to Peter's apartment. Worn out by a day that had begun in London, she had flopped onto the bed fully dressed and promptly lost consciousness. In the middle of the night she awoke refreshed and randy. She and Peter tore each other's clothes off in the dark. Sated, they went back to sleep. Peter got up early, leaving her in bed.

A key clicked in the lock and the door, only six feet from the end of the bed, opened. He came in with coffees in paper cups and a bag that she knew would contain oranges and bananas. He didn't ordinarily keep fresh fruit in his kitchen, and she couldn't begin a day without it. She got up to kiss him.

"What are you staring at?"

"You're more luxuriant."

She looked down. "Oh yes, once I put away my bathing costume, I let it grow out. I hope you like it?"

"More than ever."

She retrieved her nightgown from her suitcase and put it on. In the kitchen, she found Peter talking on his phone. He lowered it and said, "It's my boss, Assistant Deputy Vice-Chancellor Roger Merck. He wants to talk to you."

"Me?"

"Joel told him you were here." He held the phone out to her. "Relax, he's a nice guy."

She took the phone and said hello.

"Ms. Radleigh, sorry to bother you so early. But we have a little problem here that maybe you can help with. Have you heard from your brother?"

"I'm afraid not."

"Hmph," said Roger.

"He's supposed to be at a meeting on campus, Joel said."

"Well, that's the thing. I'm at the meeting, and he's late."

"Oh."

"His lawyer and accountant are here, so we're proceeding with business, but—"

"They don't know where he is?"

"No. There's an event scheduled for two o'clock, signing ceremony and photo op, and it's kind of a big deal. The chancellor will be here. It's important for Don to attend."

Renata said she would pass on the message and rang off. As she handed the phone back to Peter, she explained, finishing, "This is odd. Where *else* could he possibly be when the deal is being finalized?"

"I wish I knew."

"Let's try his apartments again."

"I already did. Swung by while I was buying breakfast. But there is another possibility of where he might have spent last night. I should have thought of it before."

"The gardening girlfriend. Of course."

* * *

In Parkdale the great spruce-up had begun. Crews were at work painting the front doors of the apartment buildings green and gray, which Peter told her were the Adams U colors. Surveyors were at work, peering through little telescopes on tripods and setting stakes in the grass. Men in hardhats and yellow vests were painting stripes and codes on the pavement to indicate where the underground utilities lay.

Peter pulled the car over in front of a three-story brick building. A stocky, fair-haired woman was trimming the yews planted along the front of it. "That's Hannah," he said.

Hearing the car door slam, she looked up at Renata. As they approached, she continued to stare at her.

"You're Don's sister," she said. "He showed me your picture. You were playing somebody called Musetta. You had a blond wig and your tits were practically falling out of your dress."

People didn't ordinarily refer to Renata's tits on first meeting her, but she badly needed the help of Don's girlfriend, so she smiled and said, "That sounds like Musetta, all right. I'm pleased to meet you, Hannah."

"And you're Peter. I remember meeting you. What do you want?"

"We're looking for Don."

"Can't help you." She made a final snip and turned toward the door of the building.

"May we come in?" Renata asked. "We want very much to talk to you."

"If you think it's worth the climb."

They followed Hannah's broad, jeans-clad rump up to the second floor. She had a pair of clippers and a phone holstered on her belt, and keys carabineered to a belt loop. She let them into her apartment and closed the door. It had a deadbolt lock and the key was in the lock. She turned it, as if to make sure no one else could get in, and sat on a well-worn couch. Her attitude suggested that an invitation to sit would not be forthcoming, so they took the initiative and sat on rickety chairs opposite her.

"We're sorry to bother you, but it's most awkward," Renata said, still striving for the pleasant note. "I've come all the way from London to see Don, and now we can't find him."

"He didn't mention to me that you were coming."

"I didn't actually tell him."

"It's not surprising that he isn't instantly available, then."

She was leaning back, legs crossed, eyelids lowered, an expression of indifference on her wide, freckled face. Whatever Don had told her, it had not disposed her in favor of his sister. She kept quiet and let Peter try his luck.

"When did you last see him?"

"Last night. I had a party for the local community gardeners. He dropped by."

"He didn't stay the night?"

"No."

"Did he say where he was going?"

"I don't require any excuse or explanation from him for not staying the night. The gardeners were still here. We had a lot to talk about. Chancellor Reeve told me himself he's enthusiastic about making garden beds available to his students. He said I could have as many vacant lots as I want. I was more interested in that than in where Don spent the night."

"It's just that he didn't go home."

"He has a place in Lindell Terrace, too."

"Oh," said Peter. "You know about that?"

She rolled her eyes. "You must think I'm really dumb. Or he's really sneaky. Nights are noisy here. Honking, shouting, occasional shots. He sleeps better in the Central West End."

"Well, he wasn't there either."

"You trying to wind me up? Get me worried he spent the night with another woman? It won't work. We don't have an exclusive relationship anyway."

"I don't understand," Renata said. "You mean, you have other boyfriends, or he has other girlfriends?"

"The first question is none of your business, the second I don't know the answer to. But I wouldn't be surprised. Men are men. You think this guy's been celibate while you've been away?" She flicked a hand at Peter.

His eyes opened wide and he said, "I … um …."

Renata put out a hand, palm up. "Don't say a word." She glared at Hannah. "Why are you being so nasty?"

"I'm getting annoyed by your questions, okay? What gives you the right? I know what happened last spring. Don was falsely accused. You cleared him. Great, but now you think he can't run his own life. So you're going to do it."

Renata did not know how to respond. She looked at Peter for help.

"Hannah, Renata's worried about her brother. Can you blame her? There was a lot of hostility toward him at the party yesterday afternoon. You must have felt it."

"People were envious. That's what happens when one person is smart and lucky and makes a lot of money. Everybody thinks he cheated somehow."

"They're not wrong." Peter was about to go on, but noticed that Renata was trying to catch his eye. She must be thinking there was a way to describe their suspicions that would go down better with Hannah.

She said, "The man Don is working for is some kind of big-time crook. He found out somehow that Adams was going to buy Parkdale. He's far away and nobody knows his name. He's willing to kill people to keep it that way. He tried to have me killed. That's why I have to talk to Don now."

Hannah rolled her head back till she was looking at the ceiling. She was still for a long moment. Abruptly she pitched forward, putting her forearms on her knees. "All *right.* You've managed to get me worried, too. Come on."

She rose and headed for the door. Renata and Peter rose, too. He said, "Where are we going?"

"To the last place I saw Don."

"But you said you last saw him when he left here," Renata said.

"I lied."

She twisted the key, unlocking the door, and walked out. Peter and Renata exchanged a look and followed. He took the opportunity to whisper to her, "Actually I *have* been celibate while you've been away."

"I didn't ask. Thanks for telling me."

22

HANNAH HAD AN OLD pickup truck. Its bed was empty but redolent of mulch. Renata was in the passenger seat, with Peter behind her in a sideways jump seat. Hannah was hunched over the wheel, lips compressed. She made Renata think of a cyclist bracing before starting up a steep hill.

Finally she spoke. “When Don left my place last night, I followed him. That’s where I’m taking you. I don’t know if he’ll still be there.”

Renata did not know what to say. She looked in the mirror, trying to catch Peter’s eye.

Hannah laughed raucously. “You two are hilarious, with your significant looks. ‘What do you make of that?’ ‘Shall I talk to her now?’ ‘No, you try it.’ And after one of you talks, the appreciative look from the other one. ‘Well said!’ ‘Another good one!’ Don used to say, the world doesn’t think much of them, but at least they’ve got each other.”

“Charming,” Peter said. “We’ll have to double-date sometime.”

“Oops, I’ve offended The Man. He’ll sulk for a while. Over to you, Renata. What have you got to say to my humiliating confession?”

"Perhaps you were more worried about him than you let on before," Renata said.

"Even worse. I was jealous. I was stalking him."

Hannah drove with the same vigor she brought to every other activity, wrenching the wheel to left or right, thrusting the long gear shift lever forward or hauling it back. They crossed the highway bridge to the Central West End.

"Every relationship has a clock," she went on. "Including yours. You'll find out. I could tell Don's and mine had just about timed out. And I've got nothing to complain about. He's been good for me.

"There wasn't much left of me when my ex got done. I was just mooching around the apartment. Too scared of the neighborhood to go out the door. My kitchen faucet had a leak that kept getting worse. Finally I had to call. And this English guy shows up at the door, says he's my new landlord, here to fix the—what did he call it?—the 'tap.' Only he didn't really know how and I had to help. He let me—unusual for a man. It took ages and when we got it done we laughed and hugged.

"He took me out to eat a lot. I only eat locally sourced fresh vegetables, so that means they had to be expensive restaurants. He never whined. He's a charming guy. And a great lay. And he talked me into taking on the community garden. Now the phone's ringing off the hook. People are always coming to the door. So it's not like he's leaving me with nothing."

Renata asked gently, "When you followed him, where did he go?"

"Oh, I got what I deserved. He walked up to a door, and before he reached it, it opened. She was waiting. I got a good look at her. And I thought, *No need to wait around. He's staying the night.*"

Peter said, "Was she about five seven, slender, medium-length dark hair, possibly smoking a cigarette?"

Hannah looked at his reflection in the mirror. "You've seen him with her too?"

"Yes. And she was at the Adams party."

"Was she? I didn't notice her then."

"I talked to her. She's on the faculty She wouldn't tell me her name, but she did tell me two things. One, that she and Don had never met. Two, that the Parkdale buy was a complete surprise to her."

"The first was a lie, and you think the second was too?" Renata asked.

"It's possible. One thing I'm pretty sure of. Whatever her interest in Don was, it wasn't romantic."

He put his hand on Hannah's shoulder. Renata expected her to shrug it off, but she didn't. In fact she looked somewhat comforted.

They passed through a bustling corner of the medical center and turned onto one of the residential streets of the Central West End. They drove past tall trees and well-maintained old houses. Hannah parked in front of a row of small, brick, attached houses with a running terra cotta frieze. As they waited for Peter to wriggle out of the back, Hannah scanned the curbs. "His Jag's gone," she said.

They went up the front walk and Peter knocked on the door, which opened promptly. The mystery woman was all Peter had promised, Renata thought. She had just the sort of coiffure Renata would have adopted if she could have afforded a weekly trip to the salon and a beautifully made-up face with eyebrows waxed into tapering pointed arches. She was wearing green corduroys and a gray turtleneck. She calmly looked them over, and her eyes came to rest on Renata.

"You're Renata Radleigh."

"Yes," said Renata, surprised. She was sure they had never met.

"I've seen you at Saint Louis Opera. Several times. You were Flora in *La Traviata*. And the year before, Siebel in *Faust*. And the year before that, you were in something Italian. Don't tell me …."

It took her ten or fifteen seconds to recall that the opera had been *Madama Butterfly*, and during that time, she just let them wait. She was a professor all right.

She was complimenting Renata on the way she had handled the role of Suzuki when she broke off. "Wait a minute. *Radleigh*. Is Don your brother?"

"Yes."

"It never occurred to me before. There's no family resemblance."

"As it happens, we're looking for Don," Peter said.

She turned to him as if she had forgotten he was there. "You're the PR man."

"Peter Lombardo. This is Hannah Mertz. Your turn."

She smiled and said, "Dana Carmichael."

"And your appointment?"

"Professor of comparative literature and associate dean of the faculty. But I'm afraid I don't know where Don is."

"He was here last night," said Hannah.

"Yes. How did you know?" The professor gave her crooked, sardonic smile. "I have a feeling this conversation is going to get complicated. Come in."

They stepped into a dim room, smelling strongly of cigarette smoke and rather overcrowded with comfortable sofas and armchairs, colorfully patterned rugs, and large landscape paintings in ornate frames. She waved them to chairs and sat down.

"I'm expecting some of my grad students in about twenty minutes, so we'll have to get right down to business. Peter, I've just remembered that I told you before I didn't know Don. I slipped up. How embarrassing." She did not look embarrassed.

"No need. I knew then you were lying."

"I had a feeling you did. Do you mind telling me how you knew?"

"I was following Don Tuesday, when he met you at the bar."

Her gull-wing eyebrows took flight. Her gaze shifted to

Hannah. "And you must have been following him last night. Pavement artists everywhere! You recognize the reference, of course. What, none of you? It's *Tinker Tailor Soldier Spy.* Don and I are both huge fans of John Le Carré."

"What else do you have in common?" Peter asked.

Dana reached for a brushed silver box on the coffee table, extracted a cigarette, lit it, inhaled, and exhaled. Renata could see the plus side of smoking. This routine allowed her to put the discussion on hold for a minute while she thought about how much to tell them.

She said, "You said you were looking for Don. He's missing, then?"

"There's a big meeting on campus to close the Parkdale deal. He's not there."

"That is strange. I have to tell you, I can't imagine where else he would be."

"Why did he come see you last night?"

"Because I invited him." She took another puff. "But I'd better start at the beginning."

She sat back and crossed her legs. Evidently she had decided there was no harm in leveling with them. "I belong to an informal group of deans and department heads. We call ourselves Cambridge Circus. Le Carré again. Our purpose is to try to find out, by any legal means, what Chancellor Reeve is going to do next."

"Is that necessary?" Peter asked.

"The chancellor comes from the military, as you know. He doesn't believe in collegiality. He believes in chain of command. After a number of nasty surprises, we decided we would have to becomes spies."

"Nasty surprises?"

"Budget cuts, basically. Are we going to have to merge departments? Eliminate tenured positions? Terminate full-time faculty and turn their courses over to adjuncts? It's nice to know these things in advance. Especially when you have to fire your friends."

"So you can oppose them?"

"So far it's been so we can cope. Opposition is the next step."

"I don't get the budget cuts. Adams has a fifteen-billion-dollar endowment," Peter protested.

"The chancellor would prefer to spend money elsewhere. Kutar, for instance." Dana put out her cigarette. "Anyway, when an Englishman suddenly popped up in Parkdale and started buying apartment houses as if they were going out of style, we noticed. We wondered if he might be hoping to sell them to Adams."

"That was pretty shrewd of you," Peter said.

"College professors aren't as dumb as people think. Several million dollars spent on real estate would mean the chancellor's number-crunchers on the phone, telling us to tighten our belts another notch. So I volunteered for the job of pumping Don for information."

"What did you find out?"

"Nothing. Don was more than polite. He enjoyed talking to me. Fencing with me. That was where *Tinker Tailor* came in. I kept asking if he had a 'mole' at Adams University. Naming my suspects. We had a fine time. But his line was, he had no reason to believe Adams was going to buy any buildings from him."

"Did you ask him about his source of capital?" Renata asked.

"Did I ever! He never let anything slip. Your brother's a very clever man."

"You're wasting your time, complimenting him to her," said Hannah. "The things Don is good at, she has no respect for."

"I've been wondering where you fit in," said Dana. "You're the girlfriend, aren't you?"

Hannah said nothing.

"I hope I haven't caused you any distress. We were having clandestine meetings, but there was nothing going on between us. He's not my type."

"I don't view you as a threat. I just think you're contemptible. Plying your feminine wiles."

That brought Dana's eyebrows into play again. "Let me be absolutely clear. I would unhesitatingly go out on the street and peddle my ass, if it would save Adams University. I've been here since I was a freshman. BA, MA, PhD. I love this place. Now it's being ransacked by an egomaniac who thinks he has a vision."

Peter said, "When you told me yesterday that the announcement of the buy was a complete surprise to you—"

"That was the truth. I'm sorry to say."

"But why did you want to see Don again, after the announcement? I would think you'd be pissed off at him."

"Actually, I never liked him better than last night. He was high as a kite. Not booze so much as exhilaration. But he did accept my invitation to come by out of a sort of compunction. Even brought me a bottle of wine, because I'd picked up most of the bar tabs. He seemed to be in the mood for an indiscretion. I was certainly hoping so.

"I'll tell you what I told him. He was sitting where Hannah is. I said, 'Don, it doesn't matter anymore, so just tell me. Who tipped you off that Adams was going to buy Parkdale?' "

They waited. She enjoyed their suspense for a while.

"He said, 'I'll answer, because I don't want you to suspect any of your colleagues unnecessarily. There never was a mole. I dealt directly with the chancellor.' "

"I said, 'Come on. The chancellor himself tells you what he's going to do?' He replied, 'No, I tell him what he's going to do.' "

"What could he possibly mean by that?" asked Renata.

"I don't know. And I've thought about practically nothing else since. I considered Don as, well, rather a lightweight. Maybe I was wrong."

The three of them waited, but that was all she had to say. Peter rose and put his card on the coffee table. "If anything does occur to you," he said.

Renata was also on her feet. “When he left, did he say where he was going?”

“No. Only that he was tired. I suppose he went home.”

23

As they returned to the truck, Peter called Roger Merck, who said that Don still had not appeared. His lawyer and accountant were representing him, but it was vital that Don show up to sign the contracts and appear with the chancellor in the photo op, which was now only an hour away.

Peter clambered into the backseat of the truck, as before. Renata sat in the passenger seat looking at Hannah, who drove in silence. She looked more severe in profile, when you could not see her wide forehead and freckled cheeks, only her strong nose and jutting jaw. Renata tried to think of something friendly to say, something that would make her open up. But as they crossed the highway back to Parkdale, nothing had occurred to her, so she resorted to, "Well, Hannah, what do you think?"

"About Don saying the chancellor takes orders from him?"

"Yes. Can it be true?"

"Oh, you know, Don says things just because he likes the sound of them."

Renata jumped.

Hannah gave her a sideways look. "Isn't that one of your cheap shots?"

"Yes, it is. I wasn't aware I'd said it to Don himself. "

"You agree with the *très soigné* professor. Don's a lightweight. This is just a real estate speculation to him. He doesn't care about saving Parkdale or the community gardens or anything but the money. And he's done God-knows-what to get some kind of hold over Chancellor Reeve."

"Hannah, enough," said Peter. "You're wrong."

"That's not what you think?"

"It's what *I* think. To the letter. But Renata thinks Don's trying to save the neighborhood. Only the man who's putting up the money is lying to him and using him." To Renata, he asked, "You *do* still think that, even after what Dean Carmichael said?"

"I'm even more sure," Renata replied. "How could Don get … leverage over the chancellor of Adams University? No, it's something this London billionaire—this murderer—has done." She turned in her seat. "And allow me to point out, Peter, that Don *has* saved the neighborhood."

They were back in Parkdale now, passing one of the buildings where a crew was painting the front door in Adams green and gray. Hannah gave her raucous laugh.

"Yeah. He did that, didn't he?" She turned to Renata. She was smiling.

Renata smiled back. "Only we're not making any progress in finding him."

"Dean Carmichael thought he was going home when he left her," Peter said. "Do you have the key to his apartment, Hannah?"

"Why do you ask?"

"We might find something that will give us a clue to his whereabouts."

"So you're going to search the place?"

"Yes."

Hannah was silent as she pulled up in front of Don's building. She didn't turn off the engine. After thinking a moment, she reached for the carabineer on her belt loop. "I'll give you the key. I have other stuff to do and … anyway, I don't want to be around when you're searching."

She detached the key and Peter took it. Then she pulled out her phone. "Can I have your number, Renata? If I hear from Don, I'll call."

"Of course," Renata said. "Thank you."

As the truck drove off, Peter led her around the building to a line of one-car, doorless garages. He pointed to the one at the end. "That's Don's."

"No Jaguar, unfortunately." Peering into the empty garage, she saw beer cans, newspapers, and flattened cardboard boxes. "A lot of rubbish."

"Don lets a street person named Wayne sleep there on wet nights," Peter said.

"You see? He has his kindly side."

"All part of the act."

They went up the fire escape to the second floor, where he unlocked the door. They stepped into a galley kitchen. "As clean as it was when Don brought me here five days ago," Peter said. "Our beer bottles are still in the sink."

"Don doesn't use a kitchen much." She shut the door behind her. "I don't blame Hannah for bowing out. This is giving me a very creepy feeling."

"We don't have much choice."

"But what if we find something awful? Like a … a gun."

"Renata, this is America. There's a gun in every home." He went on into the living room. "Looks the same as when I was here."

She walked around the living and dining rooms, which were comfortable and impersonal, like rooms in a good hotel. "There's nothing here from his house in Webster Groves. He had quite a good collection of old opera posters. He must have sold the lot and started over."

"I guess he didn't want anything that reminded him of those days."

"But having his favorite things around meant so much to Don. There were things in his house he'd brought from London. From our old family flat."

"There's that," he said, pointing. "It looks British."

She walked over to the front door and looked down at a stout mahogany barrel embellished with strange copper lozenges and medallions. "Yes. Isn't it hideous? This stood in our foyer. A Radleigh heirloom. It's an umbrella stand. I didn't recognize it with no umbrellas."

"We don't have much use for umbrellas in St. Louis."

"It doesn't rain?"

"We don't walk."

Renata looked around unhappily. "Where do we start? Shall I slit open sofa cushions or something?"

"I don't think this room is very promising. Let's look for an office."

They found a bedroom that had been converted to an office. Peter looked around. "Nice and neat. No clutter."

"Yes, Don's always been good at keeping up with his paperwork …."

Peter glanced at her curiously. "You were going to add …?"

"Nothing."

"No, go ahead."

"I was going to add, it's an exception to his general haplessness. But if Hannah were here she would say that's another of my cheap shots."

"Cheap people deserve cheap shots." He went over to the desk. "Landline hooked up to an answering machine. Kind of old-fashioned."

"Probably for the tenants. He doesn't want them ringing his mobile with maintenance requests."

Peter sat down at the desk. "I'll try to get into his computer. What kind of passwords does he like?"

"Kings of England, with no space and an Arabic numeral. His favorite is George4. I'll check the bedroom."

It had occurred to her to search his night table for his address book. Don was proud of his wide circle of acquaintances. He had an old, leather-covered, gilt-edged address book, stuffed with business cards and scraps of paper bearing telephone numbers. It would have been a helpful find, but she had no luck. Peter was playing back phone messages, and at one point she heard her own voice, sounding very British and very nasty, ordering him to ring her back "immejitly." Then there was silence, and a moment later Peter appeared in the bedroom doorway.

"Did George4 work?" she asked.

He shook his head. "I went through the entire Hanoverian dynasty. The answering machine was more useful. The last message he'd listened to came in at eleven thirty-three. Then there was one he hadn't picked up at eleven fifty-seven. That was yours, by the way."

"Who were the others?"

"Just tenants with problem toilets. But now we know when he was here."

"He didn't stay very long, it sounds like."

"Possibly he came home just to meet with someone."

"I've an idea who might know. As someone who lives in a basement flat."

"Check with the downstairs neighbor?"

"Yes."

She headed for the back door, but in the living room the umbrella stand caught her eye and she stopped. "Peter? I've just remembered something."

"Go on."

"We had to take that thing in for repair once. It was lined in copper that wore through. And the man in the shop got quite excited. He'd found a secret compartment."

"Who would put a secret compartment in an umbrella stand?"

"The Victorians loved to hide things." She knelt and ran her hands over its surface until she found the catch and pressed. A panel slid open. Inside was only one object, a blue-backed U.S. passport.

Renata was disappointed. "All that fuss for his passport?"

Peter picked it up and riffled through it. "Not his, exactly. This is the passport of Warren Hughes. Who bears a remarkable resemblance to Don."

"Oh Lord. I suppose I should have known. A fake passport does rather go with offshore bank accounts and shell corporations, doesn't it?"

"No stamps. He hasn't traveled on it. Maybe he uses it for identification when he's in the Cayman Islands or Ruritania or wherever." He held it up to the light. "I'm no expert, but it looks like an awfully good job."

"I'm sure his employer in London can afford top-flight forgers."

"I hate to say it, Renata, but just having one of these in your possession is a federal crime."

She took the passport from him and rubbed it against her shirt.

"What are you doing?"

"Getting your fingerprints off it. This thing gives me the willies. I mean Don having it. He would have thought it was rather a lark. Secret agent Don." Holding it carefully by the edges she dropped it in the compartment and pushed the panel shut. She felt relieved that she couldn't even see the seams.

Once they were out of the apartment with the door locked behind them, she felt a little calmer. They descended the fire escape and she knocked at the door of the apartment under Don's.

It was answered by an African American man with a graying moustache framed by parenthesis-shaped grooves and glasses held together by a safety pin through one hinge. "Sorry to bother you," Renata said. She could see sandwich makings on the counter behind him. "We're trying to find Don. I'm his sister."

The man nodded. "You talk like him."

"Yes. You can tell when he's upstairs, can't you?"

"Oh yeah. That is, unless I have the TV on. Don's got heavy feet."

"Did you hear him last night? Just before midnight?"

"Yep. I was watching Colbert, but they were louder than the TV."

"They?"

"Don and some guy were shouting at each other. I was getting ready to call the police when it stopped."

"Stopped? You mean they quit yelling and went back to talking normally?"

"No. The other guy just left."

Peter asked, "Did you see him?"

"Well, yeah. Once I was thinking of calling the cops, I got kind of interested. I was looking out the window instead of watching the TV. I saw him go out and get in his car. It was a black guy. He had one of those hairdos like the football players have—you know, that sticks out from under their helmets?"

"Dreadlocks," Peter said.

"That's it."

"But it wasn't anybody you've seen around the neighborhood."

"He wasn't from the neighborhood."

"How do you know?"

"He was wearing a suit and tie. Like Colbert."

"And Don?"

"I didn't see him, but he must've left soon after. It got real quiet."

They thanked him and continued down the stairs. Renata said, "You have an idea who that man was."

"Imani Baraku. A professor at the Adams School of Public Health. He's an activist, well-known around the campus. He's taken the side of the Parkdale residents Adams is going to kick out so they can move in their students and employees."

"Oh! So that's what he and Don were arguing about."

"Must have been. He told me he was going to try and derail the deal. I should have taken him more seriously."

"Let's go talk to him."

Peter glanced at his watch. "We better head for the medical center. It's almost time for the signing ceremony."

"Oh, God, let's hope Don's there," Renata murmured.

24

As they drove back to the Central West End in Peter's WeCar, Renata asked, "Do you know this Baraku fellow personally?"

"Yes. He's the kind of faculty member who makes a lot of trouble for a PR department."

"What's he like? I mean, do you think it's possible he would … harm Don in some way?"

"No. He's fully committed to his causes, but he doesn't take things personally. I'm surprised he even got into a shouting match with Don. Of course, Don can be pretty high-handed with black people."

"That's not fair, Peter. Don is high-handed with white people, too."

"True."

The medical center was one of the few places in St. Louis where the traffic was as thick as in London. Peter picked his way through the tangle while Renata kept glancing at her watch. Finally he pulled over to the curb and switched off the engine. A sign caught her eye as she got out.

"It says Adams U Police will tow."

"That's okay. It's Adams' car."

She followed him through a revolving door and along a

corridor. Double doors stood open to a big room with glossy paneled walls and a green and gray carpet into which the Adams seal was woven. A group consisting mostly of men in suits were helping themselves to an ample buffet. They seemed jovial enough. Renata looked around for Don but didn't see him. Instead she spotted the white-fringed bald head of Joel Rubinstein. He wasn't wearing a suit, but he had put on a shirt with a collar. Seeing them, he started across the room. At their questioning expressions, he frowned and shook his head.

"Don's not here," Renata said gloomily.

"Never showed up. His lawyer is in a confab with the university bigwigs now."

"Otherwise the deal is done?"

"All that's left is the signing and the grip and grin with Chancellor Reeve."

"Everything went smoothly, except for Don?"

"No, I wouldn't say that. About an hour ago, that guy—your boss—came in."

"Roger Merck?"

"Yeah. He said Professor Baraku was outside, with a delegation from the neighborhood, demanding to address us. He wouldn't take no for an answer, Roger said. It was let him in or call the riot police. So in they came."

"And?"

"They pooped our party. I recognized a couple of my tenants. We all did. Baraku kept his speech short and to the point. Said we should leave Adams' money on the table and go back to managing our buildings. We 'owed it to social justice.' "

"Anybody say anything in reply?"

Joel shrugged. "I thought of saying, I'm sixty-seven years old and want to play with my grandchildren. But it didn't seem adequate."

"What happened next?"

"Oh, the professor kept his word. They all filed out of

the room while we looked at our feet. Then we got back to business."

A voice boomed out, "Pete!"

It was a large black man with a round face and white hair. Peter introduced Renata to Vice-Chancellor Merck.

He asked her, "Have you heard from Don?"

"No."

Roger lifted both hands and let them fall. "I give up. He's not going to make it to the ceremony. The chancellor will be here in a moment. In fact, do you mind walking with me? I've got to go out to meet him."

They nodded to Joel and set off down the corridor.

"You can't wrap up the deal without him?" Peter asked.

"That's taken care of."

"How?"

"His lawyer sent a photo of the signature page to his cellphone. He signed it, photographed it, and sent it back. Our lawyers agreed that makes it legal. But I have to tell you, I'm very disappointed. He's the largest landowner in Parkdale. He should be here to shake the chancellor's hand."

"I should like to speak to this lawyer," said Renata.

"He's left. But I'll give you his card." Roger reached into his pocket for a stack of business cards, which he sorted through as he walked.

"He didn't say anything about where Don was?" she asked. "Why he couldn't be here?"

"Oh, he was most apologetic. But he didn't know anything."

They came out on the street. Roger found the card and handed it to her. She thanked him and he headed for the curb, where a small honor guard of assistant provosts, vice-chancellors, and uniformed security men was waiting to welcome Reeve to the medical campus.

A man was standing a short distance away, leaning unobtrusively against the side of the building. Peter looked at him twice and said, "Imani."

So this was Professor Baraku. She hadn't expected the activist to be so pleasant-looking. He shook Peter's hand and smiled as he was introduced to her. "You're Don's sister? You don't look at all like him."

"So they tell me."

"What happened to your delegation, Imani?" Peter asked.

"They got discouraged and went home. I don't blame them."

"But you're lingering here. Hoping for a word with the chancellor?"

"He's my last resort."

"You talked to Don late last night," said Renata.

He gazed over her head while he considered. "I don't know how you would know that, but I see no reason to deny it."

"In fact you had an argument."

"Of course. The neighbors." He was nodding to himself. "It did get loud for a while. Starting when I said to Don that for him, saving the neighborhood seemed to mean driving out all the people who lived there like so many cockroaches. Negotiations went downhill from there."

"Imani, here's the thing," Peter said. "We can't find Don. As far as we can work out, you're the last person to have seen him."

"I see. If you're accusing me of something, Peter, I'll have to ask you to be more specific."

The polite wariness of his tone made Renata feel bad. She stepped forward and put her hand on his arm and looked him in the eye. "We're not accusing you, Professor. We just want information. I came all the way from London, and it's terribly important that I see my brother."

"I noticed he wasn't with the other landlords at the meeting. It's possible he's decided to make himself scarce because of something he said to me last night."

"What?" Peter asked.

"Well, we'd been shouting at each other for a while. Don had made it clear that he wasn't being moved by my arguments. But I still wouldn't leave. So he told me I was wasting my time and should quiet down. That's what 'put a sock in it' means, right?"

She nodded.

"I said that if his fellow landlords were as unyielding as he was, I would turn to Chancellor Reeve. Don laughed. He said Reeve would never back out of the deal. That I had no idea what I was up against. That something much bigger than Parkdale was at stake."

Renata and Peter looked at each other.

"He knew the moment the words were out of his mouth that he shouldn't have said them. All the hot air just whooshed out of him. Left him limp as a popped balloon. Of course I tried to get more out of him, but he was through talking."

"Is that why you're here now, Imani?" Peter asked.

"Well, yes. If I can get a moment with Reeve, I'll ask him what's really at stake. Not that I expect an answer. But maybe it'll make him hesitate to sign the contract. Buy me and the folks in Parkdale some time."

A large sedan was pulling up at the curb. Roger, smiling, opened the back door. A lean man in a dark suit got out. Its empty right sleeve was neatly pinned to his coattail. She caught only a glimpse of him before the assistant provosts and vice-chancellors closed in.

"Chancellor!" Baraku called out in a stentorian tone. "A word, please."

Reeve looked vaguely in his direction, smiled and waved, and headed toward the building, flanked by administrators and guards. Baraku went toward him. One uniformed man turned to face him.

"I just want a word with Mr. Reeve."

"Sorry, the chancellor can't spare a moment right now."

"It's urgent that I talk to him now."

He tried to sidestep, but the guard, a young man with short blond hair, moved with him, raising his arms. "That won't be possible, sir, but you have other options."

Reeve was stepping into the revolving door. Baraku tried again to get by.

Again the guard blocked him. "You can reach the chancellor by email or phone. Or make an appointment to see him."

"I'm on the faculty. I'm an associate professor—"

"Then you'll have no problem getting an appointment."

"I must see Reeve now. Who is your superior?"

"Please step back."

"I demand to see your superior. Really, you don't want the responsibility. This can't be resolved at your level."

The young man's eyes hardened. "Hey, my *level* is just fine for dealing with guys like you."

He pushed Baraku back with both hands. Baraku stumbled and sat down hard. The security guard had already turned his back and was stepping into the revolving door. Peter helped Baraku up. The professor straightened his glasses and glanced at a scrape on the palm of his left hand.

"I'm sorry," Renata said.

He gave her a quick half-smile. "No harm done. At least not yet."

25

As Peter drove westward, Renata sat beside him with her mobile in one hand and the lawyer's business card in the other. She wasn't doing anything with them. Peter glanced over.

"Are you tired?"

"Discouraged."

"Don't be. We haven't even called Don's tradesmen yet."

"His who?"

"Isn't that what you Brits call them? The folks who support the elegant Don lifestyle. Tailor, hair stylist, manicurist, tanning salon, dry cleaner, golf pro …."

"There's no point. I've realized that we're not going to find Don. Because he's hiding from *me*."

"But how could he even know you're here?"

"I'm not sure. Still, I have the feeling he's avoiding me. It's a feeling I've had before."

In heavy silence, they drove the last few blocks to Peter's building. A police car was parked in front of it. As they pulled over to the curb, a tall black cop got out, putting on his cap. He approached Renata's window.

"Ms. Radleigh?"

"That's right."

"I'd like you to come with me, please. Or you can follow in your own vehicle if you prefer."

"What's this about?"

"A Jaguar sedan, registered to Donald Radleigh."

It was only a few minutes' ride. They followed the police car into the car park of the Delmar Station of MetroLink, St. Louis' light rail system. One of the red, white, and blue trains was pulling away as they came to a stop. She could see the curvaceous maroon rump of the Jag in the line of parked cars. Its doors, boot, and bonnet were open. Several uniformed cops were inspecting it. A black man in a suit approached them. He was tall and had a barrel chest that would have done credit to a Wagnerian bass-baritone.

"Hello, Muldaur," Peter said. "What's up?"

Ignoring Peter. the man walked up to Renata. "Is this your brother's car, Ms. Radleigh?"

"Yes." Looking at it, she noticed that the front wing window was broken.

"An hour ago, a security guard saw a guy trying to steal it. This kind of car attracts attention. He'd broken in but couldn't get the engine going. He ran off and the guard called it in. We've been trying to contact your brother, but no luck. Can you help us?"

"I'm afraid I don't know where he is," she said.

Muldaur was wearing sunglasses. She had two small images of herself to gaze at, but she could not see his eyes. "I understand you came all the way from England to see your brother."

"How did you come to understand that, Muldaur?" asked Peter.

"Spoke to Joel Rubinstein."

"Solid police work. You've done a lot in an hour. Found anything interesting in the car?"

"It's a crime scene, Lombardo. Searching it is routine."

"You being called to the scene of an attempted car theft is not routine."

"I'm not interested in talking to you right now. Ms. Radleigh, you came to see your brother, but haven't seen him. How come?"

Her twin reflections looked startled and confused. She did not know who Muldaur was, but Peter obviously did, and there was no love lost. She gave a noncommittal shrug.

"You mean he's missing?" Muldaur asked.

She said, "Well, we haven't found anyone who's seen him since last night."

"Your brother is a missing person. And instead of reporting him to the police, you chose to entrust the investigation to a former reporter for a defunct small-town paper?"

"He's not missing," Peter said. "His lawyer was in contact with him a few hours ago."

"Can his lawyer produce him?"

"Probably not."

"Get back in your car. We're going to Seventh District to file a report."

It was dark by the time the police were finished with them.

Renata was sitting on a wooden bench in the grimy lobby of the police station when a door opened and Peter appeared. They had been questioned separately. In fact she hadn't laid eyes on him in a couple of hours.

He came up to her but did not sit. "We're free to go."

"Such lovely words." She rose and followed him out to the car.

As he got in behind the wheel, Peter said, "From the questions they asked me, it sounded like you decided to tell them everything."

"I didn't exactly *decide*. Oh, Peter, I'm a mezzo-soprano, not a lawyer. I'm rubbish at fencing with the police. I hope I didn't put you in difficulties?"

"No. I mostly leveled with them about who we talked to today and what they said. When they asked me about what happened in London, I said I had no personal knowledge so I wouldn't answer."

That's a good line. I wish I could've used it."

"How did they react to what you told them about London?"

"They weren't interested in the murder of Neal Marsh. Or of the man who chased me by the canal."

"Unsurprising. Those crimes happened four thousand miles outside of their jurisdiction."

"The real estate deal did interest them. They were disappointed that I could tell them so little about Don's boss. I didn't see that man Muldaur again, did you?"

"No. But I had the feeling a few times that he was on the other side of the one-way glass."

"Who is he? Police?"

"No, but he used to be. He and Mayor Skinner were rookies together. Later they went to Saint Louis U law school together. When Skinner was chief of police, Muldaur was his right-hand man. When the mayor retired and started a security company, Muldaur was his partner. Now he's the mayor's chief of staff. If he's running this investigation, it's political. Mayor Skinner wants to get his hands on Don."

"Why?"

"Obviously the mayor is interested in Adams buying Parkdale. Beyond that I can't say."

"I've made a frightful balls-up, haven't I? I started out thinking I could keep Don out of trouble. And now I've put the police on his trail."

"Renata, he didn't leave you much choice."

"Telling the police about the things he's done. The things he's *said*. That he tells the chancellor what to do. That this deal is bigger than Parkdale."

"Don't feel bad. The cops can't do much with that kind of statement. It's too vague."

"But when you repeat these things to the police and the tape recorder is running ...."

"Are you beginning to doubt that Don is just a pawn?"

"He has no idea what he's gotten into. He's being used. The man in London is pulling the strings, telling Don as little as possible."

"Uh-huh."

She peered at his expression in the dim light from the dashboard and failed to read it. "You think he's a full partner in crime—I mean, whatever the crime is?"

"Let's say I'm rooting really hard for him to justify your faith."

They reached Peter's apartment building and parked. He switched off the lights and engine but did not open the door. "Another thing I'm wondering about. Why did he abandon his beloved Jag in a MetroLink lot?"

"Because it's so conspicuous," she replied. "He's lying low. Do you have another idea?"

"MetroLink goes to the airport. The contracts are signed. The money will soon be on the way to the offshore bank—"

"No. He hasn't finished the job."

"What else is there for him to do?"

"I don't know. But he's still here." They opened the doors and got out. Renata peered around her in the darkness. "I've had the feeling all day that he's just 'round the corner."

26

Next morning, Peter changed the sheets. In the night they had made, as Renata put it, utter beasts of themselves. He was surprised not to find scorch marks. She was in the kitchen making breakfast. He smelled warm bread and brewing coffee. She was humming, something she did quite unconsciously. As one would expect, she was a world-class hummer.

Clamping a pillow under his chin as he wiggled it into a pillowcase, he had an inner burst of pure happiness. An unutterable thought struck him: all Don's troubles were worth it, if they brought Renata here. For a luxurious few minutes he daydreamed about the future, when she would be an administrator at some American opera company and he would write advertorials and they would live together all the time.

At breakfast he said, "I'll be spending the day in Parkdale. Adams PR is running a bus tour of the neighborhood for media people and local urbanists."

"You're going to make some money? Lovely." She was peeling an orange. "I know you're relieved. The Don problem is in the hands of the police. You're hoping they catch him."

"Maybe jail would be the safest place for him."

"Yes, well, I can't take such an … objective view of the

situation. And I certainly can't mooch about the flat all day, alone with my thoughts. I think I'll go down to Saint Louis Opera. Chat up some people. Maybe they'll offer me a part next season."

"Good luck."

"Thanks." She made an effort and smiled. "And do remember to dress properly for the Adams people. No mixing plaids and checks."

Peter went out to a stiff wind and leaden skies. Indian summer seemed to have ended. He returned the WeCar to the garage and caught a bus. Adams Medical Center had an excellent shuttle bus system, and a loop to Parkdale had just been added. His first stop when he got there was Don's apartment building. As he expected, an unmarked police surveillance van was parked across the street.

Peter reported to work. His role was limited to glad-handing and passing out press releases. A professor from the Urban Studies Department stood at the front of the bus and did the narration. Seeing a crew installing a blue-light security phone, he told the driver to pull over. Everyone climbed out to inspect it. Joel Rubinstein, hunched in an old army fatigue jacket, sidled up to Peter.

"Hope I didn't do the wrong thing by answering Frank Muldaur's questions about Renata yesterday."

"No, it's okay. What brings you here?"

"That's a good question. Habit, I guess."

"You ought to be sleeping late this morning."

"I tried. But I'll have to learn how." His long gray hair was loose and the wind was blowing it around. He looked forlorn.

"C'mon, Joel. You're one of the idle rich now. Get used to it."

"You're right. I ought to be trading in the truck for a BMW. Hiring a wealth manager. Instead of walking around here, watching other people working on my buildings." He laughed. "*My* buildings."

"You've left them in good hands."

"I know. I've been saying that a lot. This is the best thing that could have happened to Parkdale. One landlord controls the whole area. And not just any landlord, but Adams University, which has the highest principles and the deepest pockets. But I have to tell you, I was just watching some guys repainting the front door of one of my buildings gray and green, and I didn't like it."

He shrugged and walked away, his head down against the wind. Peter re-boarded the bus. They drove to a vacant lot, where Hannah and the assistant dean of students explained how it was going to be made into a community garden whose beds would be offered to the students moving in next spring. Both women had to hold down their skirts against the wind. *How odd to see Hannah wearing a skirt*, Peter thought. As he fell in behind the urbanists and reporters to climb back on the bus, she approached.

"I want to talk to you."

"Have you heard from Don?"

"No. From the *cops*. How could Renata go to the cops?"

"She didn't. They came to us."

"Well, she shouldn't have cooperated. I *trusted* Renata. I helped you guys yesterday. I even gave you Don's key."

"I'll make sure to get it back to you."

"A lot of good that will do. Renata told me she believed in him. That he wasn't a criminal. So why'd she sic the cops on him? You tell her from me—"

Peter firmly raised his hand, palm out. "There's no need to tell her anything. She already feels as bad you could possibly want her to feel."

He turned away and got back on the bus. It headed for the main drag where the tour was to finish, in typical Adams style, with an ample repast. They pulled up in front of Herb's BBQ restaurant. Herb was out front, in his pink pig suit, waving a sign advertising his special to passing cars. He removed its head to welcome them. They regaled themselves with ribs, beans, and potato salad, followed by ice cream sundaes, which Ethan brought over from Cold Comfort.

Afterward, Peter saw the party off and caught the shuttle back to the medical center. He went to his old office, Medical Public Relations, with a vague idea that he ought to report to someone. His former colleagues welcomed him back, but nobody was much interested in the bus tour, or for that matter in Parkdale. Life at Adams U was fast-paced, and the PR department was gearing up for the arrival this evening of Sheikh Abdullah, the favorite nephew of the Sultan of Kutar, who would confer with the chancellor about the new Mideast campus. Peter borrowed a computer to write a report on the bus tour and email it to Roger Merck, then headed for home.

A shuttle would take him most of the way. As he boarded, he spotted the Bob Marley hair and Brooks Brothers sport coat of Professor Imani Baraku. He was sitting alone at the back. He looked at Peter but did not smile. This was unusual.

"Imani? Mind if I join you?"

"Not at all, provided we talk about football."

Peter swung into the seat beside him as the bus started off. "I guess that must mean you're busy following up Don Radleigh's little hint."

"Who do you think should start for the Packers at QB?"

"The chancellor won't back out of the deal. More is at stake than Parkdale. That's what you said yesterday. Have you found out anything since?"

"Peter, you work for Roger Merck."

"Ah, you have."

"We were discussing the Packers."

"Sorry, my game is baseball. How about some general university gossip? What do you think of Sheikh Abdullah arriving this evening?"

"You're not going to draw me on the Kutar Campus. That's above my pay grade."

"Some of your colleagues on the faculty are awfully passionate. They think it's a bad deal."

Baraku shrugged. "Reeve calls it the 'world' university. But it'll be in Kutar, a country with a population of four hundred thousand, who have a per capita worth of seventeen million dollars. Not because they earned it. Not because they have ideas or skills or do work. Just because they're sitting on a lot of oil. They drive their air-conditioned SUVs to shopping malls while people of color imported from other countries do all their work for them. But their Sultan is a benevolent despot. He knows the oil will run out. Then his people are going to have to work. They'll need ideas and skills. He wants Adams to supply these things."

"Sounds like a great deal for Kutar. What about for Adams?"

"Obviously, not all my colleagues are convinced. But the chancellor is working on them."

"Are you out to get the chancellor, Imani?"

"Peter, I'm out to keep roofs over the heads of the Parkdale tenants. That's all. Now, if you won't talk about football, let's talk about reality TV."

27

IT WAS STARTING TO rain as he reached home. Renata was just back, taking off her coat. She had dressed up for her visit to the Saint Louis Opera, in a deep-red dress with a wrap bodice that hinted at the splendors of her bosom.

"You look great."

"Oh, thank you. I've had a splendid day. Mike Joyce—you remember him, the head of production—took me to lunch and said there was a good chance for a part next spring."

"Which opera?"

"I daren't talk about it yet. I'm afraid I'll jinx it. Anyway, I have to practice now."

"Oh."

This was an issue for the couple. Renata, though candid in conversation and uninhibited in bed, was very shy about practicing. She preferred to be alone with her voice. Since she practiced for a couple of hours every day, this was an inconvenience. During their weeks together last summer, he'd felt obliged to go out, whether he wanted to or not, so she could practice. Once he asked her why he was forbidden to hear her sing an aria, when in a few weeks she was going to sing it to a thousand people.

"Then it will be *ready*," she snapped.

After that he made sure to decamp whenever she brought out her keyboard.

She was bringing it out now, so he said, "I'll, uh, take a walk."

"Oh, Peter, no. It's started to rain. Just go about your business and ignore me."

Evidently she had made a resolve. He could tell that she felt uncomfortable, so he turned his back, sat at the computer, and started on his email.

She went into the kitchen, where for a long while she made sounds like baby talk. Then she played notes in ascending order on the keyboard and sang crisp though meaningless syllables. Her singing voice, which made her normal speaking voice seem like a pale shadow, strengthened and deepened. Eventually he could not resist tiptoeing over to peer around the doorframe.

She was standing at the counter, a glass of water and the keyboard before her. Her eyes were closed. She sang the same passage repeatedly, shifting her stance or altering the way she held her head. Sometimes she made extraordinary grimaces or pressed her fingers into her throat or cheek. Between attempts she muttered criticism or encouragement in Italian. She didn't know that Peter was in the doorway. Or that she was in the same world.

He went back to his desk. She had told him once that she'd switched from piano to voice because it wasn't enough for her to be the musician; she wanted to be the instrument, too. She gave her all to the making of sweet sounds—mind, heart, and body. He sat down and gazed blindly at the screen, entertaining somber thoughts. His fantasy of this morning faded. It seemed unlikely that Renata would give up singing to be an administrator.

Later, as she cooked dinner—she was a very good cook—he watched the local news. If Don was under arrest, they might as well hear about it, but happily there was no mention of him. Instead there was the arrival of Sheikh Abdullah at Lambert-

St. Louis Airport. He was shown descending the steps from his private jet, with the wind whipping his white dishdasha and ghutrah. Hearing that he was the sultan's nephew had made Peter expect a young man, but he was portly and gray-bearded. Reaching the tarmac, he shook hands with Philip Reeve while a line of assistant provosts and vice-chancellors looked on, smiling.

Then came an interview with Reeve, recorded in the studio. He spoke of the "global networked university," "the campus for the new century," and "the education of world citizens." The very phrases that Peter had heard mocked by Dean Carmichael regained their promise and vigor when spoken by their originator. He conjured a bright image of the youth of the world starving for knowledge and Reeve hurrying to their rescue. Still, he did not seem overbearing or arrogant. Forehead grooved with worry, eyes blue as the heart of a gas flame burning bright, he seemed to be pleading: *Have faith in me, a better world depends on it.*

After the interview, a short, slick video produced by Peter's department, showed a stretch of desert on which patches of green grass, gardens, and lines of date-palm trees miraculously appeared, followed by low buildings of steel and smoked glass, and then by computer-generated students hurrying to and fro: the soon-to-be built campus of Adams-Kutar.

Renata emerged with steaming plates and they sat down. They were halfway through their ratatouille and polenta when Peter's cellphone rang. Renata jumped. He glanced at the screen and assured her, "It's not Muldaur."

"Who then?"

"Unknown number." He pressed the button and said hello.

"Peter Lombardo?"

There was a lot of background noise, but he could not mistake the smoky voice. "Dean Carmichael."

"I'm at the Ritz-Carlton. I think you want to come over here."

"Why?"

"I just saw Don Radleigh."

Peter jumped to his feet. He said to Renata, "Don's resurfaced. Do I call the cops?"

She was on her feet too. "No! We go and see him."

"On our way," Peter said into the phone, and put it away. He patted his pockets for his keys. Only then did he remember. "Oh, shit. I returned the car."

"Bus?"

"Bike'll be quicker. But we only have one."

"I'll go."

"You don't know the way."

He was already hefting the bike on his shoulder. Renata didn't argue, just held the door open.

The Ritz-Carlton was in the posh suburb of Clayton, only two and a half miles away. It was fully dark by now and the rain was tapering off. Streetlights made long streaks down the wet pavement. He pedaled hard, the bike swaying under him, and made the most of his gears on hills. He was puffing hard by the time the lights in the Clayton skyscrapers came into view. The nearest, he knew, was the Ritz-Carlton.

Hunching over the handlebars as he did the home stretch along the Ritz's long driveway, he could see a lot of activity in the hotel's forecourt. Between a floodlit fountain and the porte-cochère was a small crowd of people, police cars, and TV news vans. Peter hopped off his bike and leaned it against the wall of the hotel, hoping it would still be there when he returned. He waded into the crowd. They were a calm, well-heeled group of protesters: Adams U faculty and students, he guessed. Many were raising signs decrying the Kutar Campus. The sheikh must be staying here. After a delay that had his heart pounding extra hard from frustration on top of exertion, he found Dean Carmichael leaning against a pillar, talking to a small knot of people. He burst into the group.

Recognizing him, she said, "I saw him go in the hotel—only for an instant, but I'm sure it was Don."

"When?"

"Right before I called."

Less than twenty minutes had passed, then. He was probably still inside. "What was he wearing?"

"A long, light-colored raincoat. And carrying an umbrella."

"Thanks."

Peter trotted under the porte-cochère toward the line of doors to the lobby. They were blocked by Clayton cops standing shoulder to shoulder. They weren't wearing riot gear, just no-nonsense expressions. One of them told Peter that if he couldn't show a card key, he couldn't go in. He tried to persuade the man he was arriving to check in. But panting in his damp clothes, he didn't look like a Ritz guest. The cop waved him away.

He could think of nothing to do but watch the doors and hope to spot Don as he came out. Through narrow windows inset in the doors he could glimpse the chandelier-lit lobby. A few guests were peering out at the goings-on. A few yards away, Dean Carmichael was being helped up onto the bed of a pickup truck, which was serving as a podium. Even without a cigarette, she looked poised and nonchalant. Television lights brought out the luster in her dark hair. She raised a bullhorn to her lips. The husky, sardonic quality of her voice was enhanced by the amplification.

"We are here to draw a line in the sand."

There was laughter and applause from the crowd. The rain had kept the numbers down, but the demonstration was getting plenty of media attention. Camcorders were set up on tripods, and he recognized a few acquaintances from the print media. The timing was just right to make the ten o'clock news.

"Chancellor Reeve is telling everyone what a great deal he's making. And it is … for Kutar," the dean continued. "They get the rich resources of one of America's greatest universities delivered to their doorstep, like a pizza. But it's not great for Adams. The chancellor brags of how he's quote elevating our brand internationally unquote. Really, he's cheapening our brand. The Kutar Campus will be the Rolex you buy in Hong Kong that stops ticking before you get home. You cannot drop a ready-made university into an uncivilized country."

The faces of the protestors no longer looked calm. The dean was winding them up. "Our colleagues who accept the chancellor's blandishments to go to Kutar will face profound ethical dilemmas, trying to teach in a small, backward despotism that has no traditions of academic freedom, democracy, free speech, or women's rights. If we can't stop Reeve from finalizing the deal this week, construction of the campus will go forward. The work will be done by underpaid, maltreated foreign workers. If the usual Kutar safety standards are followed, about thirty of them will die in accidents. When the school opens, it will welcome students from many nations, as the chancellor says. As he doesn't say, none of them will be gay, and none of them will be Jews."

There was a bellow of rage that Peter could hardly believe came from the throats of professors. All his instincts told him this was a big story that was going to get bigger. He wished that Don Radleigh had never been born and the Springfield *Journal-Register* had never died, so he could whip out his notebook and start interviewing people.

He forced himself to snap out of it. Time was passing, and Don had not come out of the lobby doors. Suddenly Peter realized he was being stupid. By now Don knew that the police were looking for him. He wouldn't want to pass through a line of Clayton cops again if he could help it. He would try another exit.

Peter skirted the crowd. He debated for too long—infuriating, the temptation to dither when you had no time for it—whether to run or fetch his bike. Deciding on the bike, he mounted it and rode around the back of the hotel. A light was shining above a door, and a man in a white chef's smock was leaning against the wall next to it, taking a cigarette break.

“Hi,” Peter said, “have you seen a man go by? Man in a light raincoat?”

“Sorry, pal. We’re not supposed to talk to the media.”

“I’m not the media. You think the media rides a bike?”

The cook laughed. “Haven’t seen your guy.”

Peter rode on, past loading docks with closed doors, bulky central air conditioning units, and giant Dumpsters. He came to a high concrete wall and circled back. A figure was flickering through the light at the kitchen door. Peter saw the tan trench coat and rolled umbrella: Don.

The jocund cook was grinding out his cigarette. He grinned as Peter passed and shouted, “Go get ’im, bike-man!” Don heard. He looked over his shoulder and started running. If he turned right toward the front of the hotel and ran into the crowd, Peter would have to dismount. He’d be sure to lose him. Instead Don ran straight on, along the highway behind the hotel. *Mistake*, Peter thought excitedly. There was nowhere to go.

Don disappeared in the darkness. Peter rode on and came to a walkway that led to a pedestrian bridge over the highway. He hadn’t noticed it before. It was new and ADA compliant: no steps, just a smooth concrete ramp lined with chain link fences, zigzagging steeply up to the bridge. Don was halfway up it already. Peter blessed the decision to bring his bike. Don was trapped between fences; there was nowhere to go but up, and he couldn’t go as fast as Peter.

The bike was in high gear but Peter didn’t take time to downshift. Pumping hard on the pedals, he started up the ramp. Don was two switchbacks above, running in his direction.

“Don, Wait!” Peter shouted. “Your sister—”

“You’ve set the cops on me,” Don yelled back. “Fuck her and fuck you too!”

So there was no choice but to ride him down, leap on his back, and wrestle him to the ground. Peter’s blood was up and he was looking forward to it. He stood on his pedals and bent over the handlebars, giving it all he had. He swerved around a turn, having to put his inside foot down to save himself from falling, got up on the pedals again and pumped. Ahead of him, only one loop above, Don hadn't moved. He was down on his knees. Peter thought he had fallen.

Too late he saw what Don was doing: pushing his umbrella through the chain link into Peter's path. Peter started to swerve, too late. The ferrule slid between the spokes and the front wheel stopped turning. The bike upended. Peter went flying. He made a somersault and came down hard on his right foot. Fierce pain shot from his ankle to the top of his skull. He lurched into the fence and collapsed in a heap.

The world was blurry. He got to his knees and patted the ground for his glasses. He put them on just in time to see Don disappear from view, coattails flying, onto the bridge. Peter clawed his way up the fence until he was standing. He tried to take a step with his right foot and nearly fainted from the pain.

Nothing to do but hold on to the fence and hop on his left foot. He made his way to the top of the ramp, then over the rushing river of traffic, red lights on one side, white on the other. He could not see Don.

On the other side was a street of tall trees and small houses, quiet and dark. A car engine fired up. Peter saw its taillights but was too far away to read the license plate before it disappeared. He couldn't be sure it was Don anyway. He sat down on the curb and gasped for breath. Now that he had time to attend to it, the pain from his ankle grew more intense. His cellphone rang.

"Peter, I'm in a taxi," Renata said. "Almost at the Ritz-Carlton."

"Good. You can take me to the hospital."

TWO HOURS LATER THEY were sitting in the back of another taxi, on the way home from St. Mary's. Peter's new aluminum cane rested beside him, and his sprained ankle was professionally braced and bound. Holding his hand, Renata asked, "How are you feeling?"

"Terrific. They gave me some great painkillers. Even the humiliation is fading."

"Peter, I'm sorry."

"It was not you with the goddamn umbrella."

"If only I could have gone instead of you."

"You think you could have made him stop to listen to you? No way. He blames us both for the police being after him. Which raises the question. Do I report tonight's doings to Muldaur?"

"What do you think?"

"Well, it would give him a good laugh."

"Peter, I just don't know. I'm afraid we're driving Don deeper into desperation. Making him do even stupider things. I guess I don't want to go to the police again."

"Why do you think he resurfaced? What was he up to at the Ritz?"

"He went to see the sheikh."

"That could be jumping to conclusions. There are hundreds of people in that hotel."

"My feeling is, it was the sheikh."

"I have the same feeling. There's some connection between the Kutar Campus and Parkdale. But I have no idea what it could be. Those people who picked you up in London—the billionaire's gofers. You're sure they weren't Arabs?"

"Kutarians, you mean? No, they were Indian. Or I should say South Asian. They could have been Pakistanis or Bangladeshis. But definitely not Arabs."

"What about the billionaire himself?"

"Indian."

"You're sure? You said you didn't see his face."

"I heard him speak. I'm quite sensitive to anything to do with voices. I don't think I'm mistaken."

Peter yawned. "Please don't think I fail to appreciate the

seriousness of the situation. But those painkillers are really kicking in."

"Go to sleep, my love."

28

Next morning Peter was sitting up in bed waiting for Renata to bring him a cup of tea when his phone rang. He didn't much like tea, but she said it was just the thing for an invalid. He read the screen and said, "Hello, Roger."

"Pete, better get down here right away."

The associate deputy vice-chancellor's tone didn't leave room for an explanation of Peter's condition. "What's going on?"

"Big demonstration at the medical center."

"About the Kutar Campus?"

"What? No, about Parkdale."

Professor Imani Baraku was leading a protest march of tenants, Roger explained. They had already left Parkdale, bound for the plaza of the medical center. Baraku had not notified the administration. He had notified the media, though, and they were already on hand. Peter said that he was on his way.

With Renata's help, he managed to pull his pants on. She said he was in no shape to cover a demonstration, and he agreed. But he was too curious to stay home.

A block from the med school plaza, he paid off his taxi. It was a brisk, sunny day—good demonstrating weather. Leaning on his cane, he limped toward the plaza. He passed a parked school bus. Looking through the windows, he could see rows of black helmets. The St. Louis Police had been criticized for using military-style vehicles against demonstrators, so they were trying a Trojan horse ploy, putting cops in flak vests and helmets on a cheery yellow bus. It crossed his mind that last night the Clayton police hadn't felt the need to don riot gear to face the mostly white professors and students at the Ritz. But that was the kind of snarky thought that wasn't allowed him, now that he was a PR man again.

He hoped there wasn't going to be a riot. He was in no shape to run. And he knew from experience that tear gas didn't just cause tears, it caused rivers of snot to flow from the nostrils. It was hard to take notes with a sodden handkerchief pressed to your face.

The plaza was the nearest thing the fragmented medical campus had to a center. It was a street converted to a pedestrian mall, with planters full of zinnias and a large fountain. On either side rose the walls of hospitals and classroom buildings. Peter limped to a traffic bollard that would give him a good view and sat down.

The news vans from local TV stations were already here. He watched the technicians setting up cameras and raising the stout aerials on the back of the vans. Adams security men were deploying to guard the entrances to the buildings. Passersby, some in white coats or scrubs, others in ordinary clothes, were pausing to watch the developments. Looking up, he could see hospital administrators leaning out of their office windows in the surrounding buildings. He remembered the worried tenants looking out their apartment windows at the Adams party three nights ago. The role reversal would gratify Baraku.

A murmur of voices gradually detached itself from the rumble of traffic. The faraway chanting grew louder as the marchers neared. They swung around the corner into view, filling the street from side to side, and just kept coming. Baraku seemed to have mobilized the entire population of Parkdale as well as sympathetic students and faculty. Photographers scurried around in front of them. Now Peter could make out the chant: "SAVE OUR HOMES!" They were carrying signs, too, and he noticed their slogans addressed and decried Reeve, not the university.

Once the marchers were in the plaza, taking up a respectable portion of the large space, it became clear that this was not going to be merely a mill-around-and-shout demonstration. Nobody was going to throw rocks at windows or challenge the guards at the building entrances. Imani Baraku had something more purposeful in mind, and he was a past master of organizing demonstrations. Marshals with armbands and bullhorns were moving among the crowd, getting them to settle down. They were followed by assistants passing out bottles of water. Crews wheeling dollies appeared. One was a platform, intended as Baraku's dais, and the TV people were all over it, placing their microphones. The other object was more puzzling, a large rectangle with a nacreous surface. After a moment, Peter recognized it as a video screen for showing movies outdoors.

Baraku walked to the podium. His dreadlocks seemed more luxuriant today, spreading over the back of his corduroy sports jacket from one shoulder blade to the other. The crowd cheered, then fell into expectant silence.

"I need not speak for long," he began, his voice echoing from the surrounding buildings. "The people of Parkdale have already delivered one of our main messages, by showing you that they exist. Something Chancellor Philip G. Reeve would prefer for you to forget."

People roared and waved their signs or their fists.

"My other point is that Chancellor Reeve's *real* plan for Parkdale is not the one he has announced."

Peter sat bolt upright.

"The university has spoken vaguely about rehousing some residents in rehabbed, rent-controlled buildings. That statement is no longer operative. None of the former residents will be living in Parkdale. In fact, *no one* will be living there. Chancellor Reeve does not intend to restore Parkdale. He plans to destroy it."

Baraku nodded to the crew at the projector and stepped down. Peter got up and shuffled over to a spot that gave him a better view of the screen.

The shield of Adams University Medical Center appeared on the screen and sprightly string music began to play. A narrator, whose voice Peter recognized from the local PBS station, sang the praises of the med center, in phrases Peter could have recited in his sleep. Adams had more Nobel prize winners on its faculty than any other medical school. Granger Hospital was consistently rated among the top five in the country.

In the next shot, a drone camera flew over the Central West End and the traffic-clogged streets around the hospital. The narrator's voice turned grave. The med center's future was clouded, perhaps its very existence threatened, by its outmoded physical plant. The labs, clinics, and offices were housed in more than twenty-five different buildings, some old and antiquated, scattered among apartment houses and office buildings over several square miles. Staff wasted their valuable time on shuttle buses. Patients searching for care wandered the center in bafflement. And there was never enough parking. Adams was losing out in the competition for the health insurance dollar to suburban hospitals that provided inferior care, simply because they were more convenient.

The Answer: The New Medical Park!

An animated map appeared on screen. Across the highway from the medical center, a green blob appeared and quickly spread, as if a bottle of green ink had been tipped over. Parkdale's streets and buildings disappeared. The music swelled. A suburban-style hospital campus arose from the green: low-lying, sprawling buildings, woods and lawns and fountains. The narrator was extolling the concentration of services, the easy availability of care, more beds, more parking spaces ... but it was getting harder to hear him.

Most of the crowd were on their feet, shouting, raising their signs, shaking their fists. The roars gradually coalesced into a chant: "REEVE, TIME TO LEAVE!"

Peter spent the rest of the day in his old office, among his former colleagues. Everything in the world of Adams University seemed to be turning upside down, and Peter himself felt upended and backwards. He had never experienced a full-fledged media firestorm from the inside. He'd been through a couple as a reporter and remembered his indignation and contempt for the PR media-wranglers, who knew what was really going on but kept denying it, trying to palm him off with implausible assurances of good faith.

Now he was on the other end of the phone, and that was all he had to offer to termagant reporters. No matter how much they cross-examined, menaced, or feigned sympathy with him, all he could do was deny that the Medical Park was an active plan, or that Chancellor Reeve had lied. In a brief meeting before they started answering phones, Roger had told them to take this line and hold it. Such was the atmosphere at Medical PR that one of Peter's colleagues had called on the boss to promise that they weren't going to have to eat these denials in the next news cycle. Roger had solemnly promised.

No more information was forthcoming. Who had made the video? How had Baraku gotten hold of it? What was the university going to do to him? Most of all, the reporters wanted to know when Chancellor Reeve was going to face them. Peter and his colleagues had answers to none of these questions. As the hours passed he began to get very irritated with the sanctimonious reporters, and to feel solidarity with the flacks at the desks around him. These were emotions he had never expected to feel.

He even began to respect Roger Merck, whom he had always liked but not esteemed. Roger was continuing to be calm and polite under heavy pressure. Lobbies, waiting rooms, and meeting rooms were full of angry delegations. Neighborhood groups and politicians from the neighborhoods surrounding the medical center were demanding to know what other land grabs the university was plotting. At the main campus, the same tumult was going on. Everyone wanted to see Reeve himself, of course. Roger was making excuses for him, scrambling to come up with senior administrators to speak to these groups. It wasn't easy. Like the PR people, the associate provosts and vice-chancellors didn't want to take stands that future revelations would force them to back away from.

In mid-afternoon, Roger was making one of his regular rounds of the office suite to encourage the troops. Stopping at Peter's desk, he said, "Come with me."

Peter wriggled out of his current phone call and picked up his cane. As they walked down the corridor, Roger whispered, "The chancellor wants to see you."

"We're going to the main campus?"

"No, he's here. He came in early. He wanted to be on hand in case things got hairy."

Peter stared at his boss. He wondered how much hairier things would have to get before Reeve put in an appearance. But Roger said no more. His round, tan face, with its aureole of white hair, was unreadable.

They went to the other side of the building, which housed the development offices. There the atmosphere was more tranquil. One door was guarded by an Adams security officer. Roger knocked and said, "Chancellor? I have Pete with me." They went in.

It was dim in the room. The lights were off and the blinds closed. A desk was against the wall. The chancellor, sitting behind it, seemed barricaded in the far corner of the big room. He said, apprehensively, "Who's this?"

"Pete Lombardo. He's the PR man for Parkdale. You remember."

"Yes, of course." As Reeve rose and came forward, putting out his left hand, Peter remembered an especially nasty reporter trying to get a rise out of him by saying, "Is it true they're calling Reeve the one-armed bandit in St. Louis?" His hand felt clammy with sweat. Peter fought off an urge to wipe his own hand on his coattails. Reeve's normally keen blue eyes were glassy and his face had an unhealthy pallor.

Roger took his elbow and steered him to a small table in the middle of the room. They sat down and waited for Reeve. He didn't say anything. Finally Roger said, "Pete's here in case you want to ask him anything about Parkdale before the press conference."

"When is it?"

"In an hour."

"That's too soon."

"Well, Phil, it's been announced. Postponing it will make a bad impression."

Reeve said nothing.

"If you're not right on the dot, no harm done," Roger said. "Won't hurt the reporters to sit there for a while."

Reeve fixed his eyes on Peter. "There is no Medical Park," he said. "No such plan exists."

Peter nodded.

"It's crazy to think we would just abandon the med center we have. Just in the last year, we've spent $5.8 million dollars updating labs and clinics. We've just broken ground on a new pediatric research facility."

Reeve ran out of words. Peter felt the need to say something. "If you had been planning to level Parkdale, you would never have gotten up in front to the media three days ago and said what a fine neighborhood it was and how proud you were to save it."

"Exactly." Reeve was nodding vigorously. "People seem to find it so easy to believe I'm a liar. Do they think I'm stupid, too?"

"People aren't convinced you're a liar, Phil," Roger said. "They're hesitating, waiting for you to speak. You can get your credibility back."

Reeve did not seem to hear. He said, "That son of a bitch Baraku. He's been out to get me for years. He fabricated that video himself. I'm going to fire him. I don't care if he's got tenure. This is a gross ethical violation. A crime. I'll fire him and prosecute him."

"We better not say the video is a fake," said Roger quietly. "That might not stand up."

Reeve looked at him, wide-eyed. "You knew about it."

"No."

"You knew and kept it from me."

"No, Phil, I had no idea the video existed. But I think somebody at Granger Hospital made it. They're not talking now, of course, but it would fit. You know they're always complaining about competition from the suburban hospitals and not enough parking spaces."

Reeve was nodding again. "That's true. Bitching and moaning. All the time. We'll go after the bastards. They let me get blindsided. Get their CEO—what's his name—on the phone. I'm gonna demand to know who made that video and who leaked it. I'll announce it at the press conference. Full investigation. With terminations and prosecutions to follow."

"Phil, we can't pick a fight with Granger. If the media sees any daylight between the med school and the hospital, they'll exploit it. They'll get us flinging charges back and forth and everybody will look bad."

"Then what am I supposed to say? You're sending me out to face the reporters and you won't let me say anything. Cancel the press conference. There's no point."

"It's important for you to say the Medical Park is not your plan. It's not going to happen."

"I shouldn't *have* to say that. It's so unfair. I mean—my God—people want to attack me for what I've done, fine. I'll defend myself. But I didn't *do* this. It's not my fault."

"No, it's not fair. But your credibility is on the line. You have to go out there in an hour and say the Medical Park is not going to happen."

"That's not going to satisfy them. They'll throw all kinds of shit at me."

"Let them. Just keep saying it's not going to happen. Because that's the truth. The reporters will work their sources, who won't be able to confirm the story. Time will pass and nothing will happen except that we continue to rehab Parkdale. The story will slowly fade away. Phil, you can get through the worst of it this afternoon."

Reeve sat in silence, his head bowed. At length, he muttered, "Water."

Roger got up, went to the next-door bathroom, and returned with a glass of water. He waited to make sure Reeve had a good grip on it before he let it go.

"Thank you, Pete, I'll take it from here," Roger said, accompanying him to the door.

"Okay. Good luck." Peter dropped his voice. "You think he'll be ready for the press in an hour?"

"He'll be okay. It's just that he's been sandbagged. Anyone would react the way he's reacting."

As the door closed, Peter was thinking that this was the first time it had occurred to him that Philip G. Reeve was just like anyone.

29

AT FOUR O'CLOCK PETER was standing on the curb outside the public relations building, waiting for Renata. She had called half an hour before to say that Frank Muldaur had notified her that he wanted to see them in his office at City Hall immediately. She would pick Peter up in the car she'd rented. He asked her what make of car to look out for, but she couldn't tell him. Renata had no interest in cars.

It was a Ford Escort that pulled up at the curb. He got in with relief. The sports coat he had put on this morning was no longer adequate for the weather, which had turned cold and blustery. She kissed him and said, "I expect you're quite happy to escape. It must be a madhouse."

"Actually, I feel like a rat deserting a sinking ship."

"The radio said the chancellor didn't show up for his press conference."

"No. Roger had to take it. They gave him a hard time, of course."

"What's the matter with Reeve?"

"I don't understand it. I wouldn't expect a few hostile reporters to scare him. He's faced the Washington and New York press corps many times. He's testified before Congress. Not to mention fighting in Iraq. But he's come totally unstrung."

"You're sure there's nothing to the Medical Park plan?"

"He never heard of it before today."

They drove a mile in silence.

Renata said, "I'm wracking my brains. How does this fit in with everything else that's happening?"

"It doesn't. This is nobody's plan. It's a train wreck."

City Hall was a tan and brown imitation of a French chateau. Built in 1914, it looked as if it had seen better days. They went in and gave their names.

A page escorted them upstairs to Muldaur's office. The big man was wearing a crimson power tie today. He was seated behind a wide desk under a tall window, which provided a view of the Gateway Arch, a silvery band against the gunmetal sky.

"I don't have much time," he said. "Sit."

He leaned back in his chair, folded his hands over his broad gut, and gave Peter a heavy-lidded look. "What's going on at Adams, Lombardo?"

"Reeve never heard of the Medical Park plan."

"You mean you really believe what you're being paid to say? I'm not going to waste any more time on you, then. I have a question for you, Ms. Radleigh, and if you give me a straight answer it will go better for everyone, especially your brother."

"All right."

"If he calls you, what are you going to say?"

"Mr. Muldaur, I am the last person my brother would call."

"We think he's about down to his last person."

"Muldaur, what are you saying?" Peter asked.

"Only that the St. Louis Police turn out to be better at finding missing persons than you, Lombardo. Don Radleigh rented a Honda Accord day before yesterday. He probably wanted something less conspicuous than that old Jag. But he rented it under his own name, and a computer search turned it up. A patrol unit spotted the Honda early this afternoon in the parking lot of a motel on Hampton Avenue. He was registered at the hotel and they went to his room. Just in time to look out the window and see him going over the fence at the back of the motel. He got away, but now he's on foot, and they have a description of what he's wearing. So if I was your brother, I'd be thinking time was running out."

He leaned forward. The chair squeaked under his weight. He fixed his eyes on Renata's. "I want to make sure we're clear on a couple of things, Ms. Radleigh. There are no charges pending against Mr. Radleigh at this time. There are just a few questions we would like to ask him. If your brother calls, pass that information on. Advise him to turn himself in to the nearest police officer, who probably won't be far away. Then he'll have nothing to fear."

"I understand," Renata said.

Muldaur gazed at her a while longer. Then smiled and sat back, accompanied by more squeaks. "Okay. That's all. I hope you'll do as I ask."

He rose and went out a side door. Renata and Peter looked at each other, then got up and went out into the corridor.

"What do you think?" she said softly.

"I would never tell anyone they could trust Muldaur, but I think what he told us is true. The cops are closing in on Don."

"He won't contact me, no matter what. His boss has probably ordered him not to."

"I wouldn't be too sure. You saved his ass before."

Peter noticed that the corridor was unusually busy. People kept passing them, all headed in the same direction. Many were talking excitedly, either to their companions or on their phones.

"What's going on?" Renata asked. "Is there a fire drill?"

"We'll see when we get to the atrium."

"What's that?"

"It's where Mayor Skinner likes to make speeches. He also likes to have all the office workers fill the galleries. I guess this is why Muldaur was in a hurry."

The corridor ended in a gallery overlooking a spacious atrium, brightly lit by a skylight and bedecked with flags of the city, state, and nation. They joined the municipal employees lining the railing and looked down on a broad staircase. Muldaur was descending it, to join a dark-suited phalanx standing behind a podium bearing the city's seal. Below them, the well of the atrium was filled with reporters and photographers. A man stepped out of the phalanx and took his place at the podium. The employees applauded; the media people did not.

Rodney Skinner, the mayor of St. Louis, was the sort of politician the papers would have called "colorful" if he had not been African American. He had survived scandals sexual and financial as well as fiery feuds with powerful people. He was short and slender, bald and gray-bearded; he did not look at all like the ex-cop he was. But he had the voice of a giant, deep and powerful.

"I've been asked to say a few words about the Adams University situation," he boomed.

Renata and Peter exchanged a glance.

"Adams is a great institution. All St. Louisans are proud of it. I myself am as proud as a Saint Louis U man is allowed to be." He waited out the laughter and resumed. "Every once in a while, I've heard the whispers, as I'm sure you have too, that Adams doesn't return our affection. That it thinks being in St. Louis holds it back. It would like to be where the other great universities are. California. New York. New England. I never believed that. And I *sure* never believed it wanted to be in Kutar."

He drawled it out, *Kooo-taaar*, and got another laugh.

"As I say, I believed Adams cared about St. Louis. So I wasn't surprised, but I was very pleased, when Chancellor Reeve announced that he was buying one of our fine old city neighborhoods, and that he was going to set it on its feet again." The crowd was murmuring now so that the mayor had to increase his volume. He had plenty to spare. "I can see I don't have to tell you that the plan has changed."

He allowed the audience to laugh and mutter among themselves for a moment, then resumed. “I’ve been trying to call my friend Phil, get him to clear up the confusion. But he’s not talking to me. Or anyone else. Guess he figures he doesn’t need anybody’s permission if he wants to tear down the homes of a lot of city residents and build a Medical Park.”

There were stray shouts of “No way!” and “Stop Reeve!” from the galleries. The mayor held up his hand.

“I’m not going to come out against the Medical Park. It’s a complicated question. We’ll all have to study it and talk about it, soon as Phil decides to start talking to people again. But there is one thing I want to get clear right now. The med center is a nonprofit. Doesn’t pay a penny in taxes. Which means that if the Medical Park goes through, the whole Parkdale neighborhood drops off the tax rolls. The city can’t take a hit like that. We shouldn’t have to.”

Skinner straightened up and grasped both sides of the lectern. “You’ve all heard what Adams likes to call itself. The Yale of the Midwest. Fine with me. In fact, I encourage them to take note of what the Yale of the East is doing. It compensates the city of New Haven for lost tax revenue. Every year, this great university makes a voluntary payment of *eight million dollars*.”

City employees were oohing and ahhing and clapping in the galleries.

“So my message to Adams University is this: we’re happy to work with you on your Medical Park plans. But you ought to kick a little something into the kitty. And with an endowment of fifteen billion, you can afford to.”

The mayor stepped back from the lectern, lifting his bearded chin at the applause. Peter and Renata turned away without waiting to see if he would take questions. As they stood before the elevator doors, Peter said, “The Mayor is up for re-election next spring. Seems he’s decided to run against Adams U.”

“Is that smart?”

"There are a lot of people who will cheer him for going after a snooty private university that likes to throw its weight around. And now we know why Muldaur wants Don so badly."

"For what Don can tell him about the Parkdale buy?"

"Yes. The mayor's looking for dirt to use against Reeve."

The elevator doors opened and they stepped in. Renata leaned against the wall. "Don hasn't a prayer of getting away, has he?"

"I would say he's St. Louis's most wanted man."

Peter had asked too much of his injured leg today. Pain shot from ankle to hip every time he took a step, no matter how hard he leaned on his cane. Going up the stairs to his apartment, he leaned on Renata instead, which was better.

She settled him before the television, provided a stack of books on which to prop his foot, and an ice pack. She also offered to bring him aspirin. He said he'd take a shot of bourbon instead. When she brought it, he asked her what she was going to do now.

"Nothing to do but sit by the phone."

"You might want a shot of bourbon, too."

She shrugged. Renata wasn't much of a drinker. She went out of his sight, to sit on the bed. He heard the "thunk" as her cellphone dropped on the night table.

Peter sipped and watched the news, flicking among the local stations. All led with the Adams story and the mayor's statement. It was the chancellor's bad luck that the story had one of those strong visuals television news producers loved: the two videos of campuses springing up in a matter of seconds, one in Kutar, the other in Parkdale. They came across as proof of Reeve's megalomania. For proof of his hypocrisy, the newscasts showed bits of the speech from three days before in which Reeve talked about rehabbing Parkdale. Reeve's failure to go on camera and make a strong denial played out just as disastrously as Roger had feared. A couple of stations ran interviews with Imani Baraku, who seemed dazed by what he had wrought. He wanted to talk about allowing the residents of Parkdale to stay in their homes, but the reporters were only interested in the video and how he had gotten hold of it. One station interviewed the mayor of College City, the suburb where the main campus of Adams U was located. She said that if the medical center was making a compensation payment to St. Louis, the main campus should make a bigger one to College City.

Peter became aware that Renata was standing beside him. She had changed to jeans and a rain jacket. On her face was the resolute expression that he knew so well and that always struck fear into his heart. She said, "I'm going to look for Don. You can't come. You'd only hold me up."

She headed for the door. Peter scrambled to his feet, knocking over the pile of books, and hopped after her. He got between her and the door and gripped both her arms.

"You're not going to talk me out of this, Peter."

"Yes, I am."

"I can't sit here any longer waiting for the phone to ring."

"You have no choice." Peter braced his back against the door and took the weight off his bad leg. "There's nothing you can do. You don't even know where to begin looking for him."

"I know exactly. Parkdale."

"Parkdale is the last place he'd go. He'll know he's sure to get caught there."

"He has to risk it. He needs his fake passport. The one hidden in his apartment."

Peter was jolted. He'd forgotten the fake passport.

"He'll be wanting to get out of the country," she went on, "and he's clever enough to twig that the St. Louis Police have put his real passport on a Homeland Security watch list. He'd be arrested at the airport."

"Instead he'll be arrested at his apartment. The cops have a surveillance van in front of his building."

"I must talk to him."

"Why? To warn him? Renata, do you want to help him get away?"

"I know I have to talk to him. I don't know what I'm going to say."

"You'll only get arrested with him."

"Then I don't have to worry about what I'm going to say."

Peter realized that it was hopeless. But he kept on talking. "Muldaur warned you to stay out of the way. If you go to Parkdale, you will end up in jail."

"Poetic justice. I'm the one who set the cops on my brother."

"It was the right thing to do. He's a fucking crook."

"He's *not*."

Peter let go her arms and hung his head. "God, how I love you," he said miserably. "You're magnificent even when you're totally deluded."

He turned and began to limp back to his chair. "I'll have my phone in my hand. They'll let you call from Central Booking."

He heard the door open and close, and her footfalls on the stair, and she was gone.

30

RENATA SLOWED DOWN ENTERING Parkdale. Its street layout was the usual American grid, so she could tell when she was one block from Don's building. She turned into the alley that ran through the middle of the block between the backs of the buildings, switched off her headlights and slowed to a crawl. Peter had told her the police had a van in front of the building, so she would approach from the rear. Of course, by now they were probably watching the back of the building, too. Halfway along the block, she pulled into a parking space. She would go the rest of the way on foot.

It was a cold night with low clouds that threatened rain and strong, shifting winds that drove the trash in the alley toward her. Cans and Styrofoam cups clattered past her feet. Papers sailed by her head. A gust tried to snatch her cap; she caught it by the bill and pushed it down hard. She paused next to the brick wall of a garage and looked at the back of Don's building. Her right hand, deep in her pocket, held the key to his door that Hannah had given her. Once she got in, she would see if the false passport was still in its hiding place in the umbrella stand. If not, she would head straight for the airport. If so, she would wait for Don to show up.

But first she had to cross the backyard and climb the fire

escape to the second floor. There were buildings on either side; the police could be sitting at any of their darkened windows, watching. By the time she unlocked Don's door, they would be running up the fire escape to arrest her.

She heard a cough. No, a coughing fit—loud, hacking, phlegmy—that went on and on. It was coming from the other side of the brick wall. This was Don's garage, and she remembered that Peter had told her a street person slept here some nights. What was his name? Wayne, that was it.

She stepped around the wall, into the open-fronted garage. She could see big cardboard boxes lined up parallel to the back wall. Lacking Don's Jaguar, the man had made a barrier of his own. She called, "Wayne?"

His head appeared: long, lank, gray hair, wide open eyes and mouth. "I got the owner's permission," he said hoarsely, as if he hadn't spoken in weeks.

"Yes, Don's. He's my brother. Have you seen him?"

Wayne shook his head. "No. He don't park here no more."

He sounded frightened. She thought he wasn't telling the truth. She drew closer. It would be a mistake to break through his barrier of boxes, she thought, so she crouched down next to it. Her eyes were now level with Wayne's. "He was here tonight, wasn't he?"

Wayne looked away.

"Did he ask you to go up to his apartment? Get something for him?"

"No."

"No he didn't ask, or no you wouldn't do it? Please tell me. I'm nothing to do with the police. I'm his sister. I talk like him. You can hear my accent, can't you?"

He had twisted his head as far away from her as he could. "I don't know what you're talking about."

"Don's been good to you. You would have helped him if you could."

"'Course I would."

"He was here. What happened?"

"What he wanted was crazy. He said go in the front door. They won't know which apartment you're going to. They'll think you're a tenant." Wayne clawed his beard and grasped his greasy shirt. "I said no, man. Looking like this? They'll know I'm from the street. They'll think I stole the keys. They'll put me in the car and take me to the station. Ask me a lot of questions I can't answer."

"What did Don say?"

"Nothing. He went away."

"When was this?"

Wayne didn't answer.

"When was Don here?"

"Before I went to sleep."

That could have been hours or minutes. Renata thought she wasn't going to get any more out of him. She thanked him, straightened up, and went out into the wind. After a moment of indecision, she headed back to her car. She was hoping that it hadn't been long since Don had been here, that he was still in the area. She would drive around and try to spot him.

She drove slowly, scanning the sidewalks. Despite the weather, there were a lot of people out. Parkdale, having received notice of its doom, was restless. Jackson's corner boys were at their stations and doing business. Knots of people sat on the front steps of buildings or stood next to parked cars, talking. A group of teenagers swaggered down the middle of the street. As Renata drove slowly toward them, a police car pulled up next to them and the cop shouted at them to use the sidewalk. They ignored him. He drove on anyway. She carefully drove around them.

Stopping at the next intersection, she noticed a man standing motionless on the sidewalk, head bowed and fists clenched. Suddenly he threw his head back and shouted at the top of his lungs, "Fuck Reeve!" She drove on, past a parked car. A mound of nuggets rested on the road next to its door: broken safety glass. Its window had been shattered.

She was almost at the intersection with the commercial strip. Its lights and traffic were inviting, but she was more likely to find Don lurking in the alley. She turned in and drove slowly past the backs of buildings, telephone poles, and Dumpsters. Her headlights glittered on the bright steel of a shopping cart. It was being pushed slowly toward her by a hunched-over man. He was a Dumpster-diver, and the cart was packed with his finds. She flicked on her high beams. Atop the mound was a soft tan briefcase that she recognized.

Renata threw the gear lever into park and jumped out of the car. The man was turning his cart away, preparing to beat a retreat, but she grasped it with her left hand and picked up the briefcase with her right. It was a canvas briefcase with a shoulder strap and loops that held a folding umbrella. She turned it over and saw the monogram: DPR.

"It was in the trash," the man was saying. "Don't belong to nobody." He snatched it from her hands, then got between her and his cart. He was a stocky African American, or maybe he was just well padded against the cold in several layers of clothes. He had a pungent odor. Missing teeth gave him a fierce appearance. "Leave it alone," he shouted at her. "It's empty."

It had not felt empty, but trying to open it and have a look would cause trouble. "Where did you find it?"

"I forget."

"No," she said mildly. "It's on top. You found it just a short time ago. You remember."

The man scowled. He turned and pointed. "Down there. Last Dumpster at the end of the block. Never found anything but greasy napkins and paper plates in there before. From the BBQ place."

She ran to the car and backed up to the street. Turning onto the commercial strip, she drove down it to an electric sign that outlined a smiling pig.

A man in a pink pig costume was standing on the curb waving a sign that said "RIBS $12.95!" That would be Herb.

Peter had told her about him. She parked and crossed the street.

"Hello, Herb."

The pig mask, with a big grin beneath the snout and button eyes, turned her way. The man's eyes, visible through small holes in the mask, were narrowed and wary. "Who are you?"

"I'm Peter's girlfriend."

"Oh yeah. Guy from the neighborhood newsletter. Tell him to come back. Write about my booming business."

He turned, showing his curly tail, and pointed his trotter at the bright window of the restaurant. Every table was empty.

"It isn't a night when people feel like eating out, I guess," Renata said. "Maybe you should pack it in."

"I have to make the most of every day I got left before Adams U kicks me out," he said. "I owe two thousand bucks on the smoker. And that's just the beginning of my debts."

"I'm sorry."

"My fucking landlord promised me I was gonna be here for years."

"Don Radleigh?"

"What have you got to do with Don?"

"I'm his sister. I'm trying to find him. Is he inside?"

The pig head jerked as the man inside it flinched. "No," he said.

"But you've seen him."

"Not tonight."

"Yes, tonight. Not long ago."

He walked away, leaving her looking at the back of the pig head and its floppy ears as he held up his sign to a passing car, which kept on going. Over his shoulder he said, "Fuckin' Don talked me into buying that smoker instead of renting. He said, 'You'll save in the long run.' " He had dropped into a credible imitation of Don's breezy, upper-class voice. " 'You'll be in this location for years. Not you personally—you'll have franchised your concept and be living in Florida, happy as a pig in shit. Ha-ha!'"

“Hey, what’s going on?” asked a tentative voice.

It was a weedy young man, standing at the door of the next shop down. The sign above his head said “Cold Comfort Ice Cream Emporium.” He approached cautiously, hands plunged deep in the pockets of his apron.

“Go back to your customers, Ethan,” said Herb. “There’s nothing going on here.”

“Don’t have any. Is there some trouble? I told you there was gonna be trouble.”

“Shut up.”

Renata faced Ethan squarely and met his eye. He looked away. “I’m Renata Radleigh, Don’s sister. And I want to know how his briefcase ended up in the Dumpster behind this building.”

Ethan dropped his eyes and muttered to Herb, “I told you.”

“We don’t have to say anything.”

“I’m not here to make trouble for you. I’m only looking for my brother.”

Herb let the trotter holding the sign drop. With his other he waved them into his restaurant. She followed the oversize head with the ears that flopped at each step.

Inside, the place smelled deliciously of searing pork and spicy sauces that no one was going to eat. Herb lifted off the head and threw it down on the nearest empty table. His thinning hair was sweat-soaked, as was his moustache. He had heavy bags under his eyes.

“Half an hour ago, about, I was out there waving my sign and I see a guy with a briefcase cross the street. I can’t believe it at first, but it’s him, all right. So I get Ethan here, and we agree we’re gonna give Don an affectionate sendoff. Tell him what a difference he made in our lives. By the time he sees us it’s too late to run. So he gives us that shit-eating grin and says, ‘What’s it to be, tar and feathers?’ We grab him and march him across the street and into Ethan’s place. He kept up the jokes the whole way.”

"It was just the three of us," said Ethan. "I had to let my employees go."

"He hadn't been around much lately, so we filled him in on what the last few days in the neighborhood had been like. How happy we were about Adams U buying us up.

"We thought all these buildings would be full of students and hospital workers. People with lots of money and no time to cook. We had it made. And then today we find out, nobody's gonna live here. Adams U is gonna evict us and flatten the buildings. We'll be left with nothing but our debts."

"Adams U isn't going to evict you. The Medical Park isn't going to happen."

"We saw the goddamn video. That asshole Reeve had his secret plan all along. Don was denying it all, of course. Said he knew nothing about any Medical Park."

"It's not Reeve's plan and Don didn't know about it."

"Aw, come on! Don knew months ago that Reeve was gonna buy up Parkdale. You're telling me he didn't know *why*?"

She was wasting her time. She said, "What did you do to him?"

They both looked at her, then away. Ethan said, "He walked out of here on his own power. He's fine."

"But you hit him."

"No. I held him. Herb hit him."

"I wouldn't've done it if he just admitted the truth. That he was playing us for suckers all along. But he kept giving us the same shit about how he was trying to do the best for Parkdale. For us. He was as surprised as we were by the Medical Park."

"How badly is he hurt?" she asked levelly.

"He's a little bloody, that's all. You can't throw a decent punch in this fuckin' outfit."

"I let him go and he ran," said Ethan. "We didn't mean to rob him. He just left the briefcase. So we threw it away."

"It was a stupid, ugly thing you did," Renata said. "You're starting to feel bad already, aren't you? Get used to it. Don's done you nothing but good. There isn't going to be a Medical Park. Adams will rehab the neighborhood, and you *will* be happy as pigs in shit."

She brushed past Herb and went out the door. She must not allow herself to imagine Don staggering into the turbulent night, covering his bloody face with his arm. It would only upset her and there was no time. The only question that mattered was where had he gone, and she could think of only one possible answer.

She got back in her car and drove to Hannah's.

CHAPTER 31

LEAVING THE CAR AT the curb, she ran up the front walk and pressed Hannah's buzzer. As she waited, she could hear distant pops. Her English mind produced the possibilities of car backfires or firecrackers or planks dropping on cement. But no. This was America and they were gunshots. Sirens were wailing thinly, far away, as plaintive as a baby crying. Behind her a car went by slowly, blasting rap. She pressed the button again. There was no response. Some instinct made her look up, and there was Hannah at her second-floor window. She stepped back and let the curtain fall. This was the last straw for Renata. She put her thumb on the buzzer and left it there.

Hannah bore it for a surprisingly long time, but at last she came in view through the glass panel in the door, descending the stairs. Renata released the buzzer. Hannah opened the door a few inches.

"You're crazy to be out here tonight," she said. "What do you want?"

"Is Don here?"

"I haven't seen or heard from him since the last time I talked to you. Not so much as a text message."

"He's around somewhere. He has no car. He's been beaten up. Nobody in Parkdale will help him except you."

"What makes you think I will?"

Renata flinched. "Hannah, you care about him."

"Every relationship has a clock. I told you. Ours ran out, about the time the Medical Park plan got leaked."

"The Medical Park is a red herring."

Hannah ignored her. "Made me think back to my thrilling meeting with Chancellor Reeve. At the party where he announced he was going to save the neighborhood. Give me more community gardens. We chatted about how I was planting my daffodil bulbs for next spring, resting my vegetable bed next summer so the tomatoes would be especially sweet and juicy the year after that. And the great man is nodding and smiling, knowing all along, those bulbs will never sprout, those tomatoes will never be planted because my garden's going to be paved over."

"Hannah—"

"I know what you're going to say. How can I be worried about my little garden when big things are going on. But I'm fed up with men lying to me. Like Reeve did. Like Don did."

"Neither of them knew about the Medical Park plan. It's not going to happen."

Hannah shut her eyes and wagged her head, bored with the denial. "What are you doing here? You called the cops on Don. If he's out on the streets tonight, they're going to get him. They're everywhere. Isn't that what you want?"

"I want to talk to Don. Or listen to him, really. I want him to tell me everything he's done."

"You're not afraid to find out?"

"No. My brother is not a bad man. But he's been used." She hesitated. Hannah's eyes were fixed on hers through the gap between door and frame. She was listening, as she hadn't been before. Renata felt the need to tell her the exact truth. "He's *let* himself be used."

"He's not guilty," Hannah said, "but not innocent, either. I mean, not innocent enough to satisfy you."

"I'm not setting myself up in judgment."

"No. You don't think you're a judge. You think you're a priest. He's going to confess to you, and you're going to give him his penance. You're going to tell him to turn himself in."

"Don's never done what I say."

"That's not what I'm asking you."

Renata looked away from the searching eyes. But she knew the truth now and so did Hannah, so there was no reason not to say it. "I'll tell him to turn himself in."

Hannah shook her head. "Go home to your boyfriend, Renata. Let the cops finish the job you started them on. You can talk to Don in jail."

"He's not in jail yet. He's bound to come to your door. Does he have a key?"

"No. I never gave him my key. I have that to congratulate myself on, at least."

She was stepping back, closing the door.

Renata said desperately, "If you see him, call me. Please!"

"You won't hear from me. I'm going to bed. I won't answer the door. I won't look out the window. Not on this night. Go home."

The door slammed, and through the glass she saw Hannah turn away and mount the stairs. She went back to her car. Then she sat behind the wheel without turning the key. Hannah was right. There was nothing to do but go home. But that was impossible when Don was somewhere around here, running or hiding.

A hollow explosion, like a thunderclap in the small car, sounded in her ear. Small objects hit the right side of her face. When she opened her eyes, she saw a car accelerating away. Her passenger side window was gone. A mound of shattered safety glass pebbles was on the seat, along with a chunk of broken cinderblock. Someone in the passing car had thrown it through the window.

She looked at herself in the driving mirror. Round frightened eyes but no blood. The nuggets of glass had bounced off her cheek harmlessly. She had only to brush away the ones caught in her hair. She was unharmed and had no excuse for giving up. She started the engine and drove on. At the first intersection, she recognized a familiar building. It had been her first stop in Parkdale, the night she arrived. On the top floor was the apartment where Joel Rubinstein and his fellow landlords watched for drug dealers. She leaned out her window and looked up. A light showed in a top floor window. She parked across the street and went to press the buzzer.

"Who's there?"

Through the intercom distortion she recognized Joel's voice. "It's Renata."

The door release snarled and she pushed through and started climbing. Joel was standing at the top of the last flight. "Where's Peter? You shouldn't be out there alone. Even with a squad of Marines it wouldn't be a good idea."

"Why are you here, then?"

He waved her into the apartment and closed and locked the door. She noticed that the table and chairs were gone. There were two cases of beer on the bare floor, and that was all.

"I was emptying the fridge. Before I turn the keys over to Adams U. It was getting dark, and somebody called, told me kids were breaking windows and looting stores on the main drag. I figured it might be a bad night. So I'm hanging around."

He turned off the lights and went to the window. A pair of binoculars rested on the sill. He picked them up.

"What are you looking for?" Renata asked.

"Fires. I'm sort of like a forest ranger up in my watch tower. My final service to Parkdale."

Renata sank down on one of the cases of beer. She felt very tired. "Let me know if you spot my brother, will you?"

"What would he be doing here?"

"Running from the police. I won't explain, if you don't mind. Do you really think people will set fires?"

"I can hardly blame them, the way they've been jerked around the last couple of days. We all have. If only I'd turned down Reeve's offer. Tried to talk the others into doing the same. I never would've sold my buildings if I'd known they'd be destroyed."

"They're not going to be destroyed."

He lowered the binoculars and turned to her. "What?"

"Professor Baraku found a video made by some low-level people at Granger Hospital. Reeve had never heard of it."

Joel came over and sat on the box facing her. "You sure about this?"

"Peter talked to him that day. And Peter's hard to fool. Anyway, if Reeve knew all along he was going to flatten Parkdale, he wouldn't have gotten up in front of the cameras to say what a fine neighborhood it was."

"That's true. If he really was deceitful, he would have arranged not to look as deceitful as he does now. Jeez. I've been sitting here hating the guy. Now I'm going to have to feel sorry for him. 'Cause he's in the shit now."

"Yes. But Parkdale is going to be just fine."

"So I didn't make the mistake of my life."

"No."

"Well, this is going to take some getting used to." Joel straightened up and shrugged, as if a backpack full of bricks had been lifted off his shoulders. He rose and went back to the window. After a while, Renata followed.

They watched in silence. There were more yells and pistol shots. Every second car that passed under the streetlight below the window was St. Louis Police or Adams Security. The little groups that had been standing around parked cars or sitting on front steps were gone now, the people seeking shelter. The streets were left to the young men, glimpsed fleetingly as they ran from shadow to shadow.

"What a clusterfuck," Joel said. "And it's all a misunderstanding? No one's responsible?"

"Oh, someone's responsible, all right. A rich man on the other side of the world who's pulling Don's strings. He doesn't know or care that you're up here looking for fires, or that Herb is standing in front of an empty restaurant in a pig suit, or that Baraku's trying to save people's homes, or that Hannah's mourning the gardens she thinks are lost. He's never set eyes on Parkdale. But he spotted a chance to make some money off it, and that's why all this is happening."

"You mean, by buying eighty-nine buildings cheap and selling them to Adams?"

"That was just the opening move. A bigger game is going on. With higher stakes. But I have no idea what it is."

Two men ran laughing under the streetlight. Joel watched them vanish into the darkness. He said, "Hannah."

"What?"

"That must be where Don is. Who would take him in but Hannah?"

Renata shook her head. "I've already been there. She said if Don came to her she wouldn't let him in. He lied to her and she's through with him."

"Sounds like Hannah, all right. Hard-bitten, self-sufficient. But I've noticed, she likes to hear herself say those things, because in fact she's doing the opposite, and she's afraid she's making a fool of herself."

Renata ran through her conversation with Hannah in her mind. This time she heard the false notes. Joel was right.

"Oh God. He got there before me. He was up in her apartment, the whole time she was talking to me. He's there now. I'm going back."

She spun away from the window and ran toward the door. Joel followed. They ran down the stairs. As they came out he said, "My truck's right here." An old pickup was parked in front of the building. They climbed in.

As Joel accelerated and ran through the gears, Renata said, "Don's there. She won't buzz us in."

"We'll go up the fire escape."

He turned into the alley next to Hannah's building and stopped. Far down the alley, she glimpsed a running figure as the headlights went off. Something different about him from the other running men she had seen tonight. She said, "Joel, turn on your lights."

He did. The figure was gone.

"What is it?"

"Nothing. Let's hurry." But as she got out of the pickup, she realized what had caught her eye about the figure. His straight-up posture even as his legs and arms were pumping rapidly. It was the way the man had run, chasing her along the canal in London. Flathead. But he couldn't be here. She must've imagined it.

"Hannah's second floor, isn't she?" Joel asked. He was looking up at the building. Renata looked up, too. Behind Hannah's windows was a strange flickering light. It took a moment for her to realize the apartment was on fire.

Joel was already rushing up the back steps. He banged on the doors of the first-floor apartments, shouting "Fire! Get out!" Renata ran past him and mounted the next flight. She had to get out of the way of people running down—the occupants of the apartment across from Hannah's, who must have already smelled smoke. The window above her shattered, blown out by the heat. She ducked her head under the shower of glass fragments. She looked up to see a gout of flame erupt from the hole where the window had been.

The back door of the apartment stood open. She rushed into the darkness of the narrow kitchen, felt the heat, and smelled the fire on the other side of the wall. She remembered the layout of the apartment she had visited two days ago. The fire was in the dining room. The sound was eerily familiar, the rustle and crackle of burning logs on a hearth, but a thousand times louder. Fighting all her instincts, she advanced into the smoke pouring from the doorway into the dining room. Her eyes were running and she was coughing. Through the smoke, she could see the dining table and chairs in flames. A pool of fire was spreading across the ceiling.

The smoke was so thick that breathing was as useless as if she were underwater. She dropped to her knees and it was better. The floor was hot under her palms as she crawled blindly on. Her hands found a soft obstruction. A body on the floor. It was still, unresponsive—no telling if the person was alive or dead. She ran her hands over the torso, felt the breasts: Hannah.

Don was farther in, then. She swept an arm through the smoke. Her hand hit a wall. She turned into what she hoped was the entrance to the living room, shouting, “Don!” It was no use. She could barely hear herself. No hope of hearing a response. She was coughing helplessly again. She had to go down on her belly to be able to breathe.

Through streaming eyes, she was able to see again. The smoke wasn’t as thick. In the living room the sofa was on fire but the walls and ceiling hadn’t caught yet. She could not see Don. Nor the entrance to the bedroom—it must be in the thick smoke behind her. No more time to search for him. She had to hope he had gotten out. Save Hannah and herself.

She got to her feet and ran to the front door, grabbed and twisted the doorknob, cried out as the hot metal burned her hand. The door wouldn’t budge. Locked. She remembered seeing the key in the deadbolt lock, assuming Hannah habitually left it there. She felt for it, but it wasn’t there now.

She swung round and dove into the smoke, hit the floor and started crawling on her stomach. There was almost no breathable air left. She crawled back to Hannah, scraping her cheek along the floor, gulping smoky air, coughing. Her fingers found Hannah’s hair, sank into its tangles. She was going to drag her through to the kitchen and the open back door. But the ceiling of the dining room was all flame. Too much smoke. She would pass out before she reached the kitchen.

She crawled back the way she had come, into the living

room, dragging Hannah behind her. The smoke thinned a little. Flames from the sofa were licking at the smoke-blackened walls and ceiling. Any second, the paint and plaster would catch fire. Holding her breath, she rose to her knees. Grasping Hannah by the wrists with both hands, she pulled her across the room. She blinked at the front windows. The glass had been blown out and sparks were flying into the black sky. Just a few feet beyond the window were the limbs of a tree. Clusters of leaves were burning. At the window now, she smelled—or imagined she could smell—the outside air. One strong limb stretched toward her, a bridge to safety. For a terrible moment, she was tempted to abandon Hannah and leap for it.

She looked down. Two stories—less than twenty feet. It seemed farther. She saw the upturned faces and open mouths of people standing on the lawn, people who could do nothing for her. Looking straight down she saw lumpy shapes in the darkness and remembered the yews along the front of the building that she had seen Hannah trimming. The shrubs could break their fall.

Crouching, she slid her arms under Hannah's and straightened her knees. God the woman was heavy, or Renata was weak—she could barely lift her onto the windowsill. Grasping her ankles, she flipped her legs out and Hannah fell. Renata climbed into the other window, had a fleeting impression of people rushing to Hannah, where she lay sprawled across the yews. Renata sprang out and to the right to clear them, stretching out her arms and legs. She seemed to fall for a long time, long enough to register with pleasure the cold fresh air rushing against her face.

The shrubs flattened beneath her. The ends of branches jabbed her breasts and belly, though the impact was lessened by a mound of coats that must have been contributed by onlookers. She toppled to the ground and lay on her side. For a while she did nothing but breathe. All the years she had spent training her muscles to draw great draughts of air into the depths of her lungs seemed worth it now.

Eventually she became conscious of someone leaning over her, talking to her. She blinked and brought the face into focus: Joel.

"Hannah?' she said.

He shook his head. "Renata, her throat was cut."

32

At three in the morning, Renata was lying in a bed in the emergency ward of Granger Hospital. She was wearing a patient's smock, soft and worn from many washings. Her own clothes, reeking of smoke and soaked with Hannah's blood, had been cut away as soon as she was brought in, and she hoped never to see them again. Her left hand, which she had burned badly on the metal doorknob, was heavily bandaged. A lead attached to her right middle finger measured the oxygen content of her blood. A clear plastic tube running under her nose was boosting the content with every breath, she hoped. The doctors had wanted to put a tube down her throat. Worried about damaging her precious vocal cords, she had convinced them the external tube was enough.

The door opened and Frank Muldaur leaned in. "The doctors say you're well enough to chat with me for a few minutes. Do you agree?"

Warily Renata nodded.

Muldaur came in. He was carrying a large, heavy plastic bag, which he dropped on a chair. Standing by the edge of the bed, he put his hands in his trouser pockets, which dragged back his suit coat and made him look especially broad in the beam.

"I have some good news. The crime scene investigators

haven't finished their work yet, but they haven't found any human remains. They say there was no one else in the apartment."

So Don had gotten out. It was the news Renata had been hoping for, but she kept her face impassive.

"That is good news, right? Didn't you go up there hoping to find your brother?"

"I didn't know where he was."

"You were looking for him. That's why you were in Parkdale in the first place, right?"

"I won't answer any more questions."

Muldaur took his hands out of his pockets and raised them, palms up. "Renata, I'm not a cop anymore, and this is not an interrogation. Anyway, whatever your reasons for going down to Parkdale last night, all you ended up doing was rushing into a burning apartment and trying to save a woman's life, and we don't arrest people for that."

"I'm free to go, then?"

"It's the doctors holding you, not the police. I'm just here to inform you about the crime scene. Out of respect."

"Respect?"

"Yes. Your brother is a sleazebag. Lombardo is a pain, like all reporters. But you're a gutsy lady."

"Mr. Muldaur, sucking up to me isn't going to be productive. I have no information about Don's whereabouts."

"You sure? I wish you'd give it some more thought. We're looking for him a lot harder now. You know why?"

"They've given me painkillers. Maybe that's why I'm having a hard time following you."

"The crime scene team found traces of accelerant."

"You mean the fire was set?"

"Yes. Presumably to destroy evidence. But Joel Rubinstein called it in right away and the fire department got there fast. Saved the building. Preserved much of the evidence. We're pretty sure we have the murder weapon."

Renata pulled herself upright.

"It's a long kitchen knife. The wooden handle was mostly burned off. There's blood on the blade. On the kitchen counter, we found a wooden block, scorched but intact. It's a knife holder. There are five knives and six slots. The empty slot fits the blade of the murder weapon. Does that suggest anything to you?"

She shook her head.

Muldaur took a pair of latex gloves out of his pocket and began to put them on. "We know the victim was Mr. Radleigh's girlfriend. It would be a natural assumption for you to make, that he was hiding out with her."

"She was his girlfriend, yes. I had no reason to think he was there last night," Renata lied blandly.

Muldaur picked up the plastic bag and opened it. She smelled smoke. He pulled out a tan trench coat, heavily smoke-stained, with one sleeve half burned away. "This was hanging on a hook in the foyer. Is it your brother's?"

"He has a tan trench coat. I don't know if that's it."

"This one has a tag that says Burberry, Regent Street, London. That narrow it down any?"

She shrugged.

"How about this?" He opened the coat and held it out to her. Don's monogram was sewn into the plaid lining.

She said, "Those are his initials, but you don't need me to tell you that."

"No. We don't." He put the coat back in the bag and peeled off the gloves. "Any idea why he went back to Parkdale? Kind of a strange thing for him to do."

"No idea."

"But you knew to go there to look for him."

"I just couldn't think of anywhere else to go."

Muldaur smiled thinly. "Based on your non-answers, I think you already know what we think happened. Radleigh was on foot in Parkdale. Bad place to be. He needed somewhere to hide. He knocked on Hannah's door. She opened it to speak to him, but he couldn't convince her to let him in. So he pushed his way in. She fought him. He saw the knives on the counter, and—"

"My brother did not kill Hannah."

Muldaur gazed at her for a while. It was acutely uncomfortable. "You know, Ms. Radleigh? I'm not a cop anymore. That means I no longer have to do parts of the job I hated. Like convince a good woman that her lover or son or brother is a bad man. But think about it."

He picked up the plastic bag and went out the door.

Renata stepped through the door into the waiting area where Peter had been sitting for what seemed like most of his life. She had changed into the fresh clothes he had brought, but the bandaged left hand and bloodshot eyes spoke of her ordeal. He planted his cane and rose as she moved gingerly toward him. Her eyebrows rose questioningly as she looked into his eyes.

"Can't muster a smile?" she asked.

"I've had a hard night. Sounds ridiculous, saying that to you. But it's true."

"I'm sorry, love."

They embraced. Her hair smelled of smoke. He moved to put her on his left side—the side with the uninjured leg—and she took his arm and leaned on him. He leaned on his cane, and they set out, slowly and carefully. The automatic doors swished open on a cold, gray dawn.

"I do hope you've brought a car."

"The one you rented. I found it in Parkdale. It's okay except for a broken window."

"You've been to Parkdale?"

"It made a change from sitting in the waiting room."

They reached the car, parked on the side of the wide, nearly empty street. Peter settled her carefully against a fender while he brushed broken glass from the passenger seat. Then he helped her in. She drew in her breath sharply when she saw the umbrella stand from Don's apartment, lying in the foot well.

"It was at the bottom of the back steps of Don's building."

"The passport's gone, of course."

"Yes. Don must have taken advantage of the diversion caused by the fire. The cops watching his building were distracted."

He waited for her to say something, but she did not. He closed the door and went around the car. Settling behind the wheel, he headed for home. Renata still kept silent. He glanced at her. She had her eyes closed against the cold air rushing through the broken window. He asked the question.

"Did you tell the police about the passport?"

"No. It would have been pointless, since I don't remember what name was in it."

"I do. It was—"

"No, you don't."

"Oh."

"I'm not going to help them catch him for killing Hannah, because he didn't do it."

"You know who did?"

"I caught a glimpse of him fleeing the scene. Flathead."

"The man who chased you along the canal? He was *here*?"

"His employer can afford plane tickets for his hirelings. And this was the same sort of job. I mean Don was in the same sort of position as Flathead's mate, who fell in the canal. He was in trouble. Likely to be caught by the police. It was necessary to make sure he wouldn't tell them anything. Particularly who he was working for."

"What do you think happened in Hannah's apartment?"

"The kitchen door was open when I got there. Flathead must have talked his way in. All he had to say was that their boss had sent him to help Don. Flathead killed Hannah first. Maybe she got suspicious. Maybe not. Even if she didn't put up a fight, she was a witness and he had to kill her. I can't be sure how it happened. But I know exactly what happened next."

He glanced over. She was blinking in the wind and tears were running down her cheeks. He said, "Do you want me to pull over? You'd be more comfortable in the back."

"I don't want to be comfortable. Do you remember, when we went to see Hannah the morning after I arrived, the key was in her front door lock?"

"I didn't notice."

"I did, because I have the same sort of deadbolt lock, and I leave the key in it too, so I can get out in case there's a fire. Well, last night there *was* a fire. I wanted to get out the front door. But the key was gone. Don had taken it."

"I don't follow."

She folded her arms and bowed her head. "Hannah bought him a few precious seconds. While Flathead was cutting her throat, he beat a retreat. He saw the key in the lock and realized it was his chance. He unlocked the door, took the key, stepped through, and locked it again. Flathead was locked in. He would have to go through the apartment, down the back steps, and around the building, giving Don time to run away. Lose himself in the darkness."

"Flathead must have seen right away it was hopeless. He gave up the chase and set fire to the apartment to destroy the evidence."

"Yes."

Peter pulled up in front of his building and switched off the engine. Renata picked up the umbrella stand but made no move to open the door.

"Let's go inside. Warm you up."

"No. Let's finish this." She dried her tears on her sleeve. "We can assume Don is on a plane now. He's fleeing to … I don't know. Buenos Aires? Sydney? Somewhere he hopes neither the police nor his former employer will be able to find him."

"If he's in the air now, the cops might still be able to nab him, if we give them the name on the passport."

"He's not a murderer," Renata insisted again.

"No, but he is a liar and coward, and has probably committed other crimes we haven't found out about yet. Not the sort of person I would normally commit the felony of withholding evidence for."

"I'm so sorry you got dragged into this."

"I'm sorry *you* got dragged into it. He has almost gotten you killed twice. I'm keeping count."

She looked away. He suspected the tears were flowing again and she didn't want him to see. "I'm such a pessimist about most things. But I have these two fond illusions—that I still have a career as an opera singer, and that Don is not as bad as he looks. I've caused you so much worry. I don't blame you for being angry with me." She was sobbing now. She got out a handkerchief and blew her nose. She folded it away quickly, but not before he saw that her mucus was spotted black from the smoke she had inhaled.

Peter felt awful. He said, "I'm not angry at you. I'm angry at Don."

"So am I. But it's a waste of emotion. We'll never hear from him or of him again." She set the umbrella stand upright in her lap. "How nice of him to leave the family heirloom to remember him by."

"What do we do now?"

"You rest your leg and recover. I go home."

"London?"

"Yes. I'll do what I can to clean up the mess Don has left behind. Go to Detective Inspector McAllister and see if he's made any progress with his investigation of Neal Marsh's death. And the man in the canal, the one Flathead shot. Tell McAllister all I know and all I suspect. Except about the passport, of course."

"All right. I'm going with you."

"My love, I'll be perfectly safe. I'm putting this in official hands. The police will protect me if I need protection."

"Forget it. I let you out of my sight for one evening and you run into a burning building. I'm going with you."

33

There was a television at the gate in Lambert-St. Louis Airport, tuned to CNN. Waiting to board, they learned that Sheikh Abdullah and his entourage had taken off in their private jet late last night. University spokesman Roger Merck said that plans for the Kutar Campus were on hold indefinitely.

Peter was reminded to send Roger a text message, saying that he couldn't continue his PR assignment because his leg was too painful. He was surprised to receive a reply text immediately. Roger sympathized and promised to pay Peter anyway. The associate deputy vice chancellor was an awfully nice man.

There was a television at the gate in JFK, too, and they heard that the Board of Trustees of Adams University had met in emergency session. Their chairman announced the appointment of an interim chancellor. They had accepted the resignation of Philip G. Reeve. They did not add "reluctantly." The correspondent said Reeve could not be reached for comment; according to his representative, he had gone to his winter home near Pensacola for a rest.

As their plane set off across the Atlantic, Peter, who had not slept at all the previous night, dropped off, disloyally leaving Renata, an anxious flier, to sit wide-eyed and upright. He did not wake until the wheels hit the runway at Heathrow. They taxied for a long time, passing lumbering, enormous planes just arrived from or about to set off for the ends of the earth. Peter gaped through the window at the stylized kangaroo of Qantas, the swirling golden Arabic letters of Etihad, the red and blue fish, or whatever it was, of Malaysia Airlines. "I've a feeling we're not in Missouri anymore," he murmured.

At passport control they separated, Renata to the "European Union" line and Peter to "All Others." His line was longer, and by the time he emerged, she had telephoned Detective Inspector McAllister. He had identified the corpse from the canal. Orangefoot's real name was James Bartleby. He was a villain well known to police. In Britain, Peter now learned, they actually called the bad guys "villains." But no leads had yet been found to his current employer or his accomplices. Renata wanted to come in and talk to him immediately, but he said tomorrow would be better. Peter remembered reading somewhere that the wheels of British justice ground exceedingly slowly.

Peter refused a wheelchair, which was a mistake. After walking down endless corridors, his ankle was throbbing. He leaned on Renata as they staggered to the curb and entered one of the big, black, comfortable taxis of song and story. She said that it was the first time she'd taken a cab home from the airport in ten years, and when he saw the final figure on the meter, he knew why.

They walked to one in a long line of identical row houses—a terrace, Renata called it—with bay windows and steep stairs up to a door flanked by columns. A low iron fence separated the sidewalk from what Renata called the "area." The neighbors had brightened up their areas with colorful tiles and potted plants, but Renata and her roommates had only litter blown in from the street decorating theirs.

"This is a nice neighborhood," he said. "I thought you said your place was more depressing than mine."

"I pay six times as much rent as you. That's the depressing bit. But it's nice coming home with you."

"Will I get to meet any of your roommates?"

"Not sure if anyone is home."

They went under the front steps to the door of the basement flat. She unlocked the door and pushed. She had to put her shoulder into it. When they stepped into the dim, narrow corridor, he saw why. A mound of mail was behind the door.

"Several days' worth," she said. "No one's here."

They gathered the mail. It was a complicated operation, because Renata's bandaged left hand was fairly useless and Peter couldn't lower himself to the floor. They were laughing by the time they got the mail to the kitchen table. He looked around the room and recognized it from Skype.

"All junk as usual," she said. "No, hang on, here's an actual letter."

He looked at the envelope in her hands. It was addressed in handwritten block capitals. She took a kitchen knife and slit it open. There was one piece of paper, which had on it only:

DANGLY FOOT
YR AGE ZAUBER
50

Renata had gone perfectly still. He said, "What?"

"It's from Don. Couldn't be anyone else. He's writing in Radleigh family code."

"What's it mean?"

"I'm not sure. But I recognize the references."

Peter picked up the envelope. "Postmarked London yesterday."

"But he could have gone anywhere in the world. Why is he *here*?"

"It's pretty obvious," Peter said. "He decided not to run."

She looked at him, then back at the paper. After a moment

she said, "It's a rendezvous. He's asking us to meet him. What's the time?"

"Eleven thirty."

"We have to go now."

Half an hour later they were walking in Hyde Park, along a straight path lined with tall, bare trees. A bitter wind was sweeping across the flat expanse of parkland, but the sky was blue and the grass all but glowed green.

"Am I holding you up?" Peter asked. "You can go ahead."

"Not, it's all right. He's not there yet."

"Ah. That's the rendezvous?"

"That's Dangly Foot. Known to the rest of the world as *Physical Energy* by G.F. Watt."

At an intersection of paths ahead stood an equestrian statue. A naked man, hand to brow, sat leaning back and scanning the horizon atop a prancing horse. He had a saddle but no stirrups. His bare feet pointed to the ground.

"Don was quite the equestrian when he was a boy. Used to rail against Mr. Watts for forgetting to put in the stirrups."

"I see. And YR AGE ZAUBER?"

"When I was twelve my parents took us to see *The Magic Flute. Die Zauberflöte.* My first opera."

"And that's memorable because it was when you decided to be an opera singer?"

"No. I was a veteran, committed pianist. Didn't like the opera at all. I was bored and restless. Don was a little saint, our parents said. It was usually the other way round."

"So we're meeting Don at twelve?"

"Yes, but he's late."

People were streaming past the statue, but no one was lingering: mothers wheeling prams, joggers, parties of tourists gawking and taking pictures, lone, briskly striding men with backpacks.

"Is this typical?' Peter asked. "I mean, in St. Louis there's hardly anybody in the park on a weekday."

"London's chock-full of people, my love. You'll have to get used to it."

Peter put his back to the base of the statue and shifted his weight off his bad leg. Renata was too keyed up to stay still. She paced, looking up the paths in all directions, trying to spot Don. Minutes crawled past.

"What does '50' mean?" Peter asked.

"Haven't got that yet. Been ransacking my memory."

"Maybe he meant he'll be here at fifty minutes past twelve."

"I hope so. I simply won't be able to bear it if he does a bunk."

"He's wary. Obviously. Sending you a letter in code rather than a text message. Why do you think—"

"Peter, I'm too nervous to think."

She continued to pace and scan the faces of approaching people. One had windswept hair, thin face, orange vest over greasy anorak. A homeless man selling the *Big Issue*. "Oh lord," she whispered to Peter. "They never fail to glom onto me. Some days I buy five copies." As he drew near she sighed and smiled. "I'll take one, please."

He said, "Renata?"

"What?"

"Got something for you."

"Oh. You mean … a man gave you something to give to me? When?"

"Yesterday. But I didn't lose it." His voice rose and his eyes widened. He must have spent the last twenty-four hours worrying about losing it. "Be out a hundred pounds if I lost it, wouldn't I? The man said you'd give me a hundred pounds."

"He said fifty." Peter was approaching. The man shrank back as if he expected Peter to beat him with his cane. But he locked eyes with Renata again and his weathered features set in a stubborn expression. "A hundred or I won't give it you."

"Oh … all right." She dug in her purse. It was lucky that she had stopped at an airport cash point to get grocery money. She handed all of it to the man, who was fidgeting under Peter's watchful eyes. His dirty fingers grasped the £10 notes while his other hand ducked under the orange singlet and came out with an untidy sheaf of paper. He gave it to her and walked quickly away.

"It's Don's handwriting," she said. His elegant but near illegible script covered the first page, which was his boarding pass.

Peter read the pass and said, "He caught a late flight out of Chicago night before last. He's been here a full day. Can you read what he wrote?"

"It's not easy. 'Dear Renata, I must keep this impersonal and short, because you may have to hand it over to the police.' " Her insides were knotting up. She raised her head and forced a deep breath into her lungs.

"He didn't manage to keep it short. There must be ten or twelve pages."

The wind was curling the pages over her fingers. She said, "Let's find a place to sit down and read."

34

THEY WENT INTO A crowded, noisy café overlooking the Serpentine. The wind was making waves in the long, narrow, blue lake, which sparkled in the sunshine. People on the banks were feeding the ducks and geese. Renata laid the untidy manuscript on the table. Don had obviously written it on the plane, using whatever pieces of paper had come to hand.

She glanced at the first lines and said, "Well, at long last. We have the name of Don's boss."

"Who is it?"

She read, " 'This is a true and complete statement of my activities in St. Louis, Missouri, USA, on behalf of Anand Mavalankar—' "

"Mavalankar!" Peter said. "Holy shit."

"You know of him?"

"You mean you don't?"

"Peter, ordinary people aren't so well informed as you. Who is he?"

"A major international criminal. Infamous around the world for his greed and ruthlessness. Nobody knows how many deaths he's been responsible for, one way or another, but he's too well insulated to be prosecuted. The part of his activities that shows above the surface is a construction company. It's the company that was at the center of the Commonwealth Games scandal."

"I'm afraid I don't know about that either."

"Delhi hosted the Commonwealth Games five years ago. It was a fiasco, thanks mostly to Mavalankar. He won the contracts to build the stadium and other facilities, not by making the lowest bid, but by bribing politicians to accept his inflated bids. He and his extended family and associates squeezed everybody else out with payoffs and intimidation. When one of his cronies lost the food service contract, Mavalankar simply slowed down work on the whole sports complex. It wasn't going to be ready in time, and the government caved. Gave his pal the contract.

"But by then it was almost too late. Mavalankar forced his employees to work longer and longer hours. He ignored safety procedures. I think it was thirty or thirty-five workers died or were crippled in accidents. The games took place on time. But in the years since, most of the buildings have become unusable or completely collapsed, because Mavalankar used cheap materials. Hundreds of millions of dollars had disappeared into his pockets and those of his friends. Even for India, it was too much. The government mounted an all-out drive to prosecute him. But the case broke down. The vital witnesses either recanted or disappeared. No one will ever be able to prove it, but Mavalankar's *goondahs* probably murdered at least ten people."

"Goondahs?"

"The Indian word for men like your friend Flathead."

Renata resumed reading, in silence, passing each page to Peter as she finished with it. Don's resolve to write a formal statement had given way in the first sentence.

> Never been much of a writer but here goes. We've left Chicago. Soon we'll be in Canadian airspace. Now I can gather my wits and begin. Hope I don't run out of time or paper. If I were in first class the stews would provide me

with stationery. But they won't do a thing for you here in steerage.

Steerage. That's where to start. When we met at Maestro Grinevich's, I was in London to see Mavalankar, and the trip had got off to a rough start, because his people had put me in steerage. A sign that I was in disfavour with the great man.

When I walked into his office in the City, he just looked at me. It wasn't only the usual smile and handshake and invitation to sit that were missing. It was as if he'd never laid eyes on me before. He asked when he was going to see a return on Parkdale. I couldn't come up with a reply. Before, he'd always said it was a long-term investment.

He lost his temper. I'd been pouring his money into Parkdale and he was tired of it. He wanted to unload those buildings now. Did I have a buyer in mind?

I didn't. I'd made some friends on his staff and they'd warned me. You never knew where you were with him. But I wasn't prepared. I was standing in front of his desk with my knees wobbling. The longest minutes of my life went by. Then he said, So it's up to me to come up with someone? Very well.

He called the man who stands outside his door, and whose only job is to take off the Persian slippers he wears in the office and put on his street shoes—which are always bespoke from New & Lingwood, by the way. So we were going out. As we crossed the outer office he shouted for someone to ring Sheikh Abdullah, ask for the favor of an interview, and say we were on our way. It was the first I heard of Sheikh Abdullah.

He didn't say a word to me on the ride across town. Busy on his mobile. It was raining and I was looking out at the wretched people under their umbrellas. Remembering what it was like when I was one of them and saw a limousine go by. Now I was in the limo, and envying *them.* A flunky crouching on a jump seat asked me if I wanted anything from the bar and I knew I couldn't swallow so much as a sip of water. I hadn't even noticed what make of car it was.

Our destination was the sheikh's townhouse in Belgravia. As soon as I met him I began to feel a little better. He hadn't just climbed down from a camel. The voice and manners and handshake told me he'd been at a British public school. Mavalankar's filthy mood improved a bit, too. It was obvious they were old friends.

We sat down and ordered tea. Mavalankar said he'd have chai, not too sweet, and turned to the sheikh and said in the same tone, I have 89 buildings in St. Louis, USA, and you're just the man to buy them from me. The sheikh didn't turn a hair, just asked, St. Louis, where Adams University is? Mavalankar said yes, and that's who you'll sell them on to. By the time tea arrived, the deal was done.

Mavalankar suggested to the sheikh that I should act as his agent, that I was a very capable fellow. Rather dizzying to be back in good odour with him so fast. The sheikh graciously accepted my services. He explained that he and Chancellor Reeve had been working on a Kutar Campus for some time. It was the first I'd heard of it. The sheikh had taken considerable trouble, his contribution had been vital, and now he deserved a token of Reeve's appreciation. Adams would buy the 89 buildings from him, for a few hundred thousand dollars more than he was about to pay Mavalankar. To be exact, I would do the asking. In Arabia, the two principals would never lower themselves to discuss a side deal like this. Trusted subordinates would do it. I would act for the sheikh, he said, and whom did I think I should approach for the chancellor?

I had to tell them that this might be courtesy in Arabia,

but in America it would be called corruption. Safer all around if I approached Reeve directly. Mavalankar said I was trustworthy and discreet and should be given a free hand. The sheikh concurred.

Outside the house, Mavalankar clapped me on the shoulder and said, You may be representing the sheikh, but don't forget you work for me. I'm not letting you go. As long as I was here, I might as well stay the weekend. Come along to the musical evening at Grinevich's. That's when I mentioned you, and he said he'd ask Grinevich to add you to the program.

If this should be our last communication, I hope you'll remember that when I was on top of the world, or thought I was, I did you a good turn. Give me credit for that at least.

Back in St. Louis, the Adams flunkies were very tiresome. Wouldn't let me see the chancellor unless I explained my business. I checked his public schedule and found he was appearing at the opening of the university's latest do-gooder enterprise, a center for at-risk, differently abled children with special needs, or whatever. He was doing some sort of engineering demonstration involving Legos. The children were much more interested in his missing arm than the engineering. He twigged and made a joke about it and asked for volunteers to assist him. You should've seen it. A bunch of street urchins who could barely sit still, but when the chancellor gathered them round him, they were like shepherds adoring the Blessed Virgin. The man certainly does have charisma. Or did.

Afterward he was drinking lemonade with some teachers, pretending to be accessible, but his flunkies kept heading me off. All I could do was write the sheikh's name on a napkin, fold it and hand it to him as he was leaving. Couple of minutes later, a flunky returned to escort me to his car. He played dumb at first, said Parkdale was an interesting idea but would have to go through channels. I told him plainly, his friend the sheikh was asking for a personal favour and if he said no they wouldn't be friends anymore and he could forget about his Mideast campus. He lost his temper. Just threw all his toys out of the pram. Said he didn't believe I came from the sheikh. I told him he would receive a call and got out of the car. Then I rang London and arranged for the call.

The very same day my mobile rang and it was the chancellor. Singing a very different tune. He would buy the 89 buildings. In fact, for camouflage purposes, he was going to buy all of Parkdale in one fell swoop. He wanted to put it behind him, and he wanted to get off the phone with me as soon as possible.

That very day, Lombardo interviewed me. Fancies himself a tough journalist, always sniffing for a rat. Well, sucks to him and his suspicions. I told him I was saving Parkdale, and that's just what I was doing. You'll say it was a corrupt deal. But what Joel Rubinstein and his friends had been trying to do the honest way for thirty years, I pulled off in a couple of days.

I was positively livid when I got that phone message from you. This was the most delicate moment of a not quite legal deal. And it was my golden chance. The money I'd make on it would be only the beginning. Last thing I wanted was you mucking it up with your ridiculous suspicions. I rang my friend Jhumpa. She said she'd try to calm you down.

Only hours later Mavalankar himself called. I was frightened but he made a joke of it, asked me why I couldn't control the females in my family. He told me you were on the way to St. Louis, even your flight number and arrival time. I asked him what he wanted me to do and he replied it was quite simple. You could only do real mischief if you found out his name. And I was the only one in St. Louis who knew it. I need only stay away from you. Next day he called again and I said the Parkdale deal was all over bar the shouting and why didn't I just come back to London. He told me he would have something else for me to do in St. Louis. I didn't ask what it would be.

This is why I don't like to write. Not this sort of postmortem anyway. Makes one aware of all one didn't do and should have done. The sort of pointless brooding you're so good at.

I'm back after a break. Didn't feel at all like going on. Crept past rows of sleeping people to the stews' lair and managed to talk them into selling me a couple more little bottles of Scotch. Then I had a nap. But we're over Ireland now and I have to finish.

While you were dashing about St. Louis I was in a comfortable motel in the suburbs with my laptop. You'll want to know what I was doing with my last hours before everything went spectacularly pear-shaped. I was on London estate agent websites, looking for a place to live. On what Mavalankar would pay me, I could definitely afford Fulham. Maybe even Chelsea.

Remembering that made me so cross with myself I had to go back for more Scotch. Sorry. If I had more paper I would throw this sheet out, but I don't.

Now the descent into hell begins. First sign: The evening news said the police were looking for me. Something else to blame you for. I changed motels, registering under a false name, but forgot to get rid of the car I'd hired under my own name.

Then the call came. Mavalankar told me to present myself at the Ritz Carlton, as Sheikh Abdullah had an errand for me.

The top floor was entirely taken up by his entourage. Soon I was taking off my shoes at the door of the sheikh's room. He welcomed me and turned on some sort of humming machine that's supposed to foil listening devices. Then he brushed back his moustache, took a sip of tea, and said the things we discussed at our London meeting did not in fact happen. Parkdale did not change hands. I was to go to the chancellor immediately and inform him that I worked for Anand Mavalankar. That was whom the chancellor had made the deal with.

He actually expected me to salaam him and depart. But finally, much too late, I was becoming a bit curious, and I demanded to know what the hell he and Mavalankar were playing at.

The sheikh explained that he and Reeve were at an impasse. In view of the long friendship between himself and Mavalankar, it was inconceivable that anyone else should get the contract to build the Kutar Campus. But Chancellor Reeve consistently refused to do business with Mavalankar, whose reputation he found unsavoury. His resistance would cease, once I told him that he was already dealing with Mavalankar. The contracts were signed and the money was transmitted.

I won't waste space bidding for sympathy from you. You've never had a moment like that. That's one advantage of being so anxious and pessimistic, such an all-round wet blanket. You've never been led down the garden path to the edge of the cliff. Finally, I saw that this was what it had all been about from the beginning. Parkdale didn't matter. It was just a few million. The contract to build the Kutar Campus was worth a *hundred million dollars.* All this rigmarole had had only one purpose, to get Phil Reeve into bed with Mavalankar without his knowing it.

They had me where they wanted me, too. No one would believe I'd been such a fool. I had only one chance and that was to do as I was told. Give Phil Reeve the glad tidings and get out of St. Louis. Out of America.

And those were the cheerful thoughts going through

my mind when I emerged from the Ritz and looked over my shoulder to see Lombardo on his bloody bicycle bearing down on me. It did cheer me up a bit to send him flying arse over tip.

Sorry. That's the Scotch talking. I'd throw this page away too if I could.

I had the chancellor's private number and I rang it. He didn't want to meet with me. Even when I made it clear to him he had to, he wouldn't let me come to his house or the campus. And so we ended up having our fateful rendezvous in the parking lot behind a Taco Bell. For the rest of my life I think I will never be able to smell a quesadilla without being sick.

If you don't think a one-armed man can't frighten you witless you haven't see Reeve in a fury. I thought he was going to pound my head in. He said he was taking me to a man he knew in the local FBI office, from which I would go directly to jail. But then he realized that was a non-starter. He would lose control of the timing of the revelations, which was his only hope of surviving the scandal.

I thought he'd let me go but not a chance. He wanted me to know all about the man I was working for. He told me Mavalankar had made untold millions on construction projects in the Gulf. He hired poor Indians and shipped them to the Gulf where they had no rights and he could house and feed them as cheaply as he pleased. He overworked them and neglected their safety and many were injured or died in accidents. Of course all that fattened the profit margin for the investors. Mavalankar had made many friends like Sheikh Abdullah.

He said it was true, the sheikh kept insisting they give the contract for the campus to Mavalankar and he kept refusing. Reeve had people on his faculty who opposed the campus for their own selfish reasons. The news that an international human rights pariah was building the campus would be a godsend to them. He wasn't sure the project would survive it. Or he would survive it.

He had no choice but to take his licks. His virtue was lost already. When you're dealing with the Devil, it's in for a penny, in for a pound. It didn't matter that the Parkdale deal was only a few million. He fell silent and I could see his mind working, how he was going to delay releasing the news, finesse it, manage the reaction. He forgot I was there, and I just stood breathing greasy exhaust fumes.

Finally he noticed I was still on the planet. He said only, do me a favor and arrange that I never see you again, and walked back to his car.

Peter looked up from the sheet. "Well, that explains it. Why Chancellor Reeve collapsed the way he did when the Medical Park thing blew up. Why he couldn't bring himself to face the press. He knew he was done for. He could survive one scandal but not two."

"Now he's resigned in disgrace. He's finished, isn't he?"

"Yes. Poor bastard."

She had little time for the problems of ex-Chancellor Reeve. She returned to her brother's.

I'd like to go back to the stews and beg another fistful of bottles but they're busy serving breakfast and we're over Merrie Olde, so I must end.

I can skip a lot about my last visit to Parkdale. From what you told Hannah, you already knew. And by now you know I was up in her flat while you were talking to her at the door. I know you. You'd only tell me I had to turn myself in to the American police and I didn't want to hear that. I just wanted to get out of the country, back to London and my reward. I'd done such a splendid job for Mavalankar. When he rang my mobile and said he was sending someone to help me, I said oh good, and told him where I was.

This tall skinny bloke knocked on the back door and we let him in. He was very soft-spoken and deferential, asked how he could help. I was starting to tell him when he reached out, plucked the knife from the holder, and slashed Hannah's throat. A jet of her blood shot across the kitchen and splashed on the refrigerator door.

A brave man would have fought him and died. Any half-decent man would have just stood there frozen with shock and died.

I lived.

We're beginning our descent into Heathrow so I'll have to give Hannah short shrift, which is my usual form. When I went to her flat that night it was sheer desperation. I didn't expect her to let me in, after the way I'd simply dropped her. But she did. In fact she was happy to see me. I realized it meant she loved me, and was most annoyed, because I was only planning to use her to make my escape and never see her again. But she wanted the whole story. She believed me and didn't blame me. And a little while later, when I got her killed, I was out the door by the time her body hit the floor.

We've landed. I wish I had time to rewrite these pages. Even more, I wish I could burn them. But you have to know.

If you don't hear from me by dawn tomorrow it means I'm dead. Take this statement to the police. It'll be enough to set off a great media storm and international scandal about Mavalankar. But he's been able to survive that sort of thing before. So it's only my Plan B.

My Plan A it wouldn't be wise to tell you too much about, even if I had time. Basically, it's this. I've got to know someone on Mavalankar's office staff. Not that I trust her, but I think I know her price. And I can pay it, since somebody slipped up and forgot to close off my access to certain Cayman Islands bank accounts. What I'll buy is the name and address and anything else I can get on the man who killed Hannah. Then I'll go to the police. I'm an eyewitness to what he did, and the coppers should be able to lay hands on him and force him to grass on Mavalankar. I want that fucker charged with murder.

Then I'll go to prison. I know there's no avoiding it.

I think I can pull this off. But I'll admit it doesn't come as naturally to me as fleeing while Hannah was bleeding her life away. If we don't meet again, I'm sorry for the trouble I caused.

Donald Radleigh

35

Don's statement was in the inside pocket of her jacket. Her heart seemed to thump against it as they walked north, out of Hyde Park.

"Look at those people," Peter said. "What are they doing?"

They paused and Renata looked. Half a dozen people were standing at the edge of a wood, perfectly still, with their heads back and hands raised, palm up. "They're feeding the parrots who live in the woods."

"Parrots? I don't see them."

"Listen and you'll hear the squawks. They're in there, but rather shy. You have to remain still for quite a long time."

"Seems like it would be a lot easier to feed the water birds, down on the Serpentine."

"That's for tourists. These are English people."

"You're a patient folk."

"I'm certainly going to have to be." She turned and walked on. Peter limped beside her. "I don't know how I'm going to endure until dawn tomorrow."

"We may hear from Don before that. He's been here for a whole day."

"You mean *if* his plan works, we'll hear from him."

"Well, yes."

"Do you think it will work? Honestly, Peter."

"I don't know. You may be in a better position to judge."

"How so?"

"I'm guessing Don was being pointlessly discreet when he wouldn't give the name of the woman he was hoping would help him."

"You mean it's his friend Jhumpa again?"

"Yes. You've met her. What do you think?"

"When I was a prisoner in that van, she did try to persuade Mavalankar to spare me. But within a few hours, I was running for my life from his goondahs."

"Doesn't inspire a lot of confidence in her."

"No. D'you mind riding the Underground home? It'll take longer, and we've hours to kill."

"Fine."

There were many more stairs in Marble Arch Station than she remembered. Peter limped down them stoically. The train was crowded, but a pink-cheeked girl in a dark blue school uniform offered him her seat. He was flustered by this old-world courtesy, but accepted. At Ladbroke Grove Station, it was a long climb to the street. Fortunately, the walk to her bank was short. She left him in a comfortable chair in the lobby while she asked the staff to let her use a photocopier. After making a copy of Don's statement, she descended to her safe deposit box, where she left the original with her will and the rope of pearls she had inherited from a great aunt. At the post office next door, she mailed the copy to Peter's address in St. Louis. Then they set off on the uphill walk to her flat.

"Sure you don't want a cab?" she asked him.

"As you say, we're in no hurry. Say, what are these spots on the sidewalk? I've seen them everywhere."

"Gum splats."

"I didn't know there were this many gum chewers in the whole world. And all of them thoughtless. You know, I owe you an apology. And Don, I guess. It was just as you said all along. He didn't know what he was getting into until it was too late."

Renata sighed heavily. "Let's talk about something else. Please."

"Sorry. The sign across the street says 'Off Licence.' What's that?"

"A liquor store."

"Maybe we should stop in."

"Peter, you know I can't drink. Not on top of my anti-depressants. It'll put me to sleep."

"That's just what I had in mind."

"Perhaps later."

Reaching her building, they went through the low gate into the area, which was peppered with litter as usual. She patted her jacket for her key. How had it gotten into her left-side pocket? Her bandaged hand probed clumsily for it.

Peter's hand closed on her arm. She looked over her shoulder at him questioningly. He said nothing, just pulled her backwards until she was looking through the window, down into her kitchen. What she saw was baffling. She could only fall back on childhood, a dim memory of her mother defrosting the fridge. Its door stood wide open, and its contents—milk bottles, beer cans, juice cartons, jam jars—stood on the table.

"Your place has been searched," Peter whispered in her ear. "Maybe they're still in there. Let's move."

They retreated to the gate. He closed it carefully, silently behind them. "Keep walking," he said. "Which way is busier?"

"Back the way we came."

They strode down the hill, as quickly as Peter could manage. It was mid-afternoon and there were plenty of people on the sidewalk, plenty of traffic on the street. It was reassuring.

"The searchers are Mavalankar's men," she said. "The goondahs."

"Yes."

"But what are they looking for?"

"Don's statement."

"How would they know it even exists?"

"Because they've got him. I'm sorry, Renata. I can't think of any other explanation."

She stopped walking. There was an iron fence on her right, and she grasped one of its posts with her unbandaged hand and leaned on it to keep herself upright as weariness and hopelessness flooded over her.

A van pulled over and stopped. Its back door slid open and a woman leaned out. Jhumpa. She was wearing a different but equally beautiful foulard headscarf. "Get in," she said. "Both of you."

"No," said Renata. "I will not get in a van with you again."

The woman jumped down from the van, leaving the door open, and approached her. "Your brother is alive," she said. "We will take you to him."

"Don't come any closer," Renata said. "I haven't got the statement on me. It's somewhere safe."

Jhumpa hesitated, a pace away from her.

"Lady," Peter said, "tell your friends to stay in the van, or we'll scream blue murder."

She turned. The front door was open and the driver had one foot on the curb. The woman spoke curtly to him in Hindi. He held still.

"Tell Mavalankar to ring me," Renata said to Jhumpa. "Mavalankar himself. I'm sure he has my number."

Jhumpa shook her head. "You cannot speak with Mr. Mavalankar."

"If he wants Don's statement, he'll have to talk to me."

The woman returned to the van. Its door slid shut and it accelerated away.

Peter was looking around. He said, "There's a safer place to wait. Come on."

Twenty paces farther on was a Barclay's Bank with a cash point and a queue of customers waiting to use it. Peter positioned them so they were covered by the CCTV camera. He said, "I think we can believe what she said. Don's alive."

"Will Mavalankar call? Oh lord, what will I say to him?"

"You're doing fine. Continue to hang tough."

She waited, mobile in hand. Only a couple of minutes later, it rang. Nothing came up on its screen.

"Hello."

She recognized the deep, lilting voice at once. "You have already told me what I wanted to know."

"Have I?"

"Your brother said his solicitor had the statement. But someone like Don wouldn't have a solicitor on retainer. I assumed you had it. Now I know I was right."

So Don had tried to protect her. She said, "What have you done to him?"

"He is unharmed. Apart from minor bruises and possibly a loose tooth. In better shape than he deserves to be, considering what he was playing at. Your brother overestimated his own abilities. And underestimated the loyalty of my staff."

"Let him go."

"I am willing to turn him over to you. If you bring me the statement."

She lowered the phone and said to Peter, "He's offering a swap."

Peter shook his head.

She said into the phone, "I don't believe it. That wouldn't get you anywhere. Don would just make the statement again."

"Oh, you're trying to talk me out of it?" Mavalankar chuckled. "You're as stupid as you are stubborn. Now listen to me. Get the statement. I give you one half-hour. No more. The van will pick you up at—"

"I'm not getting in the bloody van." She looked at Peter. He mouthed, *Stall him.*

"We are going to meet. Just you and me. You'll prove Don is alive. And then we'll talk."

Mavalankar sighed. "I cannot be bothered to meet with you."

"That statement is very detailed. It tells all about you and Sheikh Abdullah."

After a pause, he said, "At three o'clock, you will be at—"

"No. I'm choosing the place." She thought quickly. It would have to be somewhere very public and secure. "The Royal Courts of Justice in the Strand. The lobby. Just beyond the metal detectors. In one hour."

"All right," Mavalankar said, and rang off.

36

THEY ARRIVED EARLY. LEAVING Peter outside, she entered and joined the queue for the metal detectors. It moved slowly: they were being reassuringly thorough. She had to hand over her watch before she was cleared.

London's civil courthouse had a lobby modeled on the knave of a Gothic cathedral, with rows of pointed arches and a lofty vaulted ceiling. She crossed the richly tiled floor to a bench beside a statue of a robed and wigged judge. The place was as busy and noisy as she remembered from previous visits, which was just what she wanted.

She kept her eye on the entrance. The queues were not diminishing. People were shedding their coats, emptying their pockets, stepping through the metal detectors, to be frisked by guards or sent back for another try. On the far side was a lane where employees were presenting IDs and walking through. A short broad man in a beautifully tailored dark-gray suit went through this lane, smiling as he presented his pass. He spotted Renata and approached. He had rather long graying black hair, large eyeglasses, and a tan face spotted with moles. Heavy jowls dragged his mouth down at the corners. She remembered the shark-like sickle mouth she'd glimpsed in the driving mirror of the van. This was Mavalankar.

"Litigation brings me here frequently," he said, in his deep, musical voice. "I bought a pass."

"Fat lot of good the metal detectors did me, then. Score one for you."

"Don't worry. I'm not armed."

"But you wanted me to know you could be. You're smart, I'm dumb. For a rich man, you're very fond of cheap tricks. Like the ones you played on my brother and Chancellor Reeve."

He sat down beside her. She remembered the citrus scent of his aftershave. "I don't know what you mean. And I'm not really interested." From his pocket he took the latest model iPhone, which he held up before her eyes.

"What's this?"

"What you asked for. The proof your brother is alive. Note the time code. This was shot less than an hour ago."

He pressed a key and a video began to run. It showed Don lying on a concrete floor. His face was to the wall. A shoe came into the frame and prodded his back. He looked over his shoulder, saw the camera and put up his arm to cover his face. She only saw his expression for a split second, but that was enough to reveal fear, exhaustion, and shame.

Mavalankar put the phone back in his pocket. "My men have told him he will come to no harm. But I'm afraid he doesn't believe them."

"You bastard."

"It's you who is prolonging his ordeal. Give me the statement and he's yours."

"You have no intention of letting him go. You're just using him as bait. You want to kill us both."

"Such words, in such a setting. You're making yourself ridiculous. Just walk down a corridor with me, and you will see me greeted by several queen's counselors. I'm a businessman. I don't kill people."

"You hire men to do it. You sent a couple of them after me."

"There was never any question of killing you. My men would only have sequestered you."

" 'Sequestered'?"

"Jhumpa thought you could be trusted to stay home and make no phone calls. On reconsideration, I did not. You would have been kept in a comfortable place in the country for a few days, until your brother closed the deal."

"And then they would have let me go? You expect me to believe that?"

"Why not? You think I should've been afraid you would retaliate, make trouble for me somehow?

Mavalankar looked at her, raising his heavy eyelids, pretending to shrink back in fear, his chin touching the knot of his saffron silk tie. He chuckled. "Well, now we've seen what you can do, when you put all your energies into opposing me. Not much."

"You've lost your hundred-million-dollar contract."

"Chancellor Reeve disappointed me. I thought he would be able to handle the media and his employees. But you are correct that this has been a bad business. I want to put it behind me. Which I can do as soon as I have the statement." He reached into his jacket pocket and handed her a folded piece of paper. "Here are your instructions for the meeting."

"No. We negotiate that."

He wagged his head from side to side in the Indian negative. "You have wasted too much of my time already. Follow the instructions. You and your friend Lombardo will be there at nine o'clock this evening."

"And if we're not?"

"I don't think I need go into that. You'll be there. You have no choice."

He rose and walked away.

PETER WAS WAITING OUTSIDE, his back against an iron fence, allowing him to take the weight off his throbbing ankle. The

Strand, he thought, had to be the busiest street in the world, lane upon lane of oozing cars and buses, with bicycles and motorcycles whizzing among them, and sidewalks packed with people from curb to building wall.

A little while after Renata had left him, he had seen Mavalankar arrive. A long black Bentley eased over to the curb, in front of the courthouse, followed by an SUV. Three men jumped down from the SUV and deployed, their eyes sweeping the crowded pavement. They were all white, British, clad in suits and ties. Military-trained, Peter guessed. No goondahs here. This was the security detail of an executive, not the gunmen of a big criminal. The doors of the Bentley opened and three more men in suits formed up around Mavalankar, so close that the short, broad Indian could only be glimpsed. They walked through the gate in the fence Peter was leaning against and disappeared into the tall pointed archway that formed the entrance to the courthouse.

The bodyguards returned to their cars, which stayed put. Traffic snarled, drivers honked. A policeman came and knocked on the chauffeur's window. They talked, and the policeman went away. In his days on the Springfield *Journal-Register*, Peter had seen the governor of Illinois arrive at various events with the same rigmarole. It hadn't saved the governor from being convicted on corruption charges and sent to prison. The thought had cheered Peter.

Now car doors were opening. The bodyguards re-deployed, three of them going into the archway to meet the boss, the others fanning out to watch the pedestrians. The meeting must be over. Mavalankar reappeared and the three guards hurried him across the sidewalk.

A sudden movement caught Peter's eye. A street person in a thin jacket, head down, showing cropped hair and pale scalp, was shouldering his way through the crowd, heading for Mavalankar. One of the bodyguards noticed and moved to block him. The street person kept coming. They collided and the man fell. Passersby stopped and looked and a few exclaimed *oh!* But the street person was all right. He put out an arm and pushed himself up from the pavement. His only arm.

"Holy shit!" muttered Peter.

Mavalankar was back in his Bentley and the doors slammed after the security detail. The cars' flashers went off and they moved slowly away. Reeve's intense blue eyes followed them. He did not notice Peter approaching until he was standing squarely in front of him.

"Pete," he said. "What the hell are you doing here?"

RENATA EMERGED FROM THE building to find Peter with a haggard, wild-eyed street person who looked as if he was going to fall if Peter did not hold him up. Peter himself was in poor shape to support anyone. His cane was trembling under the weight. She rushed over to take the man's left arm, which was his only one. She realized he did not smell of filth and urine. He was not a street person. "What's going on? Who is this?"

"Oh … you've never met. This is Philip G. Reeve, former chancellor of Adams University."

Reeve did not react to his name. He was shivering, his arm shaking in her grip. He seemed unaware of the woman who was supporting him. He continued to stare fixedly down the Strand.

"He's ill," she said. "Fever or something."

"I don't think so. I think it's dehydration and hypothermia."

"Hypothermia?"

"I think he was standing outside Mavalankar's building for hours. When he saw the limo and chase car, he followed them here."

"He's been stalking Mavalankar?"

Peter nodded. He said, "Chancellor?"

No reaction. He leaned closer and spoke louder. "*Chancellor*?"

Reeve's brows drew together and his forehead corrugated. "Call me Phil."

"How long since you've had anything to eat or drink, Phil?"

"Don't remember."

"Let's get you inside."

There was a Burger King over the road, which seemed like the right place to take an American in sore distress. It was the mid-afternoon lull, and the staff behind the counter had leisure to eye Peter and Reeve suspiciously as they hobbled past. To distract them, Renata went up and ordered food and drink.

She found them downstairs, sitting at a quiet corner table. Peter was beside Reeve on a red vinyl banquette. Reeve's head was resting on his shoulder. His eyes were closed, his mouth open, a line of drool running down his chin. Renata set the laden tray on the table and sat on his other side.

"He just dropped off. I don't think he's slept in a long time," Peter said. "Do me a favor and pat his jacket pocket."

Reeve was wearing an unseasonable golf jacket; she remembered he had last been heard of at his vacation home in Pensacola. She felt the hip pocket. There was something L-shaped and hard-edged in it. "I think it's a pistol."

Peter nodded. "He was trying to get a clear shot at Mavalankar."

"My God. How did he even manage to get hold of a handgun in London?"

"He was a captain in the U.S. Army. Survived one and a half tours in Baghdad before the IED got him. Getting hold of a gun wouldn't be beyond him."

"What are we going to do with him?"

"I don't know, Renata. Tell me about Mavalankar."

She recounted their talk. At one point Reeve stirred, but only to fold his arm on the table and lay his head on it. Renata unfolded the paper Mavalankar had given her. "These are the instructions. He wouldn't negotiate. The time is nine tonight. I'm sure he'll kill Don if we don't show up."

"He'll kill you too if you do."

It was Reeve who had spoken. He straightened up. He must

have been awake and listening for a while, but his eyes were still closed. He opened them and looked at the tray. Hesitantly he picked up a paper cup of water and took a sip. Then he gulped down the rest of the cup, Adam's apple bobbing and water running from the corners of his mouth. He set the cup down and said, "People who can make trouble for Mavalankar disappear."

"He's right," Peter said.

"I can't leave Don to die."

"If you're going, take me with you," Reeve said.

They both stared at him. He took the paper from Renata's hand and read the instructions. "What's the M 25?"

"The London ring road."

"So you're meeting in an empty field off a highway in the dark. You'll have a better chance of surviving if I'm with you."

"Uh … Phil?" Peter said. "Are you expecting Mavalankar to be there? Hoping for a shot at him?"

Reeve did not reply.

"We know about the gun," Renata said.

Reeve slumped against the back of his seat. "Yeah, you're right. Mavalankar won't be there. It'll be just the goondahs."

"We're not going to this rendezvous. But we do want your help," Peter said. Renata looked at him, puzzled. He had another idea, but she couldn't imagine what it was. He went on, "What we need is another venue for this meeting. A survivable one."

"Mavalankar won't negotiate," she said.

"Not with us," Peter said. "We need someone he will negotiate with. Someone he respects."

"You mean Sheikh Abdullah?" she asked.

"He's back in London by now," Peter said.

"Not exactly," Reeve said. "He'll be at his country estate."

"You know where it is? Good."

"It's a long drive. And I don't want to see Abdullah again." He shook his head wearily. "We argued about who would build the Kutar Campus for months. He kept saying it had to be

Mavalankar. They've been friends all their lives. Mavalankar named a son for Abdullah's father and Abdullah has set aside a three-year-old niece to marry Mavalankar's five-year-old nephew. Their falcons have hunted together. They have a bond we shallow Westerners can't understand. Abdullah kept giving me that crap. And I kept saying, Adams University cannot sign a contract with a man of Mavalankar's reputation. I thought I had him convinced. He knew what the campus could do for his people. Obviously Mavalankar insisted and Abdullah was weaker than I thought. I'm disappointed in him."

Renata said, "Mavalankar said the same about you."

"What?"

"That he was disappointed in you. He thought that once he had you trapped, you'd be able to make your faculty and the media accept him."

Something flared in Reeve's eyes and died down. "He said that. How interesting."

She turned in her seat so that she was facing him squarely. "Chancellor—"

"Phil."

"Please help us. You can get the sheikh on our side."

"I don't know about that. I'm tired. I haven't got much left."

"You're our only hope."

"Ms. Radleigh, I don't give a flying fuck what happens to your brother."

"If you don't help us," Peter said, "Renata will go to that rendezvous. And I'll have to go with her. Will you stand by and let that happen? Wouldn't you rather have us alive and making trouble for Mavalankar?"

"What are you gonna do, Pete? Write a nasty article about him? There have been plenty of nasty articles, and they haven't done him any harm."

"It beats standing around outside his office building, hoping to get a shot at him."

Reeve sighed, sat up, and pulled the tray over. "I haven't had a Whopper in twenty years. Smells good." He unwrapped the paper, took a bite, chewed, and swallowed. It took three more bites before he made up his mind. "Okay. Maybe I can get Abdullah on our side. He owes me one."

37

At nightfall they were driving along a quiet road in Wiltshire. They had four hours left to persuade the sheikh to arrange a new rendezvous with Mavalankar. Renata had retrieved Don's statement from the safe deposit box. Reeve had advised her that an expensive car would help them get past security, so she had hired an Audi sedan. Having two arms and being used to driving on the left, she was at the wheel, Reeve beside her and Peter in back. It began to rain, and she switched on the windshield wipers.

She glanced over at Reeve. In the light from the dashboard she could see that he was awake. The Whopper and a coffee had revived him. He'd stopped shivering and some color had returned to his angular face. He had washed up in the Burger King men's room, but was still wearing the clothes he'd left Pensacola in. The gun, she presumed, remained in his jacket pocket.

She put out a hand to the heater controls. "Warm enough?"

"I'm fine. You know, Renata? You seem like a decent person. Your brother isn't worth your trouble."

"They lied to him too. He didn't know what he was getting into until it was too late."

"He didn't *want* to know. His eye was on the payoff.

Mavalankar has used and discarded his type by the dozen. But I'll grant you this much. That night, when he told me how they'd tricked me, he was plenty scared."

"Told you that you'd bought Parkdale from Mavalankar, not the sheikh, you mean."

"Yes. I knew right away they had me. No point resisting giving the contract for the Kutar Campus to Mavalankar anymore. Buying Parkdale from him was enough to put me in the shit with holier-than-thou professors and editorial writers. I would just have to shove Mavalankar down their throats. I was awake all that night. Thinking of how and when I would make the announcements, calculating the news cycles, figuring what questions I'd be asked and what answers I would give. And by the time the sun came up, I thought I could move ahead with the Kutar Campus and keep my job. A few hours later, fucking Professor Baraku gets up in front of the TV cameras and rips the lid off my secret plan—the Medical Park. It sure was a secret to me."

"Baraku undermined your credibility when you needed it most," said Peter from the back seat. "You gave up."

"I forgot. You saw me that day. It makes me ashamed to remember that. All those months I was in the hospital, after Iraq, I used to promise myself: I will never say that I'm helpless. That I have only one arm and I just can't do it, whatever 'it' is. But after the Med Park bombshell, I *was* helpless. Unable to put up the fight everyone was expecting of me. Disappointing Roger and all my other supporters, people who put their hopes and trust on me. And I couldn't even tell them why. You have no idea what it was like."

"No," said Renata. "No one puts their hopes and trust on us. We're peons."

Reeve laughed dryly. "All right. I deserve that. I've been marinating in self-pity for the last couple of days."

"How did you manage to slip away from Pensacola?" Peter asked.

"Who'd stop me? I was free as a bird. The only people who were interested in talking to me were reporters wanting me to write my own epitaph and save them the trouble. My ex sent me a consoling text message. We get along best when we don't talk. And my sons called. But they're both in the service, deployed overseas. They couldn't come running. So there I was, alone, except for the servants in my house by the sea. You get used to having a schedule. Aides rushing you around. I couldn't stand the empty time. The silence. It was like being in a vacuum. I thought I was gonna explode. Had to go somewhere, do something." He peered through the side window. They were driving along a twelve-foot-tall iron fence, with video cameras at intervals. "This is Abdullah's property."

Renata slowed down.

"No, don't slow down yet. It's a long way to the gatehouse."

They drove on. Finally the gates came into view. The golden heraldic adornments of whatever long-dead lord had built the estate flashed in the headlights as she turned in. A powerful overhead light illuminated the car and a CCTV on a pole pivoted to focus on it. There was an intercom speaker outside her window.

" 'Some work of noble note may yet be done.' " Reeve said.

"Sorry?"

"It's what my driver said last time I visited, and the gates opened."

"It's Tennyson," Peter said.

"Figures. The sheikh went to Eton."

She lowered the window and leaned out. Raindrops flicked her face. The speaker snarled something indecipherable. She said, " 'Some work of noble note may yet be done.' "

The old gates had been fitted with new motors: they swung smoothly inward. Floodlights came on as two men emerged from the gatehouse. They were uniformed and armed. Reeve lowered his window. "Evening, gentlemen."

The nearer guard bent down for a closer look. "Chancellor?"

"It's Tobin, right?"

"Tubman, sir. We weren't expecting you."

"They should have called. I'm sorry about that, Tubman."

"It's all right, sir. But I'll have to check with the house."

"Oh." The note of surprise and displeasure in his voice was not strong, but the young guard flinched. Reeve still had authority. "Tell you what. Let us through, *then* call the house. You'll have the okay by the time we get there."

The guard looked at his mate, who said, "Sorry, chancellor, but you're not on the list, and—"

Reeve waved the men closer. In a lower voice he said, "My driver has to—what do you say?—spend a penny. She's been complaining the last five miles. We can't wait."

The guards grinned. Reeve sat back and said, "Drive."

She put her foot down and the rear tires spat gravel. Outside the floodlit area, it was pitch black. She switched on the high beams. "Aren't you the clever one?"

"I apologize. Encouraging the men in their sexist attitudes is regrettable."

His voice was stronger and more relaxed. Acting like the chancellor for a moment had raised his spirits. They followed a winding, up-and-down road, crossing a short but ornate bridge with marble gods and goddesses standing on the balustrades. Eventually the house came into view. Floodlights illuminated the sweep of drive before the steps, lofty columns, and noble pediment. It was late eighteenth-century, Renata judged. There was a good deal more of it hulking behind in darkness and mist. The men at the gate had alerted the house. Several guards were standing on the steps, watching them approach.

"It looks like they're getting set to repel boarders," said Peter.

"I can hop from foot to foot, if that will help," said Renata.

"We're in," said Reeve, with serene self-confidence. "They're not going to stop us now."

SHEIKH ABDULLAH, WITHOUT HIS ghutrah, was revealed as

having long gray hair, thinning on top. His thick, drooping moustache and the spike of beard that hung from his chin were gray, too. His skin was surprisingly pale, better suited to England than his desert land. He wore aviator glasses with thick lenses. He had broad, rounded shoulders and an ample gut that rested atop his thighs as he sat with his legs folded on a chair that had been specially made to fit that posture, with a wide, deep seat. His calves and knees lay flat on the seat, an impressive display of limberness in a man of his age. He was dressed like a country gentleman, in tan moleskin trousers and a green cashmere cardigan. He had the plummiest upper-class accent Renata had ever heard outside a theater.

They were seated in a modern addition off the kitchen wing. They had reached it through long, dim, drafty corridors. But this room was as cozy as central heating and double-glazing could make it, and she suspected that the sheikh spent most of his winter nights, when not entertaining, in here. The rain-spattered windows gave views of the long rows of pedimented windows at the back of the great house.

Contrary to what she had heard about Arab hospitality, the sheikh had neither invited them to sit nor ordered refreshments. He waved away Reeve's attempt to introduce Peter and Renata. His guards were waiting in the corridor to eject them.

"I'm not interested in the details," the sheikh said, not for the first time. "I will not interfere in any negotiations between Anand Mavalankar and these people."

The former chancellor was smiling pleasantly. He moved to a chair facing the sheikh and sat down. "You'll recall that once when you were singing your friend's praises, I got you to concede that sometimes his goondahs went too far. It's about to happen again."

The sheikh straightened up and brushed back his moustache with his index finger. "I will not betray Anand. Our fathers were friends before us and our children will be friends. You in the West—"

"Yeah, yeah. Materialistic people like us can't begin to understand the nobility of a friendship like yours with the filthy fucker. How many times did I have to listen to that? I hope you don't believe in that bullshit, because Mavalankar doesn't. You and he have made big deals together. His construction company, your connections and investment capital. Malls and hotels all over the Middle East. You've both done well out of them. If you hadn't made money together, it wouldn't matter how many times your families have gathered round the same table for *Eid-al-Fitr*. He's using you for what he can get out of you. Like the contract to build the Kutar Campus. He's cost your country a great university."

"We will find another American university to partner with."

"No, you won't. Not after what happened to me. You've never been able to grasp the concept of getting fired, Abdullah. Americans are afraid of that. On every campus in the country they're talking about the fall of Philip Reeve. No university president will so much as take a call from you."

The tired-looking eyes behind the thick lenses regarded Reeve for a while. "I regret the loss of the Adams partnership. I'm sorry for what happened to you, Phil."

"Something similar can happen to you. Don't kid yourself. You're a guest in this country. An honored guest, but that can change, if you allow Mavalankar's men to commit more murders."

Reeve flung out his arm toward Renata and Peter. "You need to know who these people are. Renata Radleigh, a well-known opera singer. And Peter Lombardo, one of my men at Adams U. People like them can't be made to disappear."

Renata and Peter exchanged an arch glance. They were coming up in the world.

Reeve went on, "Mavalankar hasn't bought as many politicians in England as he did in India. There will be repercussions. And they will reach you."

"What are you asking of me?"

"Just make sure that Mavalankar lives up to his word. The exchange will take place here, the statement for Don Radleigh. And everyone walks away in one piece."

The Sheikh unfolded his legs and stood up. He was surprisingly short. He looked at Peter and Renata directly for the first time. He said, "I will ring Anand."

NEGOTIATIONS WENT ON MOST of the night. Renata did not follow every twist and turn, because the sheikh talked to Mavalankar from his office, with the door closed. He then called in Reeve, who relayed the latest move to Peter and Renata. This much she understood: Mavalankar was outraged at the sheikh's intervention. He was still complaining when the nine o'clock time of the original rendezvous passed. Eventually he conceded. But he seemed to be fighting just as long and hard against each proposal Reeve and the sheikh made. Reeve was equally patient and stubborn. Negotiating big deals with powerful people was what he did for a living, after all, and he was bright-eyed and intent. He seemed like a different person from the one she had met on the Strand in the afternoon.

The servants came in at regular intervals to serve an elegant tea with silver and china. The Americans got their coffee. Trays of sandwiches arrived, too. Renata thought she was too nervous to eat, but she wasn't. The cheddar, chutney and tomato proved delicious.

At two in the morning, Reeve emerged from the office to inform them of new developments. "He's agreed. The meeting will happen here. On the estate. Tomorrow morning. Mavalankar will be present."

Peter asked, "Did you push hard for that last one, Phil?"

Reeve nodded. "Remember what we said before—Mavalankar arranges to be elsewhere when there's wet work to be done. If he's on hand, the proceedings are much more likely to remain civilized. Why? What are you worried about?"

"You," said Renata.

"You still have that gun in your pocket, Phil. It occurs to us that the real reason you're helping to set up this meeting is to get Mavalankar in your sights."

Reeve shook his head. "If I start shooting, they'll start shooting."

"Right," said Renata. "We could all end up dead."

"I saw the way you were looking at Mavalankar this afternoon," said Peter. "Are you sure that when you see him again, you'll be able to leave the gun in your pocket?"

Reeve sat beside them on the sofa. "Okay. I'll level with you. It's not going to be easy for me to watch Mavalankar walk away with that statement in his pocket. You can help." He looked over his shoulder, to make sure that the door to the sheikh's office was closed, and leaned closer to them. "You said earlier that you planned on making trouble for Mavalankar. Please elaborate."

"We made a copy."

"A copy?" Reeve frowned. "That possibility didn't occur to Mavalankar. Let's hope it doesn't."

"The copy's unimportant," Renata said. "As soon as Don's free, he will go to the police and make his statement all over again."

"Mavalankar thinks your brother is a broken man. That as soon as he's free, he'll crawl into the deepest hole he can find."

"Oh, I'm sure that right now Don is scared shitless," said Renata. "I would be too, if I was in Mavalankar's hands. Once he's out of them, he'll recover."

Reeve raised his eyebrows, furrowing his brow. "I've told you how your brother impressed me."

"He was a bloody fool to work for Mavalankar. But he's paid for it. Now he's as determined as you are to nail the bastard."

"You sure?"

"Yes. I have faith in my brother." She smiled wanly. "Somebody has to."

"So let's get him back," said Reeve.

38

Both sides had agreed that full light would be desirable, so the rendezvous was set for an hour after sunrise. But this was England in November, and Renata emerged from the house into faint light. Leaden overcast covered the whole sky. The rain had stopped sometime in the night. The air was still and clammy.

The four of them set off in the sheikh's electric golf cart. He was driving it himself, the wheel practically rubbing up against his belly. He had changed to corduroy trousers and Barbour jacket. He was on the phone with Mavalankar, approaching the estate in his car and still trying to chisel some advantage. The sheikh told him negotiations were over. Reeve, in the front seat, kept looking over at him, and Renata could read his thoughts: if only the sheikh had learned to be this firm with Mavalankar a bit earlier, Reeve would still be chancellor of Adams University.

In the back, she was holding Peter's hand. Her own was so sweaty she fancied they might be welded together. She whispered, "What is Mavalankar on about?"

"The negotiations have assumed a life of their own. I don't think he's planning any tricks."

"Peter, how can you be so calm? Reeve I can understand.

All those mornings of lacing up his boots, picking up his rifle, going out into Baghdad. But you're a civilian."

"Old reporter's trick you learn covering riots. You're just there to observe. Makes you feel invulnerable."

"You men are so manly. I'm absolutely terrified."

"We men aren't the ones who are going forward to meet Mavalankar. You are. But there's every reason to hope it will go as planned."

They drove past a rose garden put to bed for the winter, bound stalks in semi-circular beds centering on a statue of Diana drawing her bow. The cart stopped and the sheikh led them up a small hill. The lawn fell away from them in a gentle slope, to a twenty-foot-tall column topped by a figure of Mercury in full stride.

Reeve pointed at it. "That's where you'll meet," he said to Renata and the sheikh.

He raised his hand and swept it along the low rise that bounded their view. "Beyond that hill is the drive from the gates. Mavalankar and Don will leave the car there. When you see them on top of the hill, start walking. Don't walk faster than they do. You want to meet under the statue, not on their side of it. You got that, Renata? Mavalankar will figure you're eager to get this over with."

"He won't be wrong."

"He'll try to use that feeling to his advantage. Don't let him. Mavalankar is allowed a driver and a bodyguard, but they have to stay in the car."

Renata nodded, remembering his previous briefing. "If I see them come over the hill, I shout. You and Peter will be down here with the cart, and—"

"No."

"I thought that was the agreement."

"It was. But we chose the ground and we're going to use it."

She glanced at the sheikh, but he was listening impassively. As Peter said, the negotiations had taken on a life of their own, and during those hours of verbal combat, the pliable sheikh had moved away from Mavalankar and toward Reeve.

"Pete and I will be in the haha."

"The *what?*" Peter said.

Reeve pointed, and only now did Renata see a trench with a retaining wall in it, curving away to their right.

"A haha," the sheikh said. "The name comes from the exclamation you make when you finally see it. They were very popular in the eighteenth century. Keeps the sheep from getting into the rose garden but doesn't spoil the view, the way a fence would."

"It's invisible from the other side," Reeve said. "If Mavalankar does what he's supposed to do, he'll leave without ever knowing we were there. If he tries to fuck with us, we'll have the advantage."

The sheikh's phone played its ring tone, the first notes of the overture to *Pirates of Penzance.* He held it to his ear, listened, and reported to them. The car was at the gatehouse, with Mavalankar, his chauffeur, bodyguard, and Don. The sheikh relayed a meticulous description. It was indeed Don, and he showed no signs of ill treatment. The agreed-upon frisk established that, as also agreed, the chauffeur and bodyguard were armed, Mavalankar was not. The search of the car turned up no more weapons. All was going according to plan.

"Let them proceed," ordered the sheikh. "Close the gates. Let no one else in."

"We'll take our position, Pete," Reeve said, and grinned at the sheikh and Renata. "Good luck. See you both at breakfast."

They started walking side by side but Peter soon fell behind. The ground under the dense grass was saturated and the tip of his cane was sinking into it with every step. Reeve looked back and noticed. He got behind Peter, to step on and obscure the almost invisible punctures. When they reached the steep bank of the haha, Reeve grasped his arm. They half-slid, half scrambled down into it. Their shoes sank into a mud puddle.

Reeve peered over the stone retaining wall of the trench. "Perfect height for me. You'll have to crouch down."

He reached into the pocket of his jacket, drew the pistol, and raised it to his mouth. Gripping the slide between his teeth, he pulled it back and released it, chambering a round. With his thumb, he flicked off the safety. "I was lucky to get hold of this. Beretta M9. Fine weapon. I've used it before."

"You mean, you've shot people with it in Iraq."

"Yes."

On the hill, Renata and the sheikh waited. She was longing to ask him if he thought Mavalankar would keep his word. But that would be pointless. They stood silent until the sheikh gave an explosive sneeze. She jumped and said, "Bless you. Or … sorry, if you don't say that in Islam."

The sheikh was pulling a handkerchief from his sleeve. He dabbed his moustache carefully and smiled at her. "Let us hope He reserves His blessings for the next few minutes."

Atop the far hill, two figures appeared. She recognized Don's gait at once. He was hanging his head so that he appeared no taller than Mavalankar. She and the sheikh started walking. She remembered that at this point she was to take out the buff envelope containing Don's statement. She did, holding it in her right hand. When Don raised his head and recognized her, he froze for an instant, then bounded forward. Mavalankar grabbed his elbow and pulled him back.

As they descended the gentle slope, the ground became soggier. Mavalankar's pace slowed. He had to hold Don back again. Renata longed to break into a run, to get to Don as soon as she could. But she remembered Reeve's advice and slowed her own step, matching the sheikh's. Both of them were facing front, careful not to glance toward the haha.

When they were twenty paces apart, Don locked his gaze with hers. Funny how eloquent were the eyes of someone you knew well. Her brother's spoke of his regret and resolve.

She glanced at Mavalankar. His eyes told her nothing. He

was wearing a long, fawn-colored mackintosh and green Wellington boots. He looked warm, dry, and comfortable.

They reached the base of the Mercury column and stopped. No one spoke. Renata held out the envelope and Mavalankar took it. Don started forward. Mavalankar caught his arm again.

"Not yet, I want to see what I'm getting." He slid the manuscript out of the envelope. "This is what you wrote? Your first page was your boarding pass?"

Don shut his eyes with disgust at the mildly amused voice. He hated to look at Mavalankar, to talk to him, and Mavalankar knew it. "Yes."

"How many pages did you write in all?"

"No idea."

"It's thirteen pages," said Renata. "They're all there."

Mavalankar paged through to the end, and held the last page up to the light. Then he read slowly, looking up often to savor the wretchedness on Don's face. " 'I think I can pull this off. But I'll admit it doesn't come as naturally to me as fleeing while Hannah was bleeding her life away. If we don't meet again, I'm sorry for the trouble I caused.' Then your signature. And that is the end of what you wrote?"

"Yes."

Smiling, Mavalankar put the statement back in the envelope, folded it, and shoved into an inner pocket of his mackintosh. He looked at Renata. "Did you photocopy it?"

Renata's heart sank. There was nothing to do but lie and hope to be believed. "No."

"But how do I know that?"

The sheikh said, "You should have raised that point earlier. It's too late now."

"No, it isn't. I'm not satisfied I've got the only copy."

He firmly grasped Don's arm again. His other hand dropped into his coat pocket, then re-emerged. Renata had the feeling he had a phone in his pocket and had just sent a signal.

"What did you just do?" demanded the sheikh.

"Nothing. You're coming with me, my friend. We'll hold onto the both of them until we verify we have all the copies. Then we'll let them go."

"No, you won't," said the sheikh. "You'll kill them. And you're dragging me into your crime. Just the way you did before."

Renata looked up. A man was coming over the top of the hill. It was Flathead, wearing the same soft tweed cap he'd worn when he chased her along the canal. He was carrying some sort of short rifle. He bore down on them with the upright posture and rapid stride she remembered.

In the trench Peter said, "It must be the fucking bodyguard. He's got some kind of machine gun."

"Heckler & Koch MP, I think. Fires ten rounds a second. Step in front of me."

Peter obeyed and Reeve's forearm settled securely on the small ledge where Peter's collarbone met his shoulder muscle. "This is a long shot with a pistol. Hold your breath."

"Chancellor, remember what we said. Don't shoot Mavalankar. He's too close to Renata."

"I went to West Point, son. You don't have to tell me to shoot the guy with the gun. Now shut up and don't breathe till I tell you."

The man kept on coming. Peter held as still as he ever had in his life. It seemed that Reeve was never going to fire.

The pistol going off so close to his ear was deafening. Peter flinched, but it didn't matter, the bullet was away. The running man pitched forward, rolled, rose to his knees. The gun was still in his hand. Reeve fired again and blew his brains out the back of his head in a long, dark-red plume. He collapsed.

"Now you can breathe."

The instant Reeve's arm lifted from his shoulder, Peter jumped to the retaining wall and tried to scramble up it. To no avail. His bad leg collapsed and he fell back into the mud at the bottom of the trench. Reeve was trying to get up the earthen bank, but his feet slipped in the mud and he went down on his hand, then toppled onto his side. Instead of trying to rise, he rolled onto his belly, dug in his toecaps, knees and elbow, and began to crawl up the bank. It was the only way, Peter realized, and it was going to be too slow. Renata was on her own.

Mavalankar saw his man go down. He swung round to give the sheikh a shocked and disbelieving look. That he had tried to double-cross the sheikh did not make it any more credible to him that the sheikh would double-cross him. Then he dropped Don's arm, turned, and ran.

Renata went after him. She called out, "Don! Get the gun and follow me!" But she did not look back to see if he was doing it.

Mavalankar's run was the awkward waddle of a heavy man, the tails of his mackintosh flying around him. But his boot soles gave him traction on the wet ground and he was moving deceptively fast. Renata was not gaining. As they went up the rise, the footing got drier and her longer stride began to tell. She closed the gap and jumped on his back.

They tumbled head over heels. As she got to her knees and raised her head Mavalankar's hand flew at her and drove his thumb into her eye. The pain made her scream. She lurched backward. He came at her, head-butting her. She fell back, tasting blood. When she opened her eyes, Mavalankar was half a dozen strides away. She could no longer see his legs. He was over the crest of the hill and would soon disappear from view. She scrambled to her feet and went after him.

Once over the hill, she saw the driveway and the car, a Land Rover. Mavalankar was running toward it, halfway down the hill. It was steep, and she had to throw her weight back to keep her footing. The driver was climbing out of his seat, staring at his boss open-mouthed.

"Shoot her!" Mavalankar yelled at him.

The man's hand came out of his jacket with a gun in it. He crouched to brace his elbows on the bonnet. Renata thought of putting Mavalankar between herself and the gunman but he was too far below. Then she thought of throwing herself to the ground. Maybe the gunman would miss. Or wouldn't even fire if she stopped chasing his boss.

But thinking didn't seem to matter. She was not going to let Mavalankar escape. She was getting closer to him. And to the gunman.

A flurry of pops.

She lurched to a stop. Realized she was not hit. A few steps away, Mavalankar had also stopped and was looking over his shoulder. Don was standing atop the hill with the machine gun in his hands. He fired another burst, aiming at the car. The driver ducked. The burst had no other visible effect. Don fired again. Another flock of bullets flew harmlessly away.

Mavalankar turned and ran on. Renata ran after him. The driver braced his elbows and aimed at her.

Another flurry of pops, and the windscreen and windows of the car exploded. Its doors were riddled with holes rimmed in bare steel. Hunched over, using the car as cover, the gunman wriggled into the driver's seat. Keeping his head down, he started the engine.

"No!" Mavalankar roared.

The gunman put the car in gear and drove away slowly, his punctured rear tire flopping on its wheel rim.

Renata straightened up and took a deep breath. She realized that her eye hurt like hell. Covering it, she approached Mavalankar. But his gaze was on Don, walking slowly toward him, the machine gun leveled at his stomach.

"I am unarmed," Mavalankar said. "I won't resist."

Don let the gun muzzle drop. "What a shame. Just when I'd got the hang of this thing."

Epilogue

Gretel accused Hansel of eating all the strawberries, and he riposted that she had eaten as many as he. The children bickered on, to the accompaniment of Engelbert Humperdinck's rippling, teasing music. Hansel wore a short blond wig and lederhosen, and galumphed around the stage in boyish fashion, but the figure was recognizably womanly, and the full, mellow voice was that of a mezzo-soprano.

Renata was performing on a bare platform, before a roughly painted backdrop of a forest, to the accompaniment of solo piano. The lights in the auditorium were as bright as onstage, so the guards could keep an eye on the audience. This was the refectory of Her Majesty's Prison Wayland, in Norfolk.

Some of the denim-clad men seated on rows of benches were talking to each other. Others were asleep. Many, though, seemed to be enjoying the performance, none more than a man near the back who was smiling and wagging his head in time to the beat. Don's blond hair was cut short and his skin was sallow. He had put on weight. But he was still a good-looking man.

Or so his sister thought. She had spotted him the moment she stepped on stage but had not smiled at him, because her professional standards were the same in one of HM's prisons as at Covent Garden. They would have a chance to talk after the performance, while the costumes and props were being searched prior to being packed in the lorry. The staff of the Fidelio Foundation, the troupe Maestro Vladimir Grinevich had organized to tour prisons and young offender institutions, had worked long and hard to arrange the appointment, because it was taking place outside regular visiting hours.

The visiting room was thus empty when the Radleighs met a couple of hours later. It was a large, windowless room, with well-worn tables and chairs, and the Christmas decorations only pointed up its bleakness. Still, there were no barriers between prisoners and visitors. When the guard brought Don in, they were permitted a hug.

"I've been polling the audience," he said as they took chairs on either side of a small bare table. "Rave notices all round for the opera. But there were complaints about you."

"Were there?"

"One bloke summed up the prevailing sentiment. He said, we hardly ever get to see a beautiful woman in here, and when we do, she's dressed up as a boy."

Renata laughed, mostly with surprise. She wasn't used to receiving compliments from Don. They exchanged season's greetings, then sat smiling at each other in strained silence, until he said, "Heard anything from DI McAllister?"

The siblings had always had an awkward time getting a conversation rolling, and often resorted to shop talk. When Don had worked for the Saint Louis Opera, it had been the classical music business. Now it was the Mavalankar litigation.

"McAllister's as slow and dogged as ever. Still trying to connect Mavalankar to the goondahs who killed Neal Marsh, and the ones who chased me along the canal. Apparently, if you pay someone to attempt a murder, you can be charged with any other murders he commits along the way."

"So they're hoping to charge Mavalankar for the man who

got shot in the canal? What a splendid law. Good luck to them. Heard any good outrage out of India lately?"

Renata did have some good outrage, which she had picked up from the website of a Delhi newspaper. The Indian politicians whom Mavalankar had bought never tired of denouncing his British and American prosecutors as politically motivated, racist, and imperialist. The politicians he had not bought wanted him extradited to India to face numerous charges. Nonetheless, he remained locked up in a high security prison in South London.

Don was in a low security prison, because he had pled guilty to minor charges like entering the UK on a forged passport. He was being rewarded for his cooperation in the prosecution of Mavalankar for conspiring to defraud Philip Reeve and Adams University. Now he explained to Renata that the case was being delayed by a jurisdictional wrangle between St. Louis and London prosecutors. "Wherever they end up holding the trial," he went on, "I hope my testimony can do ex-Chancellor Reeve some good. It was jolly decent of him to help wrest me from Mavalankar's clutches after what I'd done to him. I owe him one."

Don turned to face the wall. "And you, of course. More than one."

Renata faced the other wall. The siblings shared a quintessentially English moment of paralyzed embarrassment. She appreciated his expressions of gratitude but had no idea what to say to them. To her relief, he grinned and said, "Did you know Geoff Archer was bunged up in here for a while?"

"You mean the corrupt Tory politician and hack writer?"

"None of your Labourite nonsense. I mean Lord Archer, peer of the realm and bestselling novelist. He wrote a book in here, they tell me. I may follow suit if I can find the time."

"Your schedule still as busy as ever?"

"Lord, yes. I can hardly squeeze in the ordinary police anymore. It was MI5 last week. And before that the FBI and

Interpol. My favorite interrogator, though, is Geraldine."

"Who's she with?"

"Circuit attorney's office in St. Louis. She's trying to build a case against Mavalankar for Hannah's murder."

"Oh," said Renata.

"Geraldine has a lot of problems. Not with my testimony, of course. But she can't get anyone to testify to Mavalankar's involvement. Even if she can charge him, there will be problems with extraditing him. Britain shouldn't extradite people to jurisdictions that have the death penalty, and Missouri does. That's what the nambie-pambies will say anyway. Can't say I see their point."

"How are you bearing up otherwise?"

He folded his hands on the table and looked down at them. "It's an odd sort of life. You go into a room and the recorder is switched on and you run through your crimes and follies yet again. I'm all right, as long as I'm in the room with the interrogators. But when I'm back in my cell …."

He gazed at his hands for a long moment, then said, "I think of Hannah a lot."

They tumbled into another well of silence. It lasted until Renata noticed that the guard, standing by the door, was looking at his watch. He would call time soon and she couldn't leave Don like this.

"My calendar's filled up nicely," she said.

"Has it indeed?"

"I'll hit the road in the new year. Lyon, Cologne, Hamburg. Rather small parts, but it's a living."

"Saint Louis will want you back."

"Possibly."

"Tell your agent to make sure they don't skimp on the per diem. They're bad about that."

It always cheered him to give her professional advice, and he talked on happily until the guard broke in, telling them time was up. They hugged again. Then the guard took him away, and a moment later another guard appeared to lead her to the car park.

They were finishing loading the lorry, and the singers were dispersing to their cars. They exchanged waves as Renata walked to her hired Vauxhall. She opened the door and said, "Want me to drive?"

"No," Peter replied. "I want to get used to this lefty routine."

He started the engine as she fastened her belt. As they drove across the wide lot, he asked how Don was doing.

"Bearing up, I suppose. He didn't ask about you, which was just as well. I feel so guilty not telling him you're here."

"You would have felt guiltier if you had told him. You'd be imagining him in here imagining us sipping egg nog under the mistletoe."

"True."

They stopped at the gates, presented their identification for the last time that day, and drove off across the Norfolk countryside, which was, Peter told her, flatter than the Midwest. She said, "You still haven't told me how you can afford to pop over to London for Christmas."

"No. I haven't."

"I've guessed."

"I was afraid you would. Let fly."

"You're back at Adams PR."

"Yes. I'm ashamed of myself, but it's nice being solvent again."

"I'm happy for you. You'll be able to move to an apartment like the one you used to have."

"I'm not rushing that. I'll wait until something becomes available in Parkdale."

She turned to look at him.

"No, really," he said. "It's a much-envied perk of being employed by Adams U to live in Parkdale, which gets more beautiful by the day. You'll see, come May."

"Saint Louis hasn't offered me a part yet."

"They will."

"Don says so, too."

"We're optimistic on your behalf. I'll go so far as to predict the next time you're involved in murder and treachery, it will be onstage only."

"Amen to that," said Renata.

DAVID LINZEE WAS BORN in St. Louis, where he and his wife currently reside. Earlier in life he lived near New York, where he sold several stories and published mystery novels from the '70s through the '90s: *Final Seconds* (as David August), *Housebreaker*, *Belgravia*, *Discretion*, and *Death in Connecticut*.

Moving back to St. Louis, Linzee turned to other forms of writing, selling articles to the St. Louis *Post-Dispatch* and other publications and teaching composition at the University of Missouri-St. Louis.

Retired from teaching, Linzee has continued to write more than ever. He also serves on the boards of various community organizations and has been a supernumerary at the Opera Theatre of Saint Louis.

Linzee is a former marathon runner (two in New York, one

in St. Louis). He prefers to cycle rather than drive, and also enjoys scuba diving. Eager travelers, he and his wife have been to Ecuador, India, and Israel, but his favorite destination is London, explaining why English characters keep popping up in his novels.

For more information, go to www.davidlinzee.com.

Made in the USA
San Bernardino, CA
18 March 2017